The Lily Garden

BOOKS BY BARBARA JOSSELSOHN

The Lilac House
The Bluebell Girls

The Lily Garden

BARBARA JOSSELSOHN

bookouture

Published by Bookouture in 2021

An imprint of Storyfire Ltd.
Carmelite House
50 Victoria Embankment
London EC4Y 0DZ

www.bookouture.com

ISBN: 978-1-80019-424-3
eBook ISBN: 978-1-80019-423-6

To David, Rachel, and Alyssa—my loves.

CHAPTER ONE

It was on mornings like this that Caroline wished she were back in Lake Summers. Helping Maxine carry heavy oval plates piled with thick burgers or juicy steak kabobs out of the Grill's busy kitchen. Ladling Garrett "Gull" Henderson's famous chicken riggies, the rigatoni mixed with sweet peppers and smothered in his signature tomato cream sauce, into wide-mouthed pasta bowls. Giving people exactly what they wanted. Never having to disappoint.

So different from today, she thought as she eyed the résumés for the entry-level marketing position stacked on her sleek walnut desk. Today she'd be emailing countless copies of the company's form letter, saying thanks but no thanks, and good luck with your search. Telling people they weren't good enough. That there was no place for them here. Her colleague, Will, was always insisting that she took this way too personally. She owed it to the company, he said, to find the best-qualified candidate—*period*—and put the other applicants out of mind. Still, it was hard to stop thinking about the people she'd rejected since she'd taken on this responsibility a few months ago. Even some of the names stuck with her. There was Carol Bell, the newly unemployed office manager, probably in her early sixties, desperate to secure a new position, far from ready to retire. And Sidney Brotman, the former actor hoping to show that his voice-over experience had prepared him for a second career in sales. Caroline always printed out the letters and résumés. The least she could do was hold the pages in her hand as she read them, rather than merely scrolling through them on a screen.

She scrutinized today's stack, trying to estimate how many there were. Four, five dozen maybe? Each résumé painted a picture of a bright twenty-two-year-old who was convinced that a high grade point average and glowing recommendations would be enough to land a job. She was sorry they'd soon have to learn how the real world worked. That they'd soon face rejection, along with the unhappy truth that there was always someone a tiny bit better.

Shifting her gaze, she studied the framed photograph of her daughter, Lee, on the corner of her desk. It was from last spring's junior prom, Lee looking so pretty in her strapless pink dress, her choppy brown waves gliding past her shoulders, her smile lighting up her heart-shaped face. In five short years, Lee would be the same age as these applicants, another young college grad launching herself into the world. Except, of course, Lee would never be in their position. Lee's future was guaranteed. That was the beauty of being an heir to a family business. Lee's dream was to follow in her great-aunt's footsteps: first earning a business degree at Alvindale University and then working her way up to become the company's CEO.

And Caroline was proud of her daughter. Lee was amazing— smart, motivated, and personable. She deserved every success in the world. And yet, there was a piece of Caroline's heart that worried for her daughter. Was the future Lee envisioned for herself truly the best one out there? Aunt Risa was so persuasive, so good at making the family's thriving textiles business sound irresistible. Caroline had repeatedly urged Lee not to close off her options so early. But Lee had no interest in this line of conversation. The two of them were leaving tomorrow for a late-summer vacation to the East Coast to relax and sightsee, and it was all Caroline could do to convince Lee to visit a few college campuses, just to get a peek at what else besides Alvindale was out there.

Grasping the handle of her nearly tureen-sized coffee mug, the corporate name *Rantzen Enterprises* emblazoned in thick black letters around the side, Caroline pushed her chair back from her desk. The casters skated smoothly on the pricey tempered-glass floor mat. Her mug was cold since she'd poured her coffee at eight o'clock, almost two hours ago, but she didn't care. She liked the feel of something solid in her hands, something she could wrap her fingers around and hold tight. A smidgeon of ownership went a long way toward making her feel grounded. Especially in the ultra-modern office space Aunt Risa had helped design. Everything in the sixth-floor suite could either roll, swivel, nest, or otherwise reconfigure. Even the glass walls of Caroline's office were made of movable panels that could be pushed aside to enlarge the reception area for staff meetings or client cocktail parties.

She walked to the window behind her desk and looked out on the parking lot below. Hers was one of the thousands of offices in the suburban Chicago business complex, their windows reflecting the glare of the August sun, the black asphalt below glinting hot. She studied the landscaped islands alongside each row of cars, the grass neatly edged and the short trees lined up at precisely spaced intervals, the tiny pink flowers circling each tree in full bloom. She'd never thought about it before, but she wondered now who was responsible for all this conformity. Was there a gardener in an outpost checking hourly for grass that dared to stray a centimeter beyond its boundary? Someone tasked with snipping away any petal that presumed to develop a touch of brown?

Her phone buzzed on the desk, signaling that a text had arrived. Most likely it was Lee, who was coming to today's Chicago Import Forum luncheon honoring Aunt Risa. But when she picked up her phone, she saw it was from Maxine, back in Lake Summers. Maxine usually sent emails to catch up, or sometimes called on Sunday nights after she and Gull had closed up the Grill. A text from her seemed urgent, and she put down her coffee and opened it, hoping nothing was wrong.

This was in this morning's paper, sweetie, it read. *I'm so sorry to have to show it to you, but I knew you'd want to see it.*

Caroline clicked on the attached link, which brought her to a news article from the *Lake Summers Press*:

Lily Garden to be Razed Next Month

The Lily Garden, Lake Summers' decades-old homage to young love, is slated for demolition next month, according to a statement from the Mayor's office. The garden, which sits behind the library and has traditionally featured a colorful variety of lilies, daisies, zinnias, poppies, and other flowers, has suffered from neglect in recent years, as has the footbridge linking the garden's two halves. For years a romantic Eden that hosted many a marriage proposal, the garden was started three decades ago by Lily Howard, a newcomer to Lake Summers who died suddenly, leaving behind a husband and young daughter. Town officials believe the land could be put to better use.

Caroline scrolled with her thumb to the top of the article. Maxine had reported grumblings about the garden from time to time, but never before had there been such a clear plan for its destruction. She read it again, bringing the fingertips of her other hand to her forehead, her thumb pressing against her temple. So what if the garden wasn't perfect? It wasn't like Lake Summers— the one she remembered, anyway—to be so exacting. What was so bad with a little wildness? The Lily Garden had always been kind of unruly, but nobody she knew had ever considered it an eyesore. She certainly hadn't. She'd loved what an unrestrained world the garden had been, how the yellows and oranges and deep pinks had come up in their own time and reached whatever height they fancied; how they'd occasionally chosen to mingle with the azalea and hydrangea bushes along the winding dirt path on either side to the footbridge, and sometimes even crept into the realm of the slope down toward the inlet. The garden was a fairy-tale forest, magical and deliciously defiant. How could people want to take it down?

Although, she had to admit, her memories were from long ago. She hadn't seen the garden, hadn't even been back to Lake Summers, since she was twelve. She put the phone down and picked up her coffee again. Maybe the people were right, and the garden was a disaster. Maybe there'd been no one to tend it, and it was now past the point of saving.

Lily Howard. Even after all these years, it was strange to see her mother's name in print. Ghostly, like a phrase from a storybook she'd forgotten long ago, or a sound she'd heard when she was fast asleep, so she didn't know if it was real or not. She'd been only in second grade when her mother died. But she never forgot all the long afternoons they'd spent together in the garden. The recollections weren't so much stories as flashes, images: her mother in those old denim overalls and dirty Keds sneakers, her brown ponytail shiny like a fancy ribbon on a birthday present; her smile, the way her two front teeth would rest slightly on her bottom lip, making her look a little mischievous, especially when it would rain and she'd pretend it wasn't so she could continue gardening: "What rain? It's a sunny day, my sweet Caroline!" She remembered the dirt squiggles and smears that always appeared on her mother's forehead and chin. And she remembered the afternoon it started to rain as her dad showed up, and he picked up her mom and spun her around. She'd watched her mom throw back her head and laugh as her dad held her and twirled her around and around, under the early fall rain shower…

"Caroline?" came a voice from the doorway, and she jumped, sending a geyser of coffee upward from her mug. She spotted Will in the doorway just as she felt a splash—and when she looked down, a grayish-brown splotch was smack on the front of her pale-blue sheath dress.

"Oh, no!" she said, cupping the bottom of the mug with her free hand to prevent any additional drops from landing on her. "Oh, shoot!"

"Let me help," Will said, striding into her office, his legs so long that he covered the distance to her desk in two steps. He reached over her desk and took the cup. "I'm sorry, I didn't mean to scare you."

"Oh, boy," she said, as the spot took on a yellowish-green tint. "No, it wasn't your fault, it's mine. I'm such a klutz. This is why I never wear light colors. I only did today because of the lunch." It was a special event, the luncheon, recognizing her aunt as the longest-serving female CEO in the industry. The whole management team was going.

Will snapped a few tissues out of the box on the desk and handed her one. He used the others to wipe down her cup.

She patted her dress with the tissue. "It's not that big, right?"

He tilted his head apologetically. "It's kind of big."

"Maybe if I go to the ladies' room and put some water on it—"

"What? No!" he said. "That's linen, isn't it? You have to check the label. If it's dry clean only, that might make it worse."

She sighed. The irony wasn't lost to her that she was the one who'd been born into a textiles family, while he'd only joined it a year ago as head of marketing, and yet she didn't even know what fabric her dress was made of or what water might do to it.

She pushed her shoulder-length curls behind her ears and twisted them into a knot behind her head. "Okay, you know what? I'll run home and change and come right back." She reached into the bottom drawer of her desk for her shoulder bag. "What time do we need to leave here?"

He looked at his watch. "Twenty minutes."

"*Twenty minutes?* I thought the thing didn't start until noon."

"Yeah, but they're taking pictures ahead of time, and your aunt decided she wants the whole team in them. She told me to give everyone a heads-up."

"Oh, great," Caroline said. She could barely make it home in twenty minutes, let alone get there, change, and come back. She clasped her hands together below her chin. "What do you think? I can just stand like this, right? Nobody will see."

"You can't stand like that to get your picture taken. Your aunt would never allow it."

"What if I stand at an angle?" She turned her body. "It's pretty small…"

"But you can still see it." He pursed his lips for a moment. "Don't worry, I'll figure this out," he said. "Get ready to go, I'll be right back."

She nodded and watched him march back out of the office. She didn't know what he would come up with, but she expected he'd come back with a fix. Will knew how to get things done. That's the way he was. You could see it in his posture, even from the back—his straight carriage, his perfectly aligned shoulders, his long, even strides when he walked. And from the front, that perfectly trimmed blond hair and cool blue eyes could convince even the biggest pessimist that he'd come through. It was no wonder that her aunt adored him and kept piling onto him new corporate titles and ever-growing responsibilities. Everyone in the office expected Caroline and Will to become a couple. They were both single, they were both in their late thirties, they were both executives, and they both had strong connections to the boss. Even she could see how it made sense.

Although this drama over her dress reminded her of why they weren't together. Okay, she had spilled a drop of coffee—and even now she could see the discoloration fading. It wasn't as though a whole ocean had descended on her chest.

She looked back over at her phone and then pushed the button, bringing the news article back up on her screen. She felt an ache in her chest that she couldn't ignore. The article said the garden would be razed next month, and she and Lee had a whole trip planned starting tomorrow, so there was nothing she could do even if she wanted to. She had two weeks in and around Boston mapped out for them. And then they had to come straight home, Lee to attend Alvindale University's Pre-College Business Seminar for prospective college applicants, Caroline to get back to work. Late summer was Rantzen's busiest season, and her aunt wouldn't let anyone take more than two weeks of vacation in August and September. Especially not family. It would set a bad example.

Will peeked back in again, dangling something black in his hand. "Who's there for you, kid?" he said. "Martha in accounting wore a sweater today. Black, so it goes perfectly. And I think she's about your size. Button it up and no one will ever be the wiser."

He tossed it over her desk and she caught it, feeling sorry for having been annoyed before. The truth was, it was sweet that Will had found a solution for her. And wearing a sweater was definitely better than trying to hide the front of her dress for two or three hours. Threading her arms through the sleeves, she felt sorry for never accepting his occasional invitations to go out to dinner. She'd told him each time that she wasn't ready to get involved with anyone, that Lee needed her full attention. She knew that was a reasonable explanation, and she meant it. But perhaps it wasn't the only thing holding her back.

"Thanks, Will," she said. "I owe you one."

He waved her off. "And I owe *you* one for not killing me for making you spill the coffee. So let's call it a draw. Put it on, quick—here comes your aunt." He looked down the hallway and raised his voice: "Look, everyone! The most celebrated female CEO in textiles!"

"Don't be silly," Aunt Risa told him as she appeared in the doorway of Caroline's office, looking magnificent in a white pantsuit with a silky white shell, her white-blond hair styled in a tousled but neat bob, her long bangs falling in gentle curves around the sides of her face. Her complexion was smooth yet looked entirely natural, her brown eyes accentuated by delicate strokes of eyeliner, her lips a subtle berry color. She looked so elegant and so... well, not really young, Caroline thought. It wasn't that her aunt was trying to hide her age; it was more that she was the ideal—a picture of how fabulous sixty-five *could* look.

"Ready, darling?" she said. "Uncle Richard just went down to get the car. Will, would you drive too? Two cars will be sufficient to get us all there."

Caroline pulled the sweater closed across her chest to hide the stain. "Congratulations, Aunt Risa," she said. "You deserve this."

Aunt Risa winked. "Let's not get too gushy now," she said. "It's just an industry event. And a chance to honor all of us. After all, we're a team. Lee's meeting us there?"

Caroline nodded.

"Perfect," Aunt Risa said. "Come, let's not keep Uncle Richard waiting."

"I'll be right down," Caroline said, watching until her aunt and Will were gone before loosening her grip on the sweater and buttoning it up. It was true, Aunt Risa did deserve the award. She was a smart businessperson—she may have inherited the business, but she'd also transformed it. She was a good aunt to her and a devoted great-aunt and role model for Lee.

But that didn't change how Caroline felt about the Lily Garden. She needed to see it. And for some reason Caroline was sure that Lee needed to see it, too.

Picking up her phone, she switched back to Maxine's text.

Don't let them touch the garden, she responded. *I'm coming back to save it.*

CHAPTER TWO

Caroline worked through the evening to revamp their trip, which now began with an early flight to Syracuse instead of a mid-afternoon one to Boston. Still, the arrival of the sedan from Suburban Car Service early the next morning felt like a mistake, because she'd been anticipating a later departure since the beginning of the summer. She opened the front door, and the bright sunshine—which ordinarily would have made her think of taking a bike ride with Lee along Lake Michigan—seemed accusatory, like a spotlight in an interrogation room. She reminded herself that she had every right to change this trip, no matter what Aunt Risa would think. Then she nodded to the driver and turned away from the glare.

"Lee!" she called. "We have to go. Please don't tell me you went back to sleep!"

She listened to silence for a few seconds until there was the click of a door unlatching followed by footsteps on the upstairs landing. A moment later Lee appeared, leaning heavily on the banister and pulling her suitcase behind her, the wheels banging rhythmically as they crashed onto each step. Caroline winced at the clatter, even though there was no one to disturb. She and Lee had lived in the carriage house, set well behind the big house where Aunt Risa and Uncle Rich lived, since Lee was a baby. Caroline loved their little home, with just two bedrooms upstairs and a single space combining the living room and kitchen on the first floor. She liked that it was theirs alone. Aunt Risa had expected she'd move in with them after Lee's dad, Glenn, died, and while Caroline was grateful for the invitation, she'd never liked that huge house—so many rooms, so much big furniture, so many heavy drapes covering the windows and so many stodgy paintings on those endless walls. She'd reminded Aunt Risa of how noisy and disruptive babies could be, and was relieved when her aunt proposed an alternative.

"Oh my God, it's the middle of the night," Lee groaned as she wheeled her suitcase toward the door. She loosened her grip and the suitcase fell over, the handle thwacking the floor.

"It's seven thirty," Caroline said.

Lee leaned against the wall and tilted her head back, her eyes closed. "I thought our flight was at two."

"I had to change it."

"You said it was two."

"But then I told you last night I changed it." Caroline had rebooked their flights last night and then went on to rework the college tours she'd scheduled, cancel all their hotel reservations, and reserve a room at the Lake Summers Resort for their entire two-week stay instead. Fortunately, they could still get some college tours in, she'd realized, since several interesting colleges were within driving distance of Lake Summers. She initially thought they'd have to forgo a visit to Boston University, which was how they'd planned to begin their trip, but then she discovered that Boston was a five-hour drive east of Lake Summers—not a quick trip, but doable. So they could still shoot over there toward the end of the trip, assuming everything with the garden went well.

"Lee, we've got to go," Caroline said. "We'll get Starbucks at the airport. Or forget the Starbucks, you can just muscle through now and sleep the entire flight."

Lee yawned loudly. "I'm working on it, Mom," she said, running her palm up her face.

Caroline stroked her daughter's ponytail. At this time of morning, Lee could look like a little girl, with her cheeks ruddy, her mouth pouting, and wisps of light-brown baby hair framing her temples. No makeup, which was unusual for Lee—she rarely left the house without her cheeks glowing from a touch of highlighter and her eyes big and sparkling, thanks to the subtle strokes of black eyeliner she'd applied above her lashes, her technique perfected from lessons gleaned on YouTube. While she'd dressed in professional garb all summer as an intern at the Midwest Import Export Association, today she was wearing a tank top and gray sweatpants with "Alvindale University" imprinted down one leg. Aunt Risa and Uncle Rich had given her the sweatpants last weekend, a gift for the glowing reviews she'd earned from her internship supervisor. Caroline had bristled at this not-so-subtle power move.

Righting Lee's suitcase, Caroline wheeled it with her own onto the porch, and the driver helped her put them into the trunk. Then she locked the house and climbed into the backseat alongside Lee. The gravel crunched beneath the tires as the car started down the long driveway beside the big house, and Caroline silently thanked her lucky stars that Aunt Risa slept in on the weekends. She hadn't said a word to her aunt about changing the trip. Not that she hadn't thought about it. She'd intended to speak up at the luncheon or afterward. But sitting at the table in the banquet hall and listening to Aunt Risa's award speech, she'd changed her mind. The clincher was when Aunt Risa came to her concluding sentences: "The difference between colleagues and family is you get to choose your colleagues," she'd said. "But I'm lucky that my family is exactly who I'd choose to be with anyway. I'm so proud to be a Rantzen—and I know they are, too." From the stage, she'd gone on to ask the three of them—Uncle Rich, her, and Lee—to stand. Aunt Risa was so full of pride yesterday and so determined to see the family as entirely in lockstep. She would have found this news a huge betrayal.

Of course, Caroline knew it was silly to sneak off like this. She was a grown woman and could do whatever she wanted.

But everything about this trip would be anathema to Aunt Risa: Caroline's impulsiveness, her failure to run the changed itinerary by others for advice or suggestions, her refusal to seek out potential risks or downfalls of the new plan, her avoidance of significant stakeholders, of which Aunt Risa was one. Mostly, though, she knew her aunt didn't like Maxine and never would have been okay with Caroline going there, let alone bringing Lee along. So she'd hugged her aunt and uncle following the luncheon, and said she'd see them in two weeks when she and Lee got back from the East Coast. She hadn't wanted to give her aunt even a tiny opportunity to make her reconsider what she knew in her heart she had to do.

In the car, Lee lifted her head and made a "Mmmm… mmm!" sound as she pushed her feet forward and stretched her arms up, her fingers pressing against the roof. "Great," she said. "Now I'm too awake to sleep." She rubbed her eyes with the heels of her hands.

"Then tell me about the party," Caroline said. Lee's internship had ended yesterday, and her boss had taken all the summer interns to dinner at a trendy sushi place downtown and then thrown a party for them at his country club, where he'd rented a ballroom and brought in a D.J. Caroline had been wary when Lee had told her about it—"There's not going to be alcohol, is there?" she'd asked.

Lee had rolled her eyes. "Mom, what's the matter with you?" she'd said. "They know we're not twenty-one. These are important people, with kids of their own. I mean, they're arranging for cars to make sure we all get home safely. Of course nobody's serving us alcohol! What do you think?"

That was the thing: Caroline hadn't known what to think. This wasn't her world. She'd entered it when she was twelve, the year she left Lake Summers and came to live with Aunt Risa and Uncle Rich. And she'd always felt a little separate from the company, the business world. But Lee was different. Rantzen Enterprises had been a part of her life since she was born. Her early onesies had been imprinted with "Rantzen Enterprises" and the company's logo, a big, green globe with "RE" in the middle. Her cereal bowls and sippy cups had the same graphic.

Lee sat up in the car, her eyes opening wide. "Oh my God, Mom, it was so amazing!" she said. "There was a photo booth and a blackjack table where we bet mini chocolate bars… and there was a dessert bar with four types of brownies and make-your-own sundaes and cake pops and a 'smores station. God, Mom, I just love the working world!"

Caroline raised her eyebrows. "I don't think that's all the working world is about."

"I know," Lee said. "I know that. I'm just saying, the people I worked with this summer, they have such a great life. They travel and meet people and stay at fancy hotels and make deals and discover cool stuff to import, and bring it here from really exotic places… Mom, are you listening?"

"Yes, of course," Caroline said. She hadn't even realized she'd been looking down.

"Because I was talking to Gary last night, he's the guy who runs the whole internship program?" she said. "And next year they're taking the summer interns to China on a real buying expedition. And he said they don't usually take interns back for a second summer, but they think it would be a great opportunity for me. What do you think, Mom? Do you think Meems and Pops will think that's a good idea?" she added, using the names they had all settled on years ago. Aunt Risa had refused to entertain Grandma and Grandpa because she and Uncle Rich weren't Lee's grandparents.

"And yes, I know the plan was for me to start working in product development with Pops next summer, and then rotate each summer after that to other departments," Lee continued.

"I mean, that was always the plan. And I don't want to let them down. But it could give me even more experience for when I join the business if I take this China trip next summer—Mom, what is it?"

"What is what?" Caroline said.

"Why do you look like that? Like you completely hate what I'm saying? What, you don't want me to go to China? I'll be eighteen, almost nineteen by then—"

"I know you will—"

"Then what? *What?*" she said, her shoulders up by her ears, the way they always were when she was annoyed. "Why do you look like I'm saying I want to walk a tightrope over the Chicago River or something…?"

"No, I'm not, I'm not. It's only that…" Caroline said as she pressed her palms against her thighs, feeling the thin cotton of her t-shirt dress. She never liked it when Lee sounded so definitive about the future. But she liked it even less today. The two worlds Caroline had grown up in—Lake Summers and Chicago— couldn't be more different. She wished she hadn't waited so long to bring Lee to her hometown. But better late than never. Lee needed to know what else was out there.

"It's only that you don't have to have your whole life planned out now," she said. "You're still very young, and—"

There was a sharp, loud bang, and Caroline bolted in her seat. Then came a series of slapping noises, as the car listed to the right.

"Flat tire," the driver mumbled, and he put on his flashers and slowed the car. Caroline looked through the windshield. There was no visible exit ramp ahead and not much of a shoulder along this stretch of the highway, just a couple of feet between the right-hand lane and a guardrail.

"What are you going to do?" she asked.

"Change it," he said.

"Change it? Right here on the highway?"

The driver pulled to the right as far as he could and stopped the car. "What time's your flight?"

"Nine forty-five," she said.

"You'll be okay. Plenty of time. Probably best if you wait outside."

He glanced over his left shoulder, then opened his door and made a beeline for the back of the car. Still in the backseat, Caroline turned to watch behind her. She saw the lid of the trunk rise.

"God, Mom, this is weird," Lee said. "We're stopped in the middle of a highway."

Caroline nodded, her breath halted in her chest, as she watched the driver carry a jack to her side of the car. At least that was where the flat was, so he had the width of the car between him and the traffic lanes. The vehicle trembled and the driver's long ponytail flapped as passing cars whooshed by. She watched him place the jack down and go back to the trunk, then wheel a replacement tire along the narrow space between the car and the guardrail.

"Come on, honey," she said. "Let's do what he said."

She opened her door and stepped around the kneeling driver, stopping to ask if there was any way she could help. He shook his head, so she continued past him, Lee following close behind. They stood against the guardrail, the wind slapping their chests and rippling their clothes with each passing car. Caroline felt helpless, and blameworthy, too, for putting her daughter in this dangerous position. But there didn't seem to be any better choice. It would be even worse to walk along the highway toward the next exit, she thought. And she couldn't call anyone to come get them. They were already twenty minutes from home, so it wasn't as though Aunt Risa or Uncle Richard could hop right over. Not to mention that if she asked them to come, she'd be putting them in harm's way as well. She felt her arms grow jellylike. Lee was staring at the road, mouth open.

Caroline took Lee's arm and pulled her closer. What had she been thinking, secretly revamping this trip with Lee at the last minute? Suddenly the flat tire felt like divine retribution for a totally reckless decision. She wondered if she should call 911. A patrol car would be equipped with flashing lights and sirens. The officer would escort them and the driver out of danger. A tow truck could deal with the tire...

And suddenly the driver was back on his feet, bringing the flat tire and the jack to the trunk. He slammed the lid shut and jogged toward his door. Caroline gestured to Lee to climb into the back seat, and she followed behind. Inside the car, the driver tossed his ponytail behind his shoulder and turned off the flashers.

"All fixed," he said as he started the engine. He gathered speed to merge into traffic.

Caroline looked at Lee, hoping she wasn't too traumatized. Her daughter didn't take well to unexpected drama. But to her surprise, Lee suddenly burst out laughing. It started as a spritzy eruption from her closed lips and quickly turned into an all-out guffaw. That's when Caroline started laughing, too. Maybe it was the release of all that tension, relief at making it through the last ten minutes alive, but soon she was practically in hysterics, throwing her head back so it rested on top of the car seat. Lee toppled over, her head landing on Caroline's lap, and she drew her knees to her chest and wrapped her arms around them as she laughed on, easing up every few seconds and then howling and hooting anew.

"You okay back there?" the driver said. "What—you never saw anyone change a tire before?" Caroline looked down at Lee, and they both burst out laughing again. Pretty soon, the driver was chuckling as well.

Lee pulled herself back up to sitting. "Wow, Mom," she said. "That was kinda crazy."

Caroline nodded as she swiped at the tears the laughter had caused. "I know," she said. "Absolutely."

And yet, everything was okay, she thought. Flat tires weren't such a big thing. They happened all the time. She sighed, realizing that she'd panicked most likely because she was still feeling anxious about changing up the trip. She reminded herself that she had every right in the world to go to Lake Summers. The best thing she could do was to push all thoughts of Aunt Risa aside and just relax.

*

The security line was long and the flight delayed almost two hours, but eventually they were gliding peacefully above the clouds, each with a plastic cup of weak airline coffee on their tray tables. Lee was sitting cross-legged in the seat, paging through a stapled packet of pages, the top margin of each page festooned with the same bold, orange "A" that decorated many mugs and pens in Aunt Risa's home. Nearly as familiar to Caroline as the "RE" logo of Rantzen Enterprises.

"Alvindale stuff?" Caroline asked.

Lee nodded. "For the pre-college program," she said, her eyes still focused on the papers.

"Is that an assignment?"

"It's for the marketing workshop," she said. "You have to submit a business plan for a mock start-up. I'm not sure what I'm going to do."

Caroline nodded and stirred her coffee. It was great that Lee was such a good student. But the stark truth was, it didn't matter if she went to this Alvindale pre-college program or not, if she got excellent grades or good standardized test scores or not, if she'd had that selective internship this summer or had simply hung out by the lake. She'd still almost certainly get into Alvindale, because of her family's history there. And the family's donation to the university's new wing was insurance. That was how the world worked. And even if the impossible happened and she didn't get into Alvindale, she'd still have a job when she got out of college, still have a great career, still end up as CEO of Rantzen someday.

Of course, being so diligent about her future was one of the things that made Aunt Risa want Lee to take over the company. Still, there was something... not right, maybe, about watching her daughter work so hard for a future that was already hers. It was like studying for a test when the teacher had already submitted the "A." Passion was a good thing—but was it passion when the outcome was assured? Or was it merely an exercise? She wondered if Lee would ever know true passion. And would she regret it one day if she didn't?

Lee put the packet aside. "Tell me about Maxine," she said.

Caroline exhaled, happy for Lee's interest in where they were going and why. She wondered how to start. There was so much Lee didn't know.

"Maxine... is an amazing person," she said. "She helps run the Grill—it's this really good restaurant that everyone goes to. She was my mother's best friend. Well, more like an older sister, I guess. Like family."

"And she took care of you?"

"For almost five years, until I went to live with Meems."

"How did your mom die?"

"She had pneumonia."

"And what happened to your dad?"

"He died a few months after my mom. He was a builder, and there was an accident at the construction site." She looked at her lap, hoping to end the conversation there. She knew Lee would find the answer unsatisfying. Lee liked details. But Caroline couldn't bear to remember how it felt, sitting at the kitchen table that long January afternoon, the day before her eighth birthday. Still in her coat and mittens. Watching the room get dark. Waiting for her dad to get home. She had woken up in that same spot the next day. Her birthday.

Lee looked out the plane window. "What else do you remember?" she asked.

"I remember how beautiful my mom was," she said. "She had long hair and long bangs that she was always pushing aside with the back of her hand. And she had the prettiest smile, so wide. And the best laugh. And she loved to draw. She taught art classes to kids at the library, and all the kids loved her. But I was the luckiest because she was mine."

Lee picked up her coffee stirrer, then put it back down onto her tray table. She raised her arm and put it behind Caroline's neck. "Oh, Mom," she said, leaning closer so their two heads tapped together. "My mommy," she teased.

Caroline squeezed her hand. It was sweet that Lee felt bad for her. She loved that her daughter was moved by her story. But at the same time, she knew she wasn't giving Lee the full picture. It sounded sad on paper, her childhood. It was awful that she lost her parents. But she didn't remember her childhood in Lake Summers as terribly sad, not most of the time. It had been a good childhood. A wonderful one, even. She'd adored Maxine and Maxine's two boys, Jackie and Ben. She'd loved the restaurant, the Lake Summers Grill, where Maxine worked. She'd loved eating Gull's buttery grilled-cheese sandwiches at the long wooden bar while she did her homework. She'd loved stomping through the fallen leaves on the woodsy trail with Jackie and Ben on her way to school in the fall, and having snowball fights with them and the other neighborhood kids when winter came. Yes, it had been a strange childhood. But it had magic, too. It had taken her years to stop being mad at Maxine for letting her go. For letting Aunt Risa come and take her.

"It wasn't so sad," Caroline whispered. Lee was silent.

They finished their coffee, and Caroline leaned back and closed her eyes. When she woke, she noticed that Lee was drawing something. Focusing her gaze, she saw that it was a garden, a beautiful one, with a blend of green bushes of various heights and shapes, and stalks of grass, and yellow, red, and purple flowers woven in, with tall, curved trees in the background. The setting was lush, the plants neat but also a bit untamed, the grasses tall and seeming to wave in the breeze. Caroline loved that Lee had her pencils and sketchbook with her. Her artwork was always full of color and life.

"That's so pretty," she said.

Lee shrugged. "Just a sketch," she said.

Caroline closed her eyes again. Lee always brushed her off when she commented on her drawings. She wished that for once, Lee would recognize that she had other skills she might not be able to make use of in the business world.

A few minutes later, the announcement came that the plane's descent had begun. Soon they were off the plane and following the crowd through the terminal and down to baggage claim. Outside, they picked up their rental car and left the airport. They stopped for a late, leisurely lunch at a diner along the route and then set off for Lake Summers.

It was after eight when they entered the town, crossing the drawbridge that went over the Peek inlet. The sky was darkening, the sunset over. Even after all these years, Caroline remembered that there was nothing as beautiful as a Lake Summers sunset—the air fresh, the sky lavender and coral, the trees in the distance just starting to glow golden. But they wouldn't see it today. They would have to wait for tomorrow.

They could see, however, the banner up atop the doorway to the Grill.

"Welcome Home Caroline!"

Caroline pulled to the side of the road and squeezed Lee's hand as she soaked in the words. Welcome home.

CHAPTER THREE

Aaron bent down toward the doorknob and wiggled his key like a watchmaker adjusting the hairspring of a Rolex. The last thing he needed was to feel it break in the stiff old lock. Abrams Hall was mostly empty on this late-August afternoon, and he didn't know where, or if, he'd be able to find someone to help. And he didn't want anyone to get a bad first impression of him: the oaf who destroyed his lock the first time he tried to get into his office. He let go of the key for a moment, then grasped it again and took a different tack, applying gentle bursts of pressure, pushing ever so slightly harder each time. Slowly, the key eased down until the bolt snapped back. He looked inside, and he saw that his efforts had been well worth it.

The office was perfect. The heavy wood desk was chocolate in color, the tone rich and dignified. The brown leather desk chair, though scuffed, was roomy, the edges adorned with traditional brass-toned nailheads. It was an office fit for a scholar, an esteemed author, someone who'd written a dozen books and more articles in academic publications than anyone could count, and had more still inside. Someone he hardly recognized as himself. He went back to the hallway and checked the room number again, just for kicks. Yes, indeed—343. It was his office. It didn't seem like it should be. But it was.

Not that he didn't want to be there. No, this was exactly the kind of office where he'd always wanted to hang his hat. Gorson College, tucked away on the western edge of the Adirondack

Mountains, surrounded by rolling sheep meadows and lush green dairy farms, was a history professor's dream. Or, at least, *this* history professor's dream. The small school, with barely two thousand students, was more than a hundred years old, its legacy legendary. It was the kind of school where the study of humanities mattered. Where students would sit around a stone fireplace in the campus center and talk about big ideas. It was a place you could burrow into and close yourself off from the world.

Except it had email, Aaron thought, as he felt a buzz in the back pocket of his jeans. He suspected it was from Tanya's sister, and he didn't know what to do. He could refuse to answer, of course. He could ignore it. But that didn't change things. She would try again. Because even way out here in the mountains, he wasn't off the grid. Like legal documents in a court case, he was discoverable. He pulled out his phone, then paused, the screen out of sight as it continued to buzz. But no, it wouldn't be Tanya's sister, he thought. She wouldn't write him again so soon, would she? She'd said she'd wait for him to make the next move. That's what he remembered, although she might have thought of one more thing she needed to write to him. And he didn't want to read it, at least not until he had figured out a response to her first email. On the other hand, it could be an email from the dean's office. Or an update from his new landlord, another progress report about when the electricity in his house would be on…

He turned the phone over and read the notification banner. It was only an ad from a shoe store in Florida. No need for all the drama. He'd been right, Tanya's sister wouldn't break her word.

He put his phone back in his pocket, then unslung his tennis racquet and his messenger bag from his shoulder and set them on the desk. The bag's large metal buckle made a loud *plunk* as it struck the wood, and he cringed, even though there was no one else on the floor, probably not even in the building, to disturb. The lobby had been dark when he'd walked in, lit only by sunlight, with no movement visible through the frosted glass rectangles cut into the wooden office and classroom doors. He'd been told that the bulk of students wouldn't be returning for another two weeks, and even most of the faculty and staff were still on vacation. He wasn't even required to be on campus until the faculty meetings began in September, still more than two weeks away. He knocked the buckle on the desk again, this time intentionally. No administration officials would stop by, attracted by the noise, to say there'd been a mistake.

Rolling his eyes at the thought, he half sat on the edge of the desk and clasped his hands together between his jeans-clad legs. Why was he feeling so uneasy about his place here? His older brother, Neil, was named principal of a high school back in Pennsylvania last year and then superintendent of the whole district in the space of eight months, earning a leadership award. Life never proceeded logically—he knew that. He taught that, actually. History was replete with stories of people whose lives didn't make sense, who got where they were by coincidence or luck. Feeling as though you'd leaped forward before you were ready wasn't unique to him. Everyone felt that way at least once in their lives.

But not everyone had gotten an email like the one he'd received last week. Not everyone took advantage of an unexpected job offer to leap fourteen hundred miles away.

Dear Aaron. This is so hard. I can't believe what I have to tell you…

He stood back up and surveyed the office more closely, shifting from his heels to his toes as he flexed his feet inside his sneakers, his hands in the front pockets of his jeans. They'd done a nice job getting it ready. The walls were a shiny and uniform white, the smell of fresh paint unmistakable. The desk looked recently polished, and the wood floor, while visibly worn in spots, had a glossy finish, too. Someone had arranged to make it look so good. Someone wanted to welcome him, even though his was only a one-year appointment.

In the corner, he saw that his books had arrived, the two cartons he'd sent ahead neatly stacked beside the built-in wooden bookshelves that stretched the width of the wall. He'd thought he had a pretty good collection, but now he saw the quantity was pitiful. Someone arriving at the invitation of one of the country's leading experts on Greek history would be expected to have triple or quadruple the number. His books wouldn't fill even a third of the space he had. He wished he'd had time to pack up his whole bookshelf from home. But he'd left so suddenly, there hadn't been time.

Tatiana didn't want me to do this, she'd written, using Tanya's full name, the way her family always did. *But now that doesn't matter anymore...*

His face felt warm, and he rubbed his forehead with the heel of his hand. The room was close, the smell of paint more intense than he'd realized. Back in Florida, there was no such thing as a building without air conditioning, but life was evidently different in the mountains, and open windows were the way to get the air moving. He walked to the first of three tall windows adjacent to his desk and went to crank the handle. Not surprisingly after what he'd been through with the door, it didn't budge. He anchored his feet and pulled the handle again, and then he pressed one hand on top of the other and tried to push it. Still nothing. He looked around, his hands on his waist. The windows didn't appear painted shut, so there was no reason why he couldn't move the handle. They were old, yes, but they had to open. He held his breath and pushed with small spurts of pressure, just as he'd done with the key and the door lock. When it didn't move, he pushed harder, gradually putting more and more body weight into play...

"Guess you're not used to old casements," came a voice from behind him. He turned to see a tall woman in a black pantsuit, her chin-length white-blond hair tucked behind her ears, standing in the doorway. She walked toward him, the heels of her shoes clicking in precise beats, and faced the window that was giving him trouble. Reaching out, she snapped two almost imperceptible latches near either side upward. Then she grasped the lever, and it spun obediently.

He shook his head and raised his palms, a sign of surrender. How had he missed the latches?

She held out her hand. "I'm Clara Bonds. Welcome."

"Oh. Hey. Aaron Weldon," he said. He hadn't thought anyone was nearby, let alone his new boss. He shook her hand. It felt cool and unyielding. "I'm the new visiting professor from Pine Beach College," he added. "In Florida."

"I know who you are," she said, and he thought he heard an edge in her voice. "Samuel Bates hasn't stopped talking about you. I think he's gunning for you to move into his spot when he retires next year."

"Well, that's very flattering," Aaron said, feeling embarrassed at the praise, particularly since Clara didn't sound particularly happy about it. "He was my adviser at the University of Florida. I was very lucky. He had a big impact on me."

"I read your recent paper, the one on sports heroes. Very interesting," she said.

"Thanks. And I've started your book on the industrial revolution in Upstate New York," he said. "It's fascinating." The thing was, he meant it—he loved stories about the forces of change in society, about how people faced challenges, how they adapted and even thrived. But he didn't think she'd meant it when she said she'd liked his paper.

"Anyway, I hope you'll like it here," she said. "Some people find it too rural."

"Oh, I don't think it's too rural. It's amazing," he said, then caught his breath. "Amazing" wasn't exactly a sophisticated word.

He didn't mean to sound like an eager puppy, like he wanted her to pat him on the head and toss him a treat. He looked down, his sneakers catching his gaze. Why had he worn sneakers? Probably because it was summer, he told himself. And he hadn't expected to run into anybody. And anyway, why was she so dressed up? Okay, she was a department head, but still. This was a college, not a law office.

Not a law office.

I could have asked my lawyer to contact you, Tanya's sister had continued. *But honestly, Aaron, I didn't want to make this any weirder for you...*

"Yes, it's very pretty," Clara said, her arms folded across her chest, looking at the view from his window. "In a couple of months, it's going be even better. Once the leaves start changing, it's almost impossible to turn your eyes away from the window. Sometimes I pull down the blinds just to be able to get some work done.

"But don't let this warm summer day fool you," she added. "I do hope someone warned you. The winters here... well, harsh would be an understatement. They start in late October and they can last well into April. We've even had snow in May."

"No kidding," he said, trying to sound—actually, he didn't know how he was trying to sound. Appreciative of the information? Fascinated? Flexible? He couldn't shake the feeling that she came in here having already decided that she wasn't going to like him. That she wished he'd say, "Oh? Didn't know that. Guess this place isn't for me after all. Thanks, anyway." He decided to aim for flexibility. "Well, I think I'm up for it. I grew up in Minnesota. Still have family there."

"There's nothing like winter in the Adirondacks. Did you see the railings outside on the walking paths? Those aren't just for decoration. You need to hang on when the gusts kick in. And make sure you've got good winter gloves because if you can't grip the railing, you'll go flying backward. There's an art to weathering a winter here. That's how you know who the newcomers are—they're the ones plummeting down the hill."

He started to laugh, picturing dozens of professors in overcoats and plaid scarves losing their grip and sliding downward, arms and legs flailing, some even doing backward somersaults. But when he looked at her, he saw she wasn't trying to joke. He put the back of his hand to his mouth and cleared his throat.

"Thank you. Thanks for the advice," he said. "I'll check my winter gloves for sure."

She turned from the window to face him. "Have you found a place to live yet?"

He nodded, glad for a change of subject. "I'm renting a small house about ten miles east. Over in Lake Summers."

"Oh, I've heard of that. Beautiful little summer town, right? Lots of availability this time of year, I suppose. I expect you got a good deal. So, you're ready to embrace our country life, it seems. I had heard Pine Beach College is more of a city school?"

"Smack dab." He dropped his gaze downward. *Smack dab.* Who talked like that? "I mean, it's in a downtown area. No real campus to speak of. But when I say it's amazing here, I mean, curriculum-wise, too. Not just… landscape-wise. PBC is pretty new and more of an… engineering and technical, that kind of school. The liberal arts courses are mostly… not so much of a focus…" He let the end of the sentence fade. She was making him flustered. The sooner he stopped babbling, the better.

"It gets quiet in the winter here," she added. "Not at all like a city. Everyone hunkers down."

"I like quiet," he said.

"Although in two weeks it's going to be total pandemonium. The students returning and the freshmen settling in and all the parents coming to help. Like nothing you've ever seen. A cyclone."

"I like cyclones," he said. Then he shook his head, his fists balled, when he saw her turn to face him, eyebrows raised. "I don't mean that literally, of course. I just mean, I like excitement. Of students coming back, school getting started…"

She nodded. "I hear you'll be working on another paper this fall."

"Yes. Yes, I will," he said. He saw she was waiting to hear more, which meant things were about to get worse. He was still unsure of his topic, and he knew he'd have trouble describing his research. "In some ways, my idea is still pretty unformed," he said. "But I'm looking at the concept of expressions of love. Where we choose to express love, and where we promise to love, lock in our love, so to speak. Looking at the association between love and bodies of water. Why bridges and beaches and lakes are so connected with love stories. Looking at literature and history, and even verses from the Bible. The whole phenomenon of using padlocks on bridges to symbolize forever…"

She nodded and walked back to the door. "Yes. Well, I should let you settle in." He was not impressing her. "Welcome again, Aaron," she said. "It's delightful to meet you. Let me know if you need anything. We're glad to have you on board."

She left, and Aaron puffed out his cheeks, then slowly let the air out. There was always politics at play in a college, and he knew he must be in the center of a power struggle. His mentor, Samuel Bates, had been the one to reach out to him after reading in the *New York Times* about his research last fall. He said he wanted Aaron to come to Gorson, and he'd be glad to use his influence if Aaron was interested. Aaron could tell from the way Clara had looked at him, the way she'd spoken to him, that his arrival challenged her authority as department chair. And she wasn't happy about it.

Although maybe he was overreacting. He looked back out the window she had opened, the breeze too warm to be entirely refreshing. Maybe she was cold toward everyone at first. Maybe she needed time to get to know him. Maybe he was just reading her wrong. It wouldn't be the first time.

I don't even know where to begin, the email had continued. *I haven't known all that long myself. And then once I knew, I promised not to tell…*

He leaned on the windowsill, his weight on his wrists. It had been a fluke, his ending up here in the Adirondacks, so far from anywhere he'd ever lived before. But it was the story of his life, accidents and misunderstandings and flukes. He'd been teaching at PBC, and his students weren't particularly interested in his course, Ancient Greek history. What they loved was sports—and that's why he'd come up with the idea for that paper, a look at how societies have historically worshipped athletes as heroes. It wasn't a particularly revolutionary argument, just a way of engaging his students. But the paper earned him a mention in a piece on freshman education in the *New York Times,* and the offers came pouring in. He hadn't thought seriously of accepting any of them. He was comfortable at PBC. Until that email came. And he decided he needed to get as far away as he could.

He walked to his desk and sank into the chair. Taking his phone out of his pocket, he dialed his brother's number, wanting to hear a familiar voice.

"Hey, the disappearing man," Neil said. "How's it going?"

"Good, good," Aaron answered. "Pretty. Quiet. Not for long. But for now."

"Find a place to live? Ready for me to come visit yet? Joanie and the kids would love to see you. Joanie was just saying you were supposed to be coming here this week."

"Yeah. I know. Everything just happened real fast." He paused and rubbed his forehead with his fingers. "Hey Neil, I have to ask you something," he said. "And don't take anything from it. Just answer, okay?"

"Okay," he said. "What's going on?"

"Look, do you think…" He hesitated. "Did Mom and Dad… you know. Like Tanya?"

"What?"

"Just that. Did they like Tanya? Tatiana?"

"Did they *like* her?"

"Yeah, did they like her?"

"What are you talking about? That was a thousand years ago."

"It was thirteen. Thirteen years."

"And you're asking me now if they liked her?"

"Yeah. I just want to know. Did they like her?"

"Sure, they liked her. I guess they liked her. They liked all your girlfriends. Well, maybe not the one with all the piercings."

"Do you think they wanted me to end up with her?"

"Tanya? I don't know. Maybe. I think they thought you were a little young to be so serious."

"I was twenty-six."

"Yeah. Young. I don't know, I thought you were younger. But they liked her fine. I liked her, too. From what I remember. We didn't know her very well. She was in New York back then, wasn't she?"

"Do you think… do you think they would have acted like… do you think she got the impression they didn't want us together…?"

"They liked her fine. She came for Thanksgiving one year, right? Aaron, what the hell is this all about?"

"It's nothing, I'm trying to figure out… I don't know. I really don't know. Forget it." He smiled and shrugged, trying to look casual, even though his brother couldn't see him.

"You okay?" Neil asked.

"I'm fine. I'm great. I'm tired, I guess. And my house isn't ready. The electricity isn't even connected. But it'll be fine. You guys should come visit."

"We will. Columbus Day weekend."

"Say hi to Joanie and the kids."

"I will, I will. Stay in touch, okay?"

Aaron agreed and said goodbye, and then returned his phone to his pocket. He looked across the room again at his two pitiful boxes of books. They were all he had. This was how he'd been living his life since Tanya left him. Traveling light.

Except those boxes didn't tell the whole story.

There was also that email.

And a huge decision that had *forever* written all over it.

CHAPTER FOUR

Caroline pressed her hands together as she walked to the curb, her pointer fingers against her lips and her thumbs hooked under her chin. It was hard to believe: aside from the "welcome home" sign above the door, the Victorian-style building just past the Jason Drawbridge hadn't changed at all. It was still the Lake Summers Grill, the place where she'd practically lived all those years ago. She could almost feel the cushioned stool beneath her as she sat at the bar doing homework, or the soft velvet of the sofa by the fireplace where she so often curled up and fell asleep while Maxine closed out the register and Gull wiped the tables. And yet, everything also seemed the tiniest bit smaller. The white porch, the wooden door with the copper-colored doorknob, the tall windows along the façade—they looked as though someone had minimized them ten percent on a computer. Why did she remember the steps as nearly insurmountable? There was a time she'd had to grab the banister to scale them. Even the drive over the drawbridge was quicker than she expected. Main Street had never before struck her as so narrow.

And it felt… magical. Yes, that was the word—magic. As if the town had remained fixed in time and compressed in space; as if it had resisted the pull of the outside world, holding itself tightly together, the way Lee used to pull her arms up out of the sleeves of her buttoned-up winter coat and press them against her body as they walked along Michigan Avenue in December on their way to Millennium Park to see the big Christmas tree.

She'd warn Lee that it was dangerous to do that: if she tripped, she wouldn't be able to catch herself and would fall flat on her face. But Lee didn't listen, she just kept her arms inside, enjoying the illusion of power over the cold as she swayed her body from side to side so her empty sleeves flew around her.

Caroline walked forward toward the banister, her fingers still against her lips. The thing was, there was something unsettling, too, about the way the town looked. And it made her anxious, the same way she'd felt seeing Lee so vulnerable, without her arms to brace her against a fall. The whole town appeared to have been encased in a bubble. A snow globe. And that made her an outsider looking in. Yes, she could make out all the details—the colors, the textures—but now she was no longer a part of the place. She wasn't one of *them,* the people who lived here. She'd been gone too long. She hoped the feeling was temporary and would dissolve as soon as she went inside the restaurant. But a part of her feared it was permanent. Was that what happened when you left a place you loved when you were a child? Did you need to come back regularly to stop the walls from forming?

"Mom, are you *praying?*" Lee said as she opened her car door.

"What? No!" Caroline said. She turned toward her daughter and noticed that Lee looked different, too. She shook out her hand, trying to rid herself of that thought. "No, silly, I'm just looking, at—"

"Is that Caroline?" came a voice from above. She turned to see the front door wide open, and Maxine standing on the landing.

"It's me!" Caroline called back.

Maxine clapped her hands, then came running down the steps and circled Caroline's waist with her arms. Caroline returned the hug, breathing in the familiar fragrance of lavender-scented lotion. Then Maxine stepped back and grasped Caroline's hands, spreading them wide as she shook her head.

"Oh my, look at you!" she said. "You are beautiful. Just like I knew you'd grow up to be. My goodness, I have been waiting to have you back here for so long!"

Caroline squeezed Maxine's hands, remembering anew how much she'd always loved her. Like the town, Maxine felt smaller, too, her shoulders thin through the top of her white blouse, her shoulder blades feeling fragile beneath Caroline's hands when they'd hugged. Had she always been so tiny? Caroline wondered if she could have reinvented Maxine in her mind after she left for Chicago. Did she imagine Maxine bigger and stronger and more commanding because that's how she wanted Maxine to be? Because only by being strong and powerful would Maxine have been able to come to Chicago and rescue her and bring her back—as she had desperately wanted Maxine to do?

"I'm so glad to be here," she said as she looked up close at Maxine's face. Caroline could see that the years had taken their toll—the thin skin alongside Maxine's eyes was pleated, like a fan partially open, the creases numerous and extending beneath her bottom lids. Her hair was no longer the rich reddish-brown Caroline remembered, but more translucent, a mixture of gray and silver and sand. It was shorter than when Caroline was young, reaching now just below her ears in a kind of windswept style, the waves blending and then parting. Although Maxine and Aunt Risa were probably close in age, Maxine was less styled, the years of her life much more apparent on her face. They were both lovely, but in such different ways.

"So this must be Lee," Maxine said, and Lee stepped up beside them and extended her hand, just as Aunt Risa had trained her to do from the time she was eight or nine. But Maxine wasn't a handshaker. She took Lee's hand and wrapped her own two around it. "What an exciting time for you, going into your senior year of high school. I understand you'll be visiting colleges while you're in town. Smart certainly runs in the family." She turned to Caroline. "My, oh my," she said, her voice breaking. "Do you know how much she looks like your mother? Those brown eyes, that smile. It's like seeing Lily forty years ago."

Caroline looked at Lee, and she felt her throat tighten. Did Lee really look like her mother? It was hard to tell. Her mom had always seemed old to her. *Mom* age. But thinking back now, she could see the young woman her mother had been. In her twenties. Not all that much older than Lee.

"Well, you two must be exhausted, with all the traveling you did today," Maxine said, giving Lee's hand a squeeze. "And I'm sure you're hungry. Let's go on in so you can say a quick hello to Gull, and then you can go relax. He is dying to see you both."

"Oh, Gull! How is he?" Caroline said.

"He's fine. Has all those grandkids now, out in California. Keeps threatening to move out there and close up the Grill for good. He always says he won't spend another winter in this empty, frozen town. But he never leaves."

Caroline laughed. "He was always complaining. The humidity, the snow, the rain, the tourists, even the lake—too many birds."

"Not about you, though. He adored you."

"Who's Gull?" Lee asked as they followed Maxine up the steps.

"The chief cook at the Grill," Caroline said. "He made the best grilled-cheese sandwiches when I was younger. I don't know how he did it, but the cheese was so smooth and thick and the bread was crispy on the outside but soft when you bit into it. Everyone at school was so jealous of me, that I got to do my homework sitting at the bar eating Gull's grilled cheese."

"At the *bar?*" Lee said.

"Well, yes. Things were quieter during the winter, and the restaurant would be empty after school, and I'd go in and sit at the bar, with a big grilled-cheese sandwich and hot cocoa with whipped cream—"

"There she is!" came a husky voice as they walked inside. It was Gull, lifting the panel at the end of the bar and jogging toward them, his arms outstretched. In contrast to Maxine, he seemed to have expanded since Caroline had last seen him, his concave chest from the old days now broader, his waist thicker, his face wider. But he also looked mellowed, not nearly as gruff as he'd come across to her when she was young. Maybe it was because the dark, dense growth of hair he'd always had around his chin was now gray and sparser, so his blue eyes were more apparent. He was wearing a gray button-down shirt but he was missing the white, stained apron and the New York Yankees baseball cap she remembered.

"Caroline!" he said, wrapping his arms around her and patting her back. "Oh lord, it has been way too long. And is this Lee? Welcome, welcome! What do you know! Caroline has a kid all grown and going to college!"

"Gull!" Caroline said. "You look great!"

"Life's been good, can't complain," he told her. Then he swept his arm outward. "We've made a few changes since you were last here. How does the old place look?"

The restaurant was quiet, just a few occupied tables, which was typical in the evenings this late in August, when people in town for the summer would have started to take off. Uncrowded and cool with the lights dimmed, the dining room looked wonderful. Updated for sure. The old backless barstools she remembered were now tall bar chairs with classic wooden frames, and modern white ceiling fans hung from above. The wood tables looked polished and new, and one entire side wall had been replaced by glass doors overlooking an expanded outdoor deck.

"It's beautiful," she said. "Fancy, actually. What happened? I have a distinct memory of you and Maxine always complaining about the owner never wanting to spend any money…"

"Oh, we can talk about this place later," Maxine said. "These two are exhausted. Come, let's get your bags, I'll set you up in the house, and then you can decide if you want to come back here to eat or let me bring you a tray of sandwiches."

"No, no, I don't want to put you out," Caroline said. "We have a reservation up at the Lake Summers Resort. I only meant to stop by and say hello before we checked in."

"Of course you're staying with me," Maxine said. "I have the room all ready."

"But it's two weeks, other than maybe a night or two in Boston. That's way too much—"

"I wouldn't have it any other way," she said. "I've barely changed that room since you were a little girl. Oh, I guess I bought a trundle bed when Lola—that's Jackie's little girl—was born. She stays over sometimes, and I tell her stories about the pretty girl who used to live there long ago."

"Oh, I forgot that he's married!" Caroline said. "And he has the one daughter?"

"Two, actually. And twins coming this winter. He's a high-school guidance counselor now, up in Buffalo, and his wife, Beth, is a chef. They rent a little house by the lake for August. You'll see them all tomorrow. They'll be by for breakfast."

"And Ben? How's Ben?"

"He's good, too. Married with a daughter, and living in New York City, has some fancy consulting job I don't even understand. He'll be here for the Moonlight Carnival on Labor Day weekend—you're staying through Labor Day, right? So let me get you settled in. Lee looks like she's about to fall asleep—no need to come back here to eat, I'll bring sandwiches to you."

"You don't need to do this," Caroline said. "I already put the hotel on my credit card—"

"And I'll call the front desk and tell them to cancel it. You're in Lake Summers now, no such thing as a non-refundable deposit. Besides, I already made up the beds, and I don't want to have done that for nothing. Come on, you'll get a good night's sleep, and we'll send you out with a big breakfast tomorrow."

Caroline reached out and hugged Maxine. Though she had protested, she couldn't imagine anything better than staying with her, enjoying her home and her hospitality. That was far better than any hotel, even one as nice as the Lake Summers Resort. Still, she felt guilty about Lee, who was slumped in a chair, her elbow on the table and her chin on her closed fist. Lee had beamed as she looked over the resort's website while they drove from the airport, reading aloud the spa services and elaborate room service menu. She loved little luxuries, like hotel chocolates and fluffy towels folded neatly on a heated rack in the bathroom, like mini bottles of floral-scented shower gel and fragrant bars of face soap wrapped in thick, decorative paper. It had been part of the deal when she'd originally proposed the trip to Lee. Aunt Risa had taken Lee on a trip to Charleston last summer to visit some retail clients, and they'd stayed at one of the most famous hotels in the city, a place that served cheese and fruits and sparkling cider in the lobby each afternoon, and platters of fancy sugar cookies and liqueurs at night; that delivered umbrellas to their room when it rained and had icy bottles of regular and flavored water waiting whenever they returned from outside. Lee talked about that hotel still. Caroline glanced at Lee to gauge her reaction to this change in plan. She was glad to see her daughter didn't seem bothered.

She tapped Lee's shoulder to get her up on her feet and then headed out of the restaurant. Back in the car, she steered her way down the narrow alley alongside the Grill, past the long metal staircase that led to the deck and behind the restaurant, where Maxine's small, Cape Cod-style home was located. She parked close to the house, where Lee and Maxine were waiting, and she and Lee pulled out their suitcases and wheeled them to the front walk. The house had flowers in the window boxes and a bright-green door, just as vivid as it had been when Caroline lived there. What was different, though, were the automatic lights that flipped on, cool and amber in the clear night air. "I'm impressed," Caroline said.

Maxine laughed. "I'm afraid you may find some changes since you were a little girl," she said. "Not many, I assure you. But life moves on."

She opened the unlocked door and held it as Caroline and Lee stepped inside to the living room. Yes, indeed, there were changes here, too. The wood floor appeared freshly stained, and the furniture looked fairly new, the fabrics clean and bright. Yet the style of the furnishings was totally recognizable: homey and sweet. The floral sofa featured lavender peonies and yellow daffodils, and the wing chairs were an inviting plum-colored velvet. The large stone fireplace was still the centerpiece of the first floor.

"So, Lee, I thought about putting you in the guest room downstairs, which used to be Ben's room," Maxine said as she led them to the staircase. "But then I thought you'd prefer to be upstairs here with your mom. Jackie had the room across from her and oh, the pranks they used to pull on poor Ben."

"Like what?" Lee asked.

"Worms in his lunchbox. Snails in his shoes. The usual torture. But they were good to him too. Always took him with them when they went biking or to the park, or helped him with his homework. And then there were the times the three of them were in cahoots together. Remember, Caroline, how the three of you would convince Gull you'd eaten a good dinner so he'd let you make ice-cream sundaes? I was so angry when I learned about that little scheme."

Caroline nodded. "We weren't allowed to eat at the Grill for a week."

They reached the top of the steps. There was a bathroom straight ahead and two bedrooms, one on either end of the landing. Maxine led them into the one on the left and switched on the lamp on the night table. Caroline smiled when the light came on. It was still her old bedroom. Although the furniture was new, the ambiance was lovely and romantic as it had always been, with the dormer windows and long window seat. There were a dresser, desk, and night tables, all white-painted wood, and the trundle bed had a white iron headboard. The second mattress had been pulled out and set up alongside the first, both sporting rosebud sheets and pale-blue coverlets. A child-sized armchair sat in the corner beside a bookshelf filled with picture books, no doubt for Jackie's little girl.

Caroline wheeled her suitcase toward the bed. There had always been such a good feeling in this room. Such good energy. She remembered those first frightening nights after she'd moved in, the horrible nightmares she'd had about being lost. Maxine had come running when she cried out, and then sat on the foot of her bed until she fell back asleep. She thought now that it was no wonder those nightmares hadn't lasted more than a few nights. It was a room that screamed out "home."

Maxine walked around the beds and switched on the other lamp. "Well, goodnight, pretty ladies," she said. "You know where the linen closet is, Caroline, help yourselves to towels and shampoo, extra blankets, whatever else you need. I'm sure Gull has finished the sandwiches—I'll bring them so you can both have a little bite before you turn in. What are your plans tomorrow?"

Caroline looked at the calendar on her phone. "We have two college visits. The first is at ten thirty." Caroline had purposely made the next day a college tour day. It was Sunday, so it wouldn't be possible to go to Village Hall to try to speak with anyone official about the garden. And she liked the idea of spending the first full day here focused on Lee. She figured they'd have time to talk about the garden, and if she told enough stories about how important it was, Lee might actually want to help in the effort to save it.

"Okay, we'll get a nice early start, so you'll have plenty of time to get there," Maxine said. "Gull will have breakfast ready at eight. Good night, sweeties. Sleep well."

Caroline nodded and walked her to the door, then turned back into the room. Lee had already taken off her sneakers and was lying on the second mattress, her head on the pillow.

"Are you disappointed about the resort?" Caroline asked as she opened her suitcase and brought some clothes over to the dresser.

Lee yawned and shook her head. "No. It's nice here. Everything's so pretty. Everyone's so friendly."

"They're great, aren't they?"

"They really love you," she said. "I couldn't believe how Maxine looked when she was hugging you. It was so sweet. She was crying."

Lee was quiet for a moment. "How did this all happen?" she asked.

"How did what happen?"

"I mean, how did you end up here?"

Caroline walked over and sat down on the bed next to her. The same place Maxine would sit on those first nights after Caroline moved in. "I told you. My parents died."

"But what about Meems? People live with family. *We* live with family. And didn't you have grandparents? They were still alive then, weren't they?"

"I don't know much about them," Caroline said. "I didn't know much about Meems and Pops either, until Meems came to get me. I don't think they knew about me for a long time."

"But they were your grandparents," Lee said. "And Meems was your mom's older sister, right? How does a family not know about each other?" She pulled her head up, her weight now resting on her bent elbow. "I mean, my dad died, right? And what if… I mean, what if you weren't around either? Would everyone have just left me alone, too?"

"Of course not," Caroline said and tousled Lee's hair. She didn't want Lee to question the kind of person Aunt Risa was, especially since they were so close, and Lee admired her so much. And Aunt Risa had been a good aunt and great-aunt, for many years now. But Lee was smart, and she was grasping the truth—that something had gone horribly wrong with their family back then. Caroline still didn't completely understand it, even after all these years—and though she couldn't say why, she had never wanted to delve too deeply into it.

"How do you know they wouldn't have?" Lee asked.

"Honey, things were different back then," Caroline said. "My mom moved all the way here with my dad, and Meems and Pops were far away—in Hong Kong, I think—because they were expanding the business into Asia. It was hard back then, there wasn't any internet or email. It was impossible to stay in touch when you were on opposite sides of the world..." She paused. It didn't make sense, what she was saying, and Lee was going to see right through it. It wasn't as though she'd grown up in the Dark Ages. It wasn't as hard for families to stay in touch as she was making it out to be. Not if they wanted to.

Still, now wasn't the time to get into all this. She was tired and her head was fuzzy from traveling all day. She got up from Lee's bed and went to her suitcase. "Are you hungry?" she asked. "Want to get those sandwiches Maxine's bringing back?"

Lee shook her head.

"Okay, then let's get ready to go to sleep. We have another long day tomorrow."

Lee nodded and went to open her suitcase. She pulled out her toothbrush. "Just one more question, okay?"

"Okay." Caroline moved some clothes into the dresser.

"How are you so normal?"

"What?" Caroline asked.

"I mean, most people would be so damaged from all that. Wouldn't they?"

Caroline hesitated. She didn't know how to answer. The only thing she could think to do was to make a joke. "Because I'm a Rantzen, right?" she said. "Just like Meems says. Rantzens are the family we *choose* to be with." She tossed a pillow in Lee's direction. "Now come on, brush your teeth, and let's get some sleep."

A short time later they were both in bed, the night-table lamps off. But under the cover in the dark, Caroline was no longer tired. Lee had fallen asleep quickly, and she could hear her steady, soft breaths. Lee was lucky, she thought—lucky like all kids who grew up feeling safe and wanted. And Caroline had tried like crazy to make sure that was the kind of childhood Lee would have. Even though Lee's dad, Glenn, had died when she was so young, Lee had always been surrounded by a family that loved her. That was the reason Caroline had kept so close to Aunt Risa and Uncle Rich, why she lived on their property and kept working at Rantzen Enterprises even though that was never the career path she'd have chosen to take. It was to keep Lee secure. To make sure she never felt abandoned.

Getting up from the bed, she went to the dresser and changed from her pajamas into a pair of sweatpants and a tank top, and threw on a long black cardigan. She needed to be reassured like she had when she was young. She wouldn't be able to sleep here until she was.

She found a pen and paper on the desk and wrote a note so Lee wouldn't worry if she awoke.

Then she went to find Maxine.

CHAPTER FIVE

Using her phone to light the way, she tiptoed downstairs, remembering all the times she would sneak down to the kitchen with Jackie for a late-night snack. There was always a sweet and delicious treat in the fridge, usually leftovers from Gull's dessert specials: chocolate-chip cookies the size of a dinner plate, or slices of rich blueberry pie, or fudgy brownies alongside a bowl of homemade caramel sauce for drizzling on top. That's how they knew Maxine was expecting them to sneak down—the treats that were waiting. So it wasn't really sneaking at all.

She closed the front door behind her and listened for the latch to click into place. The sound was reassuring as ever: crisp and metallic and decisive. All good, it seemed to say. Padding lightly along the driveway to avoid having any pebbles slip between her feet and her flip-flops, she listened to the rhythmic crunch of gravel shifting beneath her. Sometimes at night when winter had taken hold and the wind was kicking up and the night felt so dark, when Jackie and Ben were fast asleep and Maxine had returned to the Grill to help close up, she'd steal back along this path to the restaurant. She'd curl up on the velvety sofa by the fireplace and take comfort as Maxine went about her evening routines—spritzing tables and wiping them clean with a cloth; filling salt and pepper shakers and twisting the tops back on; sashaying around Gull in what looked like a carefully choreographed pas de deux behind the bar as they wordlessly cleared the workspace, stacking dirty dishes and glasses to take to the kitchen. They both seemed born to be exactly where they were.

Reaching the metal staircase, she made her way up the steps to the deck. The Peek inlet, which ran parallel to Main Street before curving away from Lake Summers and toward New Manorsville, was visible from the far end, and she walked over and leaned on the metal railing to see it. Sometimes at night from this spot, she'd hear the water rippling, but tonight all was quiet. Behind her, though, were sounds coming from Main Street—laughter, the tinkle of a door at an eatery nearby, someone calling, "Hey you guys! Where ya going? Wait up!" and then the sound of sandals smacking the sidewalk. She turned and walked to the street-facing part of the deck. Main Street was so pretty now, with the new streetlamps—globes atop fluted metal poles—sending pools of yellow light onto the sidewalk. She could see silhouettes down the street, teenagers she guessed, still in a summer mood, trying to pretend that August would never end.

Turning her back to them, she leaned against the railing. Yes, they were nearby, those teenagers. Just steps away from the entrance to the Grill. And yet, she felt miles and miles away. In another country or on another planet, even. They were in this town, *of* this town right now, and she was from another era, a time when she belonged here and knew this town as well as anybody. She remembered how deliciously poignant late August had been when she lived with Maxine and the boys: the nights growing chilly, the stores posting fall hours or announcing their upcoming closure for the winter, their signs bearing the hopeful message, "See you next spring!" Cars would sport rooftop carriers, and suitcases would be visible through hatchback windows. The town emptied gradually—so much so, she'd sometimes wished everyone would hurry up and leave. Countdowns could be harrowing. Like the countdown the week before Aunt Risa came to take her away. "Just tell her to come already," she'd beg Maxine once she'd realized leaving was inevitable. "Just get it over with."

But Aunt Risa had work commitments. Her plans were made. She was coming on September 5th in time for Caroline to start seventh grade in her new school. Nothing would change that, Maxine had said.

Pushing herself away from the railing, she walked toward the sliding glass doors. Only one deck table was occupied, a small, square one tucked in an alcove, where a man and a woman sat catty-corner, their chairs close, a votive candle flickering before them. Their heads were nearly touching, the woman's silky hair gliding forward as their forks met on the plate. Maxine liked to close the deck early when she could, but she never interrupted couples. One time late at night, Caroline had found Maxine sitting at a table, her cheek resting on her palm and her eyes closed, while a couple sat outside. She'd curled up in the next chair and fallen asleep, too, her head on the chair's arm.

Caroline slid open the glass door and stepped into the restaurant. Maxine and Gull were standing together behind the bar, studying some papers. Gull looked up when the door opened.

"Well, looky who's still awake," he said and tapped Maxine's hand. "What's the matter, Sweet Caroline? Maxine got you on that hard trundle bed? I told her those mattresses are no good. No wonder you can't sleep."

"Oh, Gull, it's fine," Caroline said. Gull always teased as a way of showing he cared. Of course, he'd show his affection for Maxine in other ways, too—like making too much stew or chicken riggies so she would have leftovers to take to the house, or sending her home on evenings when she looked tired, even though no other employees were on the schedule and he'd have twice as much to do to close up. Caroline never fully understood their relationship. She'd always wondered if there was more to it that she didn't see.

"I thought I was tired, but I guess not so much," Caroline said. "I'm still on Chicago time. It's not even ten o'clock for me."

Maxine came around the bar, her pleated blue floral skirt free to sway without the white apron she'd been wearing before. "Lee asleep?" she asked.

"Of course. She's a teenager. She can sleep anytime, anywhere."

"That's a skill that doesn't last." Maxine chuckled. "So what can I get for you, honey? Tea? Glass of wine, maybe? I left some sandwiches for you in the house. But maybe you'd like something else?"

"No, I'm fine. I just wanted to sit here for a bit. You should be closing up, I don't want to interrupt."

"Please, we're not even close to closing. Gull's got one more pickup to prepare. And there's that couple out on the deck. I think he's about to pop the question."

"Not a chance," Gull said.

"They're awfully lovey-dovey," Maxine insisted.

"He lost his nerve."

"They're still drinking and eating…"

"But the moment's gone. I'm telling you. Or would you like to make it interesting?"

"Oh, big talker. What did you have in mind?"

Caroline laughed. She loved the banter between these two, how much they enjoyed each other. She'd wondered from time to time whether she'd ever have that. Whether she and Will could ever be that way. Could they come together, if she gave it a chance? But there was an energy, an attraction, between Maxine and Gull that everyone could see. She knew she'd never have that with Will. She'd be fooling herself if she thought she could.

Maxine waved Gull off, ultimately deciding not to bet. She turned to Caroline. "No telling how long they'll be out there," she said. "You're doing me a favor, keeping me company. Come on, the kitchen's yours. What can we get you?"

Caroline tilted her head toward the deck and raised her eyebrows. "Was that raspberry custard pie I saw out there?"

"Good eye!" Gull said. "And good timing, just one slice left. Go take a seat, the both of you."

Caroline followed Maxine to a small table, and Gull followed a few moments later with a large helping of the pie, along with two dessert plates and two forks. Then he went back to the bar and returned with two mugs and two tea bags. Caroline wasn't surprised to see they were Maxine's favorite tea, blueberry ginger. "A sweet finish always makes for a good sleep," he said as he walked away, taking a dishcloth off his shoulder and swinging it the way a cowboy might swing a rope, or a lifeguard at the pool a whistle. Tools of the trade.

"He is the nicest man," Caroline said.

"He's okay," Maxine said with a wink. She dropped her tea bag into her mug. "I hope it wasn't a mistake to put you in your old room."

Caroline shook her head. "No, not at all. I feel almost too comfortable. Maybe that's the problem. It was so long ago, and I can't help thinking how much happened since then. It's so strange to have two different parts of your life that are so unconnected."

Maxine nodded. "Like mother, like daughter. Your mom felt that way, too."

"Did she?" Caroline said. "I guess that makes sense. Although she chose to come here. I'm the one who had to leave." She picked up her fork, then put it back down. It was strange, that she had said that, about having to leave. As though she wanted Maxine to hear she was still mad at her for letting her go. She didn't mean to bring that up. And she'd never want to make Maxine feel bad—certainly not after this wonderful welcome. She turned her thoughts back to her mom. "I wish I remembered her more," she said.

"You were so young," Maxine said, and Caroline was relieved she'd decided not to respond to her quasi-accusation. "I'm so sorry you didn't get to know her better, too. She was wonderful."

"She was, right?" Caroline asked, leaning forward.

"Oh, Caroline, she was the most lovely person," Maxine said. "So much fun. Everyone loved her. All the kids in town wanted to take those art classes she taught at the library."

"I remember that," Caroline said. "I felt so lucky because she was their teacher, but she was my mom. I was the one who got to go home with her each day."

"Oh, and the things we'd do with you and Jackie and Ben, going to the lake or decorating the lawn with plastic ghosts and fake spiderwebs for Halloween, or sledding down the hill by the Public Works Building. Your dad was working so hard back then, so she was on her own a lot and I was on my own, and we were so glad to have each other. Do you remember that Halloween your mom and I dressed up as punk rockers? With the wigs and tons of eyeliner, and I was carrying around Ben's toy electric guitar? Oh, such fun. So much… fun…"

Caroline saw Maxine's eyes get watery. "Oh, no, I've made you cry twice today. I didn't mean to do that."

"No, I'm okay," Maxine said. "They're good tears, because I'm with you now. And you have to start eating, you hear me? Your mother would be furious if you left behind even one crumb of Gull's pie. I'm just so glad you're here, you and Lee. Even if it's only for a visit." She squeezed Caroline's hand on the table. "So how are your aunt and uncle?"

"They're fine. My aunt just won this big industry award yesterday."

"And the company's doing well?"

"It's doing great. Getting bigger all the time. We moved into a new office park outside of Chicago because we're growing so fast. She's adding a new South American office and another one in Australia."

"How exciting it must be."

Caroline nodded, and the nod turned into a shrug. "I guess. Not so much for me. I'm just administrative. The only reason I have a big office and a VP title is because I'm family. And the mother of the heir apparent."

"Lee?" Maxine jutted her chin forward and knitted her eyebrows. "She's still a child."

"Of course she is. But my aunt's already decided she'll head up the company someday. She's been grooming her practically since kindergarten. She's determined that Lee will go to Alvindale University, just like she did. She even made a huge contribution to build a new business research wing on the campus because she thought that would guarantee that Lee would get in."

Caroline looked down at her tea. "Let's not talk about all that. It makes me feel frustrated. Let's talk about the garden instead. What can I do—who should I talk to first?"

"I don't know if that's going to make you any less frustrated," Maxine said. "I don't know if talking to anyone will make a difference."

"But why not?"

"Oh, honey, there's been so much disagreement about what to do with that land," she said. "Things change, priorities change. All this fuss now, that it's not safe, that the slope is too steep, that people shouldn't be wandering back there."

"I never thought it was unsafe." Caroline rubbed her chin with her thumb. "I know Mom didn't either."

"Neither did I," Maxine said. "But the storms and the run-off have had an effect over the years. It's definitely steeper and more slippery. And then there was this incident a couple of winters ago. A few teenagers were there after dark and one of them took a spill down the slope and broke his arm. And everyone started worrying that if the inlet hadn't yet frozen solid and he fell in, it could have been disastrous."

"But can't they put a fence there? There used to be one, right? I remember it, a pretty wood fence."

"There was talk of a new fence, but some people didn't think that was a good enough solution. And then came this push to enlarge the library, and people started thinking if they razed the garden, they would have plenty of room to expand back there."

"But isn't there any other way to expand?"

"I suppose they could come up with another idea. But many people think this is the best choice."

Caroline sat back in her chair. "Mom didn't build the garden for herself. She did it for everyone," she said. "She saw this empty patch of ground behind the library and she knew what it could be like."

"Honey, I know. This was her adopted home. The garden was her gift to the community."

"So how can they turn their back on that? And cover up that space with a bigger building? There has to be another solution. There has to." She shook her head, remembering how her mom would bring her to the garden as soon as the first sign of spring approached. How together they'd clear out the weeds and rake the dirt and scatter seeds. How her mom would so carefully choose the flowers each year, a mix that would bloom at different times from late spring to fall. She wanted the garden always to be full of surprises, never the same no matter if you visited it every week or just a few times over the summer. "You don't make gardens for today," she'd say when April rolled around. "You make them for tomorrow and the tomorrow after that."

"Isn't there someone I can talk to?" she said. "And make my case?"

"We tried," Maxine said. "Gull and I went to every town meeting. You should have heard Gull telling stories of how your mom would come for lunch and sit at the bar and pore over catalogs and magazines to pick the most fragrant and vibrant flowers. We told them how she would go there to water the plants and add nutrients to the soil and tend to the buds. She'd stand out there with the hose every day, making sure every last flower had enough water."

"You told them all that?"

"Jackie spoke up, too—he got married in the garden. And Ben and his wife came to town and had a ceremony there for their first anniversary. And we told them how your mom and dad paid for all the seeds and supplies themselves, and they didn't have money to spare. And how she would work extra hours in the children's room at the library to make up for the time you and she spent in the garden in the afternoons. We told them about all the marriage proposals and weddings…"

"And… nothing?"

Maxine lifted her arms and let them drop to her lap in defeat.

"So what was I thinking?" Caroline said, her voice breaking. "Why am I even here?"

Maxine paused. "To say goodbye?"

Caroline listened to the words hang in the air, then shook her head. "No," she said. "I won't do that. Maxine, I can't let them destroy this garden. Mom made it because she loved it here. She created it for the future, for even after she was gone. I know that's how she felt. She gave it to the town that welcomed her in. People have to understand that. They have to know what the garden meant. And still means."

"Then go for it, sweetie," Maxine said, balling her fist. "Do it. Make noise, get them to pay attention. Your voice is more important than Gull's or mine. Call the paper, call the mayor. We're here for you, Gull and me. We'll do anything you ask us to—"

A wave of warm air drifted in, and Caroline turned to see the restaurant's front door open. A man in a hoodie and a white baseball cap, imprinted with a "Miami Open" tennis logo, stood in the doorway. He looked around and then raised his hand.

"Hey, Maxine," he called over. "Sorry, I didn't mean to get here so late."

Maxine stood. "No, you're fine," she told him. "Gull's finishing up with your eggplant parm. Go stick your head in the kitchen and tell him to get a move on."

"Got it," he said and strode toward the kitchen.

"Who's that?" Caroline asked.

Maxine sat back down. "He's a visiting professor over at Gorson, that's the pretty college on the route to Albany. Poor guy, he just moved into town and the house isn't ready. Mavis Sobel thought she could keep the summer renters through the middle of August before starting on that renovation, but there wasn't enough time. So he doesn't have any appliances or electricity yet. His furniture is stacked in the garage. He's been sleeping in a sleeping bag on the living room floor."

The man emerged from the kitchen, holding a large paper shopping bag. Gull followed behind.

"Now, eat that as soon as you get home," Gull told him. "I double-wrapped it to keep it hot, but if you wait too long, it's going to feel like you're chewing a tire. Got that? Last thing I need is you telling your colleagues up in that ivory tower that my food tastes like it was made by Goodyear."

"No worries, Gull," the man said. "All I do is rave about your food. This is going to be the restaurant of choice for the entire Gorson faculty."

"That better be true. Otherwise, you can go across the street and start eating smoothies for dinner."

"Hey, don't knock the Smoothie Dudes. Those guys make one mean Raspberry Special." He called over to Maxine. "Put this guy to bed. He's grumpy tonight."

"That's because you keep me up too late," Gull said.

"Don't listen to him," Maxine said, walking over to where the two men stood. Caroline watched from the table. "We've got a couple outside, and I think the guy's going to pop the question. We'll give him as long as he needs."

"I'm telling you, he lost his nerve," Gull said.

"Oh, you stop!" Maxine said. She patted the man's arm. "So, another late night already? Good thing you're single."

"Why would I run home, with no lights and no appliances?" he said. "I might as well stay in the office. Or on the tennis court, if I knew anyone yet who wanted to play."

"That Mavis," Gull said. "Serve her right if you slap her with a lawsuit."

"Nah," he said. "She's doing her best."

"But how are you going to see what you're eating?" Maxine said. "Would you like to stay here and have your dinner?"

"No, I'm fine, thanks," he said.

"Gull, did you put a brownie in there?" Maxine asked.

"Two. Plus the last of the cookies. And some of the garlic rolls. This boy's eating well tonight."

"You guys are too good to me," he said. "When the house is done, I'm going to have to lie and say it's not. I don't want to give up the VIP treatment." He laughed and his eyes met Caroline's. "Oh hey," he said. "I'm sorry. I didn't mean to take up so much time."

"Actually, this is someone you should meet," Maxine said, and motioned Caroline over. "This is Caroline, our very, very good friend. Caroline, this is Professor Aaron Weldon, Lake Summers' newest resident and an esteemed academic specializing in history."

"Esteemed academic, I'll have to remember that one," he said. "Hi, Caroline. Nice to meet you."

Caroline shook his hand. He seemed casual and easygoing for a college professor. She could imagine how, in other circumstances, she'd have been embarrassed to be introduced to someone when she was in sweatpants and an oversized cardigan. But she didn't feel that way at all.

"Caroline grew up here," Maxine said. "She's back for a visit. With her daughter. Who's looking at colleges, coincidentally."

"No kidding," he said. "Where's she looking?"

Caroline named the schools on their list, and he leaned toward her and nodded as she talked, his arms folded across his chest. He was clearly listening intently, and she liked that. And because he was looking at her, she couldn't help but notice his eyes beneath that white baseball cap. Large and brown. Twinkling.

"Good schools," he said. "You have a smart daughter."

"She's mostly interested in applying to Alvindale, out in Michigan," she added. "The business school. That's the family path."

"Can't go wrong with that," he said. "Still, if she's open to alternatives, she might want to consider Gorson. Small and super remote, but a great school. Gorgeous campus, excellent library, great art facilities. Top-notch faculty, too. Present company notwithstanding." He chuckled, and Caroline laughed, too. He was really very charming.

"Could they get in for a tour while they're here?" Maxine asked. "This week or next?"

"Yeah, sure… well, actually no, not so soon, come to think of it," he said. "I heard there's a program starting on Thursday for high-school seniors interested in the arts. It meets a few hours over the week, pretty low-key, mostly a chance to have a little fun. But the admissions staff is running it, so I don't think they're doing tours. Although… if she likes that kind of thing, I can call over. I think those things fill up fast, but maybe they can squeeze her in."

He looked around, then grabbed Gull's pen from the bar and tore off the receipt stapled to the bag with his dinner. "Sorry, I don't have any cards yet," he said. "So I'll just write down my number. Call me if she decides she'd like me to check."

"I will, thanks. This is very nice of you," Caroline said.

"Caroline's here for another reason too," Maxine put in, as Aaron was writing. "Her mother built the garden by the library, the one they're trying to tear down. Have you heard about that? It's an awful mistake, we've been trying to stop it for months. It's a piece of town history."

"Right up your alley, Professor," Gull said.

"No kidding? I'd definitely like to hear about that." He handed Caroline the paper. "I better get going. Would hate to have to tell people my dinner tasted like rubber."

"I'll say you would," Gull said.

"Goodnight, guys. Thanks for this. Hope to hear from you, Caroline." He raised the bag in salute and then walked out the door.

"He's a cutie, isn't he?" Maxine said as Gull went back to the kitchen. "And don't let his humility fool you."

"Oh?" Caroline said.

"He wrote some important paper that was referenced in the *New York Times*. That's what it said in the *Lake Summers Press*. We're just crazy about him. Everyone in town is."

"Well, he was very sweet to offer to make that call," Caroline said. "And I like the way that program sounded. I'd love Lee to consider a school with a good art program. She's a very good artist. You should see her drawings."

"Is that so? You know, your mother was a beautiful artist, too. Maybe Lee would want to attend the program Aaron mentioned."

Caroline considered this. "I don't know," she said. "I'd have to talk to her. She's sure she only wants to study business. Although I'm hoping that being here might open her mind a bit."

She felt a yawn coming on. "I should get back," she said. "I'm getting tired after all."

"We didn't even finish the pie," Maxine said. "Let me wrap your piece up in case Lee wants some." She went to the bar and came back with a white cloth napkin, which she draped over the remains of the slice.

Caroline accepted the plate and kissed Maxine's cheek. "Goodnight," she said. "Thanks again for having us. I'm so glad to be here."

She called a quick goodnight to Gull in the kitchen and then went back across the deck, passing the couple out there, who were still playing with their dessert. They had the right idea. The Grill in Lake Summers in the Adirondacks: proposal or no proposal, why would anyone want to leave?

Heading down the metal steps, she thought about what lay ahead of her these next two weeks. She had to save the garden, and she had to show Lee there was more to life than Rantzen Enterprises. She laughed to herself. Nothing to it. Piece of cake.

But even though she had no idea how she'd reach the first goal, she now saw a possible route toward the second.

And it would start with a conversation sometime tomorrow about Gorson College.

And then, hopefully, a call to Aaron.

CHAPTER SIX

The sunlight streamed in the next morning when Caroline awoke, forming a crisp cone shape on the ceiling. She scooted down in her bed and studied it, letting her eyes drowsily wander along the outline. It had been a long time since she'd slept here, and she'd forgotten how cozy it could be. She shifted her gaze downward to the wall beside the window. The room had surely been painted since she'd lived there, but in the morning light, she noticed it was the same color it had been back when she was young. Cornflower blue. Light but comforting. Like a cashmere sweater. Lifting her head, she looked at the clock on the night table. Six thirty—which meant it was five thirty back in Chicago. Earlier than she usually woke up on a Sunday, but she had no interest in drifting off again. Why would she, when she was only back in town for two weeks and didn't want to waste a minute?

She rolled to her side and looked at Lee, who was fast asleep, curled up in a ball, the coverlet over her head. Lee had been awake when she'd returned last night, sitting at the kitchen table and wrapped in a blanket with her knees up by her chin, devouring one of the turkey clubs Maxine had brought over.

"Oh my God, this is the best sandwich I ever ate," she'd said, tossing her ponytail behind her shoulder as she looked up at Caroline. "This bread is unbelievable—and what *is* this stuff?" She peeled up the top slice of bread to reveal a thick, bright-purple layer spread thickly onto the turkey.

"If nothing's changed, the bread is from Pearl's Café, a few blocks down Main Street," Caroline answered, putting the wrapped slice of pie onto the table. "And the purple stuff is Calio's famous cranberry chutney."

"What's chutney?"

"It's kind of a relish, or a jam, but not exactly," Caroline said. "All I know is it's delicious and Gull uses it on everything. Chutney pancakes, chutney meatloaf even. The Calios have a little farm a few miles outside of town, and they make all these amazing things, but this is the best. Gull used to send Jackie and me out on our bikes every couple of weeks to pick up a few cases. There were these big baskets"—she spread her arms wide—"that we would attach to the handlebars to carry them. They made the bikes so heavy, we could barely make it back."

She sat down opposite Lee at the table and ran her finger along a dab of chutney that had leaked from Lee's sandwich onto the plate. She pressed her finger into her mouth. "I didn't expect you to be up," she said.

"We didn't even eat dinner."

"I know, but you were sound asleep when I left. If you want something really delicious, try this." She slid the pie over and Lee pulled up the napkin and broke off a piece with her fingers. She sniffed in the aroma, and then lifted her chin high and let it fall into her mouth. "Oh my God," she said. "Mom, if we eat like this for the next two weeks, I'm never going to fit into my clothes." She took another chunk. "Maxine's still there? How late does she stay?"

"Until everything's done."

"Does she own the restaurant?"

"No. The owner lives somewhere in Pennsylvania, I think."

"She acts like she owns it. If she works that hard, she should own it." She went back to her sandwich. "What's with her and Gull? Are they married?"

Caroline shook her head. "Just very close."

"Was she ever married?"

"A long time ago. I never knew her husband."

Lee nodded as she chewed, looking deep into her sandwich. Then she lifted her chin, tossing her ponytail back again. "They're so cute," she said. "I really like it here, Mom. I was just thinking about that when you came in. I really like them."

She finished the last bite and then brought her plate over to the sink. "Why have I never been here before?" she said. "Why is this the first time?"

Caroline stood and picked up the remaining sandwiches and leftover pie. "Oh, honey, I don't know," she said. "Life was busy, I guess. There was work and school and so many choices for where to go when you had vacation time…" She wiped off the table. "I'm sorry. I wish now we had come here sooner."

"I used to wonder all the time about your mom and why she lived so far away from her family," Lee said. "But I guess this is the kind of place that someone could want to stay."

Caroline nodded. "It was the biggest adventure of her life, being in love with my dad and running away with him," she said. "I still can't get over how adventurous she was." She rubbed Lee's back. "Okay, we have a long day tomorrow," she said. "Up to bed."

She waited for Lee to leave the kitchen and then switched off the light.

Now fully awake, Caroline got out of bed and put on leggings and a tank top, then went to the closet for her sneakers. There was still a lot of time before she and Lee were expected downstairs for breakfast, and she was anxious to see the garden. She needed to see what all the fuss and complaints were about. If it was truly as disastrous as the paper made out, she wanted time to adjust before she brought Lee there.

Lee stirred in her bed. "Why are you up so early?" she said through a yawn.

"I'm going to take a run," Caroline told her. "Go back to sleep. I'll get you up in plenty of time for breakfast."

She went downstairs and took the key gently from the hook by the door. She didn't want to wake Maxine, who had probably stayed at the restaurant past midnight and was likely asleep in her bedroom off the kitchen. Outside, she proceeded down the alley onto Main Street and stopped to stretch her calves, then started on a slow jog, instinctively taking stock of what was the same and what was different. The drawbridge behind her was the same. The Grill was the same. Mrs. Pearl's was still there, visible up ahead. And Village Hall. The green where they held the summer concerts was still there. So, too, was the bookstore, and the food market, and the hot dog place, Lonny's. And the broad roof of the Lake Summers Resort was still visible up on the hill, with the mountains in the distance beyond.

She went on to enumerate the things that were different. Like the black iron benches along the sidewalk. And the streetlights with the pretty dome tops, which she'd noticed last night. The card store was gone, and the print shop, and a couple of restaurants she barely remembered, replaced by a dance school and a smoothie shop, and a running store. The new places added a modern spark, but they also left her with a sense that the town had moved on without her. She was like the teenager calling out in the dark last night: *Hey you guys! Where ya going? Wait up!*

She picked up her pace, wondering how her mother had felt, moving to a town so far from her family. She had to have missed them, Caroline thought, but she never gave the impression she was sad or regretful. She'd explained one day in the garden that Daddy lived in Lake Summers when he was a boy, and he loved it so much, he wanted to share it with them. "People are like plants, Caroline," she'd said, steering the wheelbarrow heavy with bags of topsoil and gardening tools, her face shaded by her hat's wide brim. "They can put down roots wherever they go, as long as they have love. You can't see the roots because they're hidden. But they're strong and alive, and they're what keep the flowers happy."

Keeping the flowers happy. Caroline had liked the sound of that.

Passing Village Hall, she finished her run and crossed the street to get a cup of coffee at Pearl's Café. The shop used to have just two glass coffee pots—a brown-handled one for regular and an orange-handled for decaf—warming on the counter, but now there was a range of coffee varieties in tall thermal carafes. More upscale for sure, Caroline thought. But there was still so much that was familiar, too: the screen door, which still banged shut when she walked in; the air, which still had that wonderful aroma of baked bread; the floor, which still felt gritty, even this early, with people coming in from their runs by the lake, the soles of their shoes carrying a smattering of sand. Her mom always used to order her coffee light and sweet, and would let Caroline fill her own glass of lemonade from the urn near the wall. She'd loved turning the silver lever and watching the cold liquid flow down.

She bought her coffee and went back to Main Street, taking a left at the post office and starting down Oak. The library, the first building on the right, was exactly as she remembered it—a large white clapboard house with a wraparound porch and a big red door with a large brass knocker. She walked to the back of the building, just as she and her mother used to do, usually with the wheelbarrow. There was a short lawn behind the library and a row of thick bushes. The garden was hidden just beyond that.

She went to the furthest bush on the right, which brought her to the dirt path that weaved through the garden. Starting down the path, she surveyed the scene, like a conductor observing an orchestra or a general inspecting the troops. It wasn't as perfect as when her mother was alive, but it wasn't a disaster either. Yes, there were thick patches of crabgrass and ragweed; but what was more apparent was the beautiful wave of wildflowers, orange and yellow and lavender, blending together like brushstrokes on a canvas of green bushes, a burst of color rising upward toward the morning sun. Clearly, someone was taking care of the garden now. Someone, or maybe multiple people, still cared about it.

She went further down the path until she came to the arched footbridge that rose above a small rocky dip bisecting the garden. Trying not to notice the loose planks and a handful of small holes where the wood had rotted through, she walked to the apex. This was where she and her mom would have their lunch on summer days, sitting on the planks, dangling their legs above the rocks, protected by the horizontal railings. They'd eat cream cheese and jelly sandwiches on Mrs. Pearl's thick, seeded bread, as her mom read picture books they'd borrowed from the library. The stories were often about jungles and forests, and wild animals. Or oceans. Or the darkest of nights, or ghosts. But Caroline never felt scared. She followed her mother's lead, enjoying the darkness and the unknown revealed in the books. She wondered now why her mom always chose those stories. Was it just that she liked adventure? Or was she searching for a way to understand her own life, being in a place so far from her family and everything she'd grown up with?

Leaning on the top railing, which felt a little too loose for comfort, Caroline looked toward the inlet. The slope was indeed steeper than she remembered. But she still didn't think her mom would have found it a good reason to destroy the whole garden. She'd never been one to run away from nature. Even when it would start to drizzle, the early-spring or late-summer mist chilling Caroline's fingers and the tip of her nose, the kind of weather that caused other parents to hustle their kids indoors, her mom insisted on finishing the day's work. "Whoever heard of being afraid of a little shower?" she'd say and help Caroline zip up her rain slicker. How she wished now that her mom had been a little more afraid, afraid enough to put on her own slicker that September day they were planting bulbs for next spring's garden. She wasn't feeling well, she'd been sick all week, and she didn't have her usual energy. That was the day her dad had showed up and twirled her mom around and around, her mom's sleeveless sundress so wet it clung to her, her bangs plastered to her forehead, her arms peppered with raindrops. That was the last day her mother spent in the garden. She died three days later.

Caroline took her phone out of the pocket in her leggings and looked at the time. It was almost seven thirty, and she needed to give Lee a little time to work up an appetite. Lee rarely ate breakfast, but Maxine had said Gull was planning to fix a big one, and he'd be so hurt if they didn't eat heartily. Although, she thought, maybe just the smell of Gull's cooking would get Lee's stomach rumbling. Nobody made pancakes and bacon like Gull. She continued over the bridge and through the second half of the garden, ending up back behind the library building. There, she took a few last sips of her coffee and then tossed the cup into a trash can as she headed back for Maxine's. Her head was filled with memories—but more than that, it was filled with intention. The garden was as much a part of this town as Mrs. Pearl's or the Grill. And it wasn't in such bad shape. It was still beautiful, and it had a place in this town. She simply needed to convince the right people of that.

Back at the house, the kitchen was jumping, with Gull working fry pans on the stove, and Maxine setting the table, which had extra leaves so it stretched nearly to the hallway. Coffee was brewing and oatmeal was bubbling in a cast-iron pot.

"Good morning!" Maxine said as she laid the silverware. The dishes and cups and saucers on the table were a mix of shapes and designs. Aunt Risa would never have allowed a hodgepodge like that, but Caroline loved how casual and homey it looked. "Glad you got to take advantage of the sunshine, they're calling for rain a little later. Did you have a nice run?"

Caroline nodded as she went to help, pulling juice glasses out of the cabinet and setting them beside each plate. "I went over to the garden."

"I thought you might do that." Maxine put a milk pitcher and sugar bowl on the table. "What did you think?"

"It's not in such bad shape. Honestly, I expected much worse. It's a little ragged, I guess, and the footbridge needs repairs. But the flowers were beautiful. They obviously have a groundskeeper who's done the planting and a little bit of upkeep. It just needs some weeding and trimming. I can do some while I'm here. Isn't there a garden club that can pitch in when I leave?"

"It's not if they can, sweetie. It's if they want to. People desperately want a larger library. The children's room was too small when you were a kid, and we've had so many young families move to town since then. And did you look out toward the inlet?"

"It's not so terrible. It's at the bottom of the hill, like it always was. People want a bigger library, I understand that. But it can all be worked out. Let me tell you, I've spent years watching my aunt fight import regulations and government policies and getting her way—and if she can do that, I can fight this. It's not impossible to fight City Hall."

"That's the spirit," Maxine said as she set a platter of muffins on the table.

"You bet," Caroline said with a determined nod. Then she looked toward the stairs. "I should get Lee up. She can be grumpy in the mornings if she doesn't have a few minutes to herself."

"But Lee is up. She's in the living room. Didn't you notice?"

"She is?" She walked toward the living room and looked into the alcove. Lee was on the curved window seat with her opened computer in her lap, talking to a teddy bear of a man sitting in an armchair.

"Who's that?" Caroline asked.

"Who's that? Why, it's Jackie," Maxine said, coming up behind her. "Didn't I tell you last night he'd be coming over?"

"That's *Jackie?*"

"Of course it is. Jackie! Look who's here!"

"Sweet Caroline!" he said as he jumped up from the armchair. She instantly recognized him. He had changed, to be sure, since she'd last seen him almost thirty years ago. His hair, while still dark, was noticeably thinner, and his broad chest was now softer, his belly rounder. But his eyes were still large and bright, his grin still infectious. And he still looked strong and assured, the big brother she'd never forgotten. He was the one who'd found her sitting in the kitchen by herself on the morning of her eighth birthday, still in her coat and hat from the day before, when he and Ben had come as usual to walk with her to school. "I don't think you should go today," he'd said when she lifted her head from the table. "I think I should take you home to my mom." He'd sent Ben on and then brought her back to his house, even though it meant he'd be late for school, and everyone knew that Jack Brogan was never late for school.

"Look at you!" he said and enveloped her in a hug. She wrapped her arms around his neck and hugged him back. "You look prettier than ever!" he said.

"And you're still a suck-up," she laughed.

"And you're still a badass," he said.

"Please, you two!" Maxine scolded.

"Well, she started it," Jackie said. Then he laughed. "Same old Caroline. If it was snowing I'd take you out back and challenge you to a snowball fight!"

"And I'd win!" she said and hugged him again. "So how are you? I have missed you so much!"

"I'm good. Lit, as my students say," he said. "Got a growing family—two girls and a set of twin boys on the way."

"Oh, Jackie, that's so wonderful! When are they due?"

"November. A gift for Thanksgiving. You'll meet my wife, Beth, in a minute, she went into the restaurant to get some ketchup. Sound familiar? Remember, Mom never kept enough ketchup in the cabinet."

"The problem is that you kids would put ketchup on every-thing, and now *your* kids do, too," Gull called to them from the kitchen. "Teach 'em to taste their food and they won't be pouring so much ketchup all the time."

"Okay, that's enough yelling!" Maxine said. "Come on, everyone. These ladies have a busy day and need to eat and get on the road. Gull, where are the eggs and the biscuits, where's the bacon? Lee, there's a big bowl of fruit salad in the fridge, and some of Calio's blueberry jam, can you bring them out? Caroline, the coffee should be ready, can you pour please? Who's starting with oatmeal?"

A few minutes later they were all seated at the table—her and Lee, Maxine and Gull, Jackie and Beth, and their daughters—a preschooler named Lola and a toddler named Cassie. Beth looked warm and uncomfortable, and Jackie was attentive, putting a cushion behind her back and bringing her a big glass of ice water before starting on his oatmeal.

"Caroline, Mom tells us you're trying to save the Lily Garden," Beth said. Caroline noticed Beth had called Maxine "Mom," which she found very touching.

"Jackie brought me there when we were first dating," she continued. "And it was so peaceful and tucked away, and he started telling me these quiet, beautiful stories about his childhood—and I fell in love with him. I'd never seen that side of him before. That's why we got married there. I couldn't imagine a better place." She wiped the corners of her eyes. "Jeez, look at me—I cry at everything when I'm pregnant. Please, someone, change the subject."

Jackie turned and kissed her cheek, then looked across the table. "How about we talk about colleges?" he said, gesturing with an open palm toward Lee. "I've been getting to know your daughter, Caroline. Smart girl. You did good."

"I didn't do anything," Caroline said. "She's her own person."

"Hey, Mom," Lee said. "Jackie was telling me about this electives program he started at his school. They let graduating seniors choose their own short-term internships for half the year."

"It's important for the kids who live in our district," he said. "Our school is small and rural, so we reached out to a lot of companies in Buffalo for financial support. We house the kids in hotels and give them experience with film companies, media companies, law firms even. Gives them a taste of the outside world."

Caroline smiled. This was the family she'd missed. Always thinking of others.

"And they do really well, his students," Lee added. "Two got into Harvard this year, one into Yale, and three got into Alvindale."

"Lee was telling me Alvindale's her top choice," Jackie said.

"It's got a great business school," Lee said. "I really want to go there. I'm taking their pre-college business seminar in two weeks."

"Wow, kudos to you," Jackie said. "I hear that's a selective program. Was it a lot of work to get in?"

"Not really, just a couple of essays and letters of recommendation. And for the marketing class, you have to write a mock business plan."

"No kidding. Do you have a business in mind?"

"I'm only beginning. I'm still trying to come up with a good idea."

"Well, I think the hardest part of this kind of assignment is the concept. Once you know what you're doing, the plan should flow pretty smoothly."

"Are you considering any other schools, Lee?" Beth asked. Cassie started squirming, and Beth put some scrambled egg on the high-chair tray.

"We're scheduled to visit Bearson College and Schylar University today," she said. "And we're supposed to go to Boston

University before we head back home. Plus there are a few other schools my mom is kind of making me see." She feigned annoyance, rolling her eyes, and then grinned at Caroline.

"Obviously this is not a new discussion," Caroline said. "But I believe so strongly in exploring all the options."

"It is good to see a range of schools," Jackie said, as he buttered Lola's muffin. "Even just to rule things out. Or gain a new perspective on your top choice. Information is power. That's what I tell all my students."

Caroline looked at Lee, who was listening closely as Jackie talked. He had clearly made an impression on her.

"Oh, and speaking of colleges, Jackie, Aaron Weldon stopped by the restaurant last night to pick up some dinner," Maxine said. "Caroline met him."

"Aaron stopped by? Still waiting on his house, huh? What a mess." He peeled a banana for Lola. "Wait, he's at Gorson, right? Hey, that's a great school. They're really strong academically and have an excellent reputation in fine arts. And a gorgeous campus, prettiest I've ever seen. Are you able to get over there?"

"They're not giving tours this week," Maxine said. "But he did give Caroline his number. He mentioned an art program coming up for high-school seniors. Just a few hours, a chance to have some fun, he said. Maybe you'd like to do that, Lee?"

Lee shook her head. "I don't think so," she said. "It doesn't sound like my kind of program."

"Maybe not," Jackie said. "But you want a tip? The top schools love when you show them you're well rounded. That's the kind of student they want, someone who's interested in lots of things. My Yale kid, they told him they were sold when he wrote an essay about studying opera. And one of the Alvindales—if I'm not mistaken—she actually took that Gorson program last summer."

"She did?" Lee said.

"Of course, you have to like art," he said. "But if you do, you might want to think about it. It could be fun. They have pretty great facilities there, like nothing you've ever seen in your high school. And if it's only a few hours, you'd still have plenty of time to look at other colleges and be with your mom."

"I don't know," Lee said. "I like drawing and all, but I'm not even that good at it."

Caroline started to object, but then stopped herself. She knew Lee would be embarrassed if she explained how beautifully Lee drew, how her landscapes and her portraits were so evocative. How even the garden she sketched on the plane yesterday was so detailed and so compelling. But Lee always insisted she didn't think much of her work. She called it doodling or playing around. Sometimes Caroline wondered if she downplayed her talent not because she didn't like art, but because it meant so much to her. Because she was scared of failing.

"All the better," Jackie said. "The less serious you are, the more you can enjoy the program Gorson has."

"But don't get your hopes up too high," Maxine said. "Aaron did say he wasn't sure there's still space in the program. By the way, what time is it? We don't want to hold you two up if you need to get on the road soon."

"Everyone have enough?" Gull said. "There's some more pancakes on the counter."

"I'm so full," Caroline said. "Thanks, Gull. Everything was delicious."

"Should keep you two going through the morning," he said. "Got gas in the car? It can be a long way between service stations on these roads. And be careful. They're a lot more winding than what you're probably used to."

"Gull, please," Maxine said. "She's a grown woman."

Cassie started squirming again, and Lola complained that she was tired of sitting. "Guess that's our cue," Jackie said. "Mom, need help with the dishes?"

"No, no, just go ahead," Maxine said. "I'm planning a big family dinner when Ben's in town for the Moonlight Carnival. I'll put you in charge of the dishes then."

"Okay, so troops, file out," Jackie said. He helped Beth out of her chair, then picked up Cassie from her high chair and grabbed Lola's hand. "Bookstore then lake, so Mommy can take a little rest."

"Enjoy your college visits, Lee," Beth said.

"Yeah," Jackie added as he headed to the door. "And let me know if you do get into Aaron's program. I'll be curious to know what you think."

They left the house, along with Gull, who went to start on the Grill's lunch specials. Caroline and Lee helped Maxine clear the table, and then Lee went upstairs to change.

"Beth is so sweet, and Jackie looks great," Caroline said as they started to load the dishwasher. "What a nice family."

"Beth's a doll," Maxine said. "And wait until you meet Ben's wife, Lori. She's lovely too. Let me tell you, I am one lucky mom. Don't think I don't know it."

Caroline sighed. "I missed so much, didn't I? I should have been here for Jackie's wedding. It was in the garden, of all places. And I should have known when the girls were born. I should have been back to see Ben get married, too. I guess I always thought it would be too hard, coming back."

Maxine put her arm around her shoulders. "Well, you're back now," she said. "And that's all that matters. Say, sweetie, would you like to use my shower while Lee's in the one upstairs? That way you'll get a faster start."

Caroline kissed her cheek, then went upstairs to get her clothes and her toiletries. Grabbing her things, she noticed the receipt she'd left on the night table last night with Aaron Weldon's number. She liked how Jackie had encouraged Lee to try the Gorson program not only because it would enhance her college applications, but also because she might simply enjoy it. Pure enjoyment was never a worthwhile objective in Aunt Risa's book, and Caroline was scared her attitude had rubbed off on Lee starting long ago.

She went into the hallway and knocked on the bathroom door. "Hey, Lee?" she said. "Did you want me to call about that Gorson art program? Did you want me to find out if there's a spot?"

"Um… yeah, sure," Lee said. "Why not? Could be fun. Like Jackie said."

"Okay," Caroline said, trying to sound nonchalant. The fastest way to get Lee to change her mind would be if she sounded too enthusiastic. She would wait a little while—it was still early for a Sunday—and then call Aaron Weldon.

She hoped so much he could get Lee in.

CHAPTER SEVEN

"So the science building is down the hill," the tall boy in the "I ♥ Bearson" t-shirt said, walking backward to address the dozen or so parents and students following him. Caroline watched as he checked over his shoulder every few seconds, nearly shouting, "Watch out!" each time he came close to crashing into a tree, tripping over a curb, or marching straight into the path of an oncoming car. Other parents also showed signs of tension, with clenched fists, hiked shoulders, or pursed lips. Why did the schools make their tour guides walk this way? As if there wasn't enough already to worry about. Caroline glanced at Lee, who was gazing at the gray sky, and wondered if she was even listening. She hated dragging Lee places she didn't want to go.

Now the boy was talking about the music and dance studios, and Lee had completely checked out, slowing her pace and tapping her teeth together, as she often did when she was thinking an idea through. Aunt Risa did that, too. One evening that first fall after she'd moved to Chicago, she'd worked up the nerve to tell Aunt Risa that she missed Lake Summers. She'd felt bad complaining when she lived in such a big house and had a beautiful room and plenty of nice clothes, but she couldn't stand feeling sad all the time. "Everyone's different here," she'd said. "I don't fit in." Aunt Risa had tapped her teeth together, then went to her writing desk for a sheet of paper and made a few notes. By that evening, Caroline was enrolled in swim lessons, tennis lessons, and a chess class.

Caroline had never talked to Aunt Risa about Lake Summers again. It wasn't so much that she didn't like the activities. They were fine. But all the kids she was meeting had known each other since they were young, and it was hard to make friends. Being busy didn't stop her from being so lonely.

Now she drifted back to where Lee was, a few steps behind the group. Lee looked up.

"He called her 'mom' to you," she said.

"What?"

"Jackie. He called her 'mom'—'Caroline, remember how Mom never had enough ketchup?' He said it like Maxine was your mom, too."

"Did he?" she said. "I don't think he meant it that way. Lots of people do that—they say 'Mom' when they mean 'My mom.'"

"No, I heard it," Lee said. "He was saying it like she was your mother, too."

"Well, Beth calls Maxine 'Mom,' and she's not her mom, either."

"But it's different," Lee said. "Beth and Jack are married. Beth *is* family. You're not."

Caroline tried to put her arm around Lee's shoulders, but Lee squirmed away, and Caroline regretted reaching out. Lee wasn't looking for comfort, she was looking for clarity. She wanted things to be definitive, a life where two and two always made four. Even if you had to add three and subtract seven and multiply by two and do a bunch of other things, she still wanted the result to be four. How could she accept that sometimes, when feelings were involved, it wasn't that simple?

"I'm sorry that upset you," Caroline said.

"It didn't upset me," Lee told her. "But it makes me feel a little weird. That you have this whole other family I never knew about. And they're acting like they're my family, too. I don't know what to make of that."

"But lots of people have relatives they never met before," Caroline said. "Cousins and second cousins come out of the woodwork all the time. And with these DNA tests, people are constantly finding relatives they never knew before. It's not a bad thing, honey."

"But we're not related. Don't get me wrong, Mom, I like them a lot. They're great. But I feel guilty acting like they're our family. I feel guilty about Meems and Pops." She shook her head. "I just wish I wasn't finding out about all this for the first time." She looked ahead to where the tour guide had stopped. He was pointing to the building behind him. "Great, he's probably talking about something important now, and I don't even know what it is…"

She ran to catch up to the group, and Caroline followed her. The building housed the administrative offices, and the boy was explaining how the college evaluated standardized test scores and weighted them alongside teacher recommendations, high-school grades, and extracurricular activities. Lee moved in closer. This was the discussion she was interested in. With facts and statistics, percentages and averages. Clear guidelines and formulas that made sense.

Caroline stepped away from the group, hoping the boy would finish up before the expected rain kicked in. She felt bad for what Lee was going through. It was one thing to sit with your mother on an airplane and listen to old stories, and another thing to show up someplace where your mom was well known and you were a stranger. She should have been more sensitive, especially since she knew what it was like to suddenly be surrounded by people who acted like family but felt so unfamiliar. That's exactly how she'd felt when she moved to Chicago. Lee was right: it would have been better if she'd known about Lake Summers long ago, instead of having it sprung on her now. She was at a turning point in her life, and she needed Caroline to be her rock when everything else felt fluid and uncertain. Why hadn't she thought ahead and shared her past with Lee years ago?

She went to sit on a bench a few steps away from the group. It was because of what happened that led her to move in with Maxine. It was scary and sad—so sad that she'd even closed off the conversation about her dad when she and Lee were on the airplane coming here. But now it was on her mind—that day before her eighth birthday. Even though her mother was gone four months by then, birthdays were still exciting, and she expected her dad would be planning a special surprise. That's what parents did. She wondered if her dad would bring home the cake from Mrs. Pearl's that her mom always bought, with the toasted coconut shreds on vanilla frosting. She wondered what her present would be—maybe a new bicycle or pink light-up sneakers. Or that beautiful pencil and sketchpad set they'd seen in the window of Bobbie's Palette. Or maybe he'd give her the gold necklace with the linked hearts, the one he'd given her mom the day he twirled her in the rain. He'd told her he was saving it until she was older. But maybe he'd change his mind and give it to her tomorrow.

She'd walked in the house after school that day, her last day as a seven-year-old, waving goodbye to Jackie and Ben. It was January and so cold, and the sun was starting to lower in the icy silver sky, and somehow her dad wasn't home. She always went to Jackie and Ben's house if her dad was going to be late, but he hadn't said anything that morning. She thought he was probably out getting her present or her cake. So she sat at the kitchen table as the house grew darker and colder. She never took her coat or hat off, in case there'd been a mistake, and Jackie would be coming back to get her.

The next thing she knew it was daylight, and Jackie and Ben were there in the kitchen, looking at her. Her coat was still buttoned, and her hat had slid down her forehead, so it was halfway covering her eyes.

I feel guilty about Meems and Pops. It was no wonder Lee felt bad, Caroline thought. The mystique that Aunt Risa had created around the Rantzen name, the Rantzen legacy, was inescapable. Even Maxine had seemed to acknowledge it, that last night that Caroline spent in Lake Summers. "Your aunt is such a smart and accomplished woman," Maxine had said as she tucked a wrapped box with Gull's chocolate-chip brownies, the ones with fudge stripes along the tops, into Caroline's suitcase. "And she's your family." For years Caroline had tried to understand why that meant that Chicago was a better home for her than Lake Summers. But she'd never come up with an answer. She didn't feel like a Rantzen back then.

She didn't still.

*

Lee was more engaged that afternoon, after they'd had a quick lunch at a nearby diner and then traveled an hour north to their next stop. Schylar University had a business school, which made it more interesting to Lee than Bearson, and her eyes stayed glued to the tour guide—who also walked backward, to Caroline's dismay—as she described the wide array of business classes and multiple opportunities for studying abroad. Back at the admissions building, Caroline prepared a cup of coffee from the industrial-sized Keurig machine while Lee went to speak one-to-one with an admissions officer.

Her phone vibrated in her bag as she took her first sip, and she pulled it out. She was surprised to see Will's number.

"Hi," she said. "Anything wrong?"

"No, just thinking of you. Thought I'd check in and see how it's going."

"That's nice of you," she said as she sat down on a deep-cushioned sofa in the lounge area. She hadn't expected to hear from him. They were friends in the office, but never outside of it. She'd implicitly set those boundaries, and he'd respected them. She couldn't remember a time before when he had called just to check in.

"Think Lee will be an East Coaster next year?" he said.

"I wouldn't bet on it. Alvindale is still the hot favorite."

"A girl who knows her own mind, gotta admire that," he said. "So maybe you two should ditch the rest of your visits and relax. Maybe take in a Red Sox game? Or drive up to Maine, spend some time at the beach."

"Maine? That's a trip!"

"Not really. You're right there. Just a short drive up I-95."

"No, it's not, it's all the—" Caroline caught herself, hoping Will didn't hear her gasp. He thought they were in Boston! She forgot that she hadn't told anyone back home that she'd changed her plans.

"I just mean that we may as well keep to our itinerary," she said. "But we'll have some time to relax. Not sure if we'll get to a baseball game. But we'll see…"

The door to the office opened. "Hey, Will, Lee just came out from an interview. I should go."

"Yeah, go ahead. I mostly wanted to say hi. It's going to be a quiet week in the office. Kind of boring. No coffee emergencies or last-minute sweater sprints."

"I really appreciated that. You helped me a lot."

"No problem, it was kind of exciting. A race to find the fix before the boss showed up. Anyway, good luck to Lee, and have fun. Give me a call this week, if you think of it."

"Bye, Will," she said, and then tried to control her shaky breath. She was thrown by that conversation—both the fact that Will had called and the way she had deceived him. She pushed those thoughts out of her mind as she introduced herself to the tall man with wire-rimmed glasses standing beside her daughter.

"Nice to meet you," he said as they shook hands. "Your daughter has a very impressive background. That's quite an internship she had this summer." He turned to Lee and handed her his card. "Feel free to call me if you think of any questions," he said. "I'll look forward to seeing your application."

Lee smiled and thanked him, but as they headed back to the car, she made it clear she didn't think either college they'd seen today was right for her. "The first school was too small and had none of the classes I want," she said. "And okay, yes, this place has a business school, but they don't have enough economics electives, and also not enough language courses, which is what I'm going to need if I'm to start off in the Asia division, which is what Meems thinks. And the business school is on another whole campus. And they don't even have a separate business library…"

Lee continued, and Caroline decided not to respond, just to let Lee talk. She never intended to pressure Lee to like these schools, only to encourage her to keep an open mind. But Lee liked having her future set. And she could be combative when she felt cornered, just as Aunt Risa could. The best response to either of them when they got this way was simply not to engage.

Back in Lake Summers, Caroline parked the car, and they ran through the drizzle upstairs to the Grill. Maxine was behind the bar, talking to a middle-aged man with thick silver hair, who was sitting opposite her finishing up a burger and a beer.

"Well, hello, my travelers," she called and waved them over. "How was today? See anything good?"

"Not really," Lee said. "Is Jackie around? I wanted to ask him a question about my mock business plan for Alvindale."

"Sure, he's on the deck," Maxine said. "Now's a good time to nab him. Beth took the girls back to the house."

Lee went out to the deck, and Maxine motioned Caroline closer. "Caroline, this is Nick Peters, he's a teacher at Lake Summers Middle School. And this is Caroline, who I was telling you about."

"So *your* mom built the Lily Garden?" Nick said. "I always wondered about that. Maxine here mentioned you were in town, and I was remembering the ceremony they had there on the tenth anniversary of 9-11. They read my uncle's name that day and the names of others from around here who died. It was quite beautiful."

"Oh, I'm so sorry about your uncle," Caroline said.

"Thanks," he said, nodding. "It's a long time ago now. But I've been going back to the garden every year on 9-11. Just to remember him. I couldn't believe when I heard they're tearing it down. I'm a teacher, so I know what parents are saying, how dangerous they think that slope is. Still, it's unfortunate they can't fix it somehow."

He finished his beer, then stood and reached into his pocket. "Thanks, Maxine, good burger as always," he said and tossed some bills on the bar. "Nice meeting you, Caroline. Enjoy your visit."

"I will, and thank you for telling me that," Caroline said. She'd loved hearing that story. It made her feel closer to her mom. Even if the feeling would only last a moment.

He nodded and left, and Maxine cleared his dishes off the bar. Then she took a pitcher of iced tea from the mini refrigerator behind her. "Did you get in touch with Aaron?" she asked as she poured Caroline a glass.

"I left a message this morning. Thanks," Caroline said, accepting the tea. She took a sip, then reached for a cocktail napkin off the pile nearby and put her glass on top of it. She watched the wet spot it formed expand.

"What's wrong?" Maxine asked. "I thought you'd like meeting Nick."

"Yes, I did, absolutely," Caroline said. "It's just…" She paused. "It wasn't the best morning. Lee's all confused. I'm starting to regret bringing her here and making her look at colleges she isn't even interested in." She shrugged. "I should never have combined this trip with all the college stuff. I should have brought her here to meet you all long ago."

Maxine lifted her eyebrows. "Why didn't you?"

Caroline shook her head. She didn't want to make Maxine feel bad, by admitting that being here made her remember that birthday morning. "It's not that I didn't think about it. But it never seemed a good time."

She paused, then continued. "You know, I got a call while Lee was being interviewed," she said. "From a friend from work. Well, he's more than a friend, or at least he wants to be. And he's a very sweet guy. But I haven't wanted to date at all. Not while Lee is still home."

"Well, you deserve a life of your own, too, you know."

Caroline twisted her glass on the napkin. "But you know the strangest thing? He knew about the trip I'd originally planned. I'd told him all the stops we were going to make, all the schools we were going to visit. But I didn't tell him that I changed everything. He thinks we're in Boston. And so does Aunt Risa, for that matter. I was with them all on Friday and I didn't tell them anything. Even when he called today, I didn't tell him the truth. Why is that?"

Maxine licked her top lip. "Were you scared they'd be mad?"

Caroline thought for a moment, then shook her head. "No, not mad. But they'd have tried to discourage me. Both of them. Why, though? Why are they so afraid of my past? And why am I so afraid of them? That I feel I have to lie to them?"

Maxine reached over the bar and stroked her forearm. "I don't know, honey," she said. "I guess that'll take some thinking."

Just then Gull came out from the kitchen, an order pad in his hand. "Hey, look who's back," he said as he walked to the bar. "I've got good news. Samantha Mackel just called. She wanted to place an order, and when I mentioned that Caroline's in town about the garden, she said she'd like to talk to her."

"Who's Samantha Mackel?" Caroline asked.

"She's the editor of the *Lake Summers Press,*" Maxine told her. "Oh, this is wonderful news!"

"Why? You think she might do an article?" Caroline asked.

"Can't say for sure," Gull said. "But she's been writing about this library thing for months now, and she sounded very interested in hearing you speak about your mother." He tore a page off the order pad and put it on the bar in front of her. "There's her number. She's hoping you can come by her office a week from tomorrow. I told her I'd pass along the message."

"Thanks, Gull," Caroline said and stood to kiss him on the cheek. He waved her off and headed back to the kitchen, although Caroline knew him well enough to be sure he was glad for the affection.

"How about that!" Maxine said. "This would be big. Everyone reads the *Lake Summers Press.* This really could be the break you're looking for.

"And who knows?" she added. "Maybe by talking things out with her, you won't only save the garden. Maybe you'll get some clarity, too. For yourself and for Lee."

Caroline looked over her shoulder and out the glass doors, where Jackie and Lee were sitting. Yes, that's what she wanted. Clarity.

If she could save the garden and get clarity, that would make this a very, very good trip.

CHAPTER EIGHT

Aaron placed his toasted bagel and cup of iced coffee on the countertop and pulled four dollars out of his pocket. The girl behind the register accepted them, her chin resting on her other hand and her gaze barely lifting as she dropped two quarters into his palm. He laughed to himself as he pocketed the change and headed toward the exit of the student center café. It was that kind of Sunday, the atmosphere warm and loaded with moisture after a sunny morning, the precipitation morphing between a drizzle and a hazy mist. He stopped to take a few swallows of coffee through the sip-lid, although being motionless didn't have the intended effect, as a few drops leaked out and landed square on his t-shirt. He groaned and put the wrapped bagel down so he could swipe uselessly at them with a napkin. Good thing the shirt was navy blue. He went to the tall windows that faced the main part of campus. Library or office? His house was out of the picture, as his landlord had texted that morning to say the kitchen appliances wouldn't be installed until Thursday. The electricity would be spotty at best until then, she'd added, which meant there wouldn't be any wi-fi either.

He gingerly took another sip. Left or right? It didn't matter, the campus would be deserted whichever way he went. The high school program didn't start until Thursday, and dorms didn't open for returning students for another two weeks. Plus, with the weather so steamy, even the summer students living off-campus wouldn't be showing up to hang with friends or play volleyball on the quad the way they did last week, the net tied to a couple of perfectly spaced trees. In Florida he would have jumped on a side, the kids thrilled to have him. Or grabbed one of the kids from the tennis team to hit a few balls. He wouldn't have joined in the game here, though, since no one knew him yet; but still, it would have been fun to see the kids play.

Looking out over the empty quad, he sighed and shook his head. Why was he suddenly so restless? He'd never before minded the stillness of a campus in the summer. It was part of the routine, the exquisite rhythm of college life: Freshmen became sophomores, fall term led to spring, finals had their moment and then life grew quiet until the new semester started. Summer had always been a productive time. Without the distraction of students, there were hours upon hours to read and research and plan. But now, he was finding it hard to be alone. He wasn't concentrating on his work. He couldn't stop thinking about Tanya.

His hands full, he lifted a shoulder to adjust the strap of his messenger bag. Last August, when Florida's humidity was off the charts, he'd done the research for his "heroes" paper, the one that landed him here. He had to follow up with a paper equally great. He'd been warned by the dean at his old college about sophomore slump, second-book syndrome, or whatever you wanted to call it—when your second work doesn't live up to the promise of your first. He didn't want to let down his old mentor, Samuel, who had evidently advocated so strongly for him for this visiting professorship. He didn't want to go back to Florida next summer with his tail between his legs. And he'd already squandered so many hours, with the move and the delays in getting into his new home. With thinking and thinking about that email.

He took another sip and started for the library. He was in the mood to see people, and if there were any signs of life on campus on this muggy day, it would likely be there, since that was one of the very few air-conditioned buildings on campus. Plus, he'd reserved some books online, and they'd probably be available by now. Not to mention that he didn't want to risk seeing his boss, Clara, in the history building. He was hoping to avoid running into her until he could speak more coherently about his new research. And he was in jeans and sneakers again, his button-down shirts and regular shoes still in suitcases that wouldn't be unpacked until he could settle into his new house.

He headed down the hill as the rain began, the wetness of the grass penetrating the front of his sneakers, reaching inside to his toes. Tanya had loved the rain. That afternoon they got caught in a sudden downpour, one of those crazy Florida storms that drench everything but last only two or three minutes, she'd been making fun of herself for loving how the water felt on her skin. "I must have been a fish in a previous life," she'd said.

"Uh-huh," he'd replied, shaking his head as they ducked beneath an awning outside a bookstore. It was their senior year at the University of Minnesota, and they'd gone to Miami for spring break so he could meet her parents. They were heading to the florist shop because he wanted to buy them some flowers. He shook his head again to get his wet hair away from his face, and he saw the drops fly toward her, and she giggled and lowered her chin and held up her hands to block them. Then he'd pushed wet strands of her jet-black hair away from her eyes and let his hands drop to her shoulders, his thumbs grazing that impossibly smooth dip between her collarbones.

"A mermaid," he'd said. "That's what you were once. From a whole other world." And he leaned toward her, pressing her back against the building's brick façade, and went to kiss her. But then the door of the bookstore had opened, the bell above the entrance jingling. She'd turned her head and pressed the back of her hand against her mouth. She never liked it when he kissed her in public. And without a kiss to absorb his attention, he'd thought about what he'd just said, the mermaid thing, how it was the dumbest thing he'd ever said in his life. His friends would have laughed their heads off if they heard him. His dad, a poet, would have groaned, and his mom, a physics professor, would have appreciated the sentiment but told him he could do so much better. But he had no judgment when he was with her. No filter. He was beyond all help when it came to her.

He reached the library patio and made his way inside. The first floor was nearly as quiet as the rest of campus, with just two kids behind the circulation desk looking as bored and wilted as the girl at the café register. But the air was dry and cool, and the furnishings, the colors, were calming: the soft ivory of the bookshelves, the pale gray of the carpet, the sand-colored sofas. He stopped at the desk to pick up the books he'd reserved, then walked up the central staircase to the third floor, which he'd discovered last week was his favorite. He liked the spaciousness of the long, blond-wood tables.

He picked a table and settled in at one end, placing his bagel and coffee in front of the chair. If his mom were here, she'd imagine his breakfast weighting his side of the table now, with no counterbalance at the other end. She'd imagined that end of the table flying up into the air, and then the whole table tumbling over, striking the nearby stacks—causing all the books to fly off the shelves—before landing upside down. It could happen, his mother would have insisted. One thing could go wrong and cause utter chaos, as long as it was weighty enough. Put a pebble on the end of a table and all is fine; put a truck on it and suddenly, disaster. The thought of his mom's theory about life made him remember what he'd read last week about bridges and bodies of water and love—his next project that he'd tried to explain to Clara. There was an article that described how Paris officials were banning lovers from attaching "love locks" to the bridges, out of concern that the weight of the locks could soon cause the bridges to collapse. But how many more locks would it take? One? A dozen? A hundred? What was the tipping point?

That's what he needed to know, he thought as he looked at his breakfast. What had set her off? A word, a look, a touch? Calling her a mermaid? No, that had happened years before. Calling her something else? He had no idea what terrible thing he could have said. Or was it his lock, the one that he'd bought to surprise her, the one that was supposed to mean everything? Was that the one that might have made a Paris bridge collapse? Or just the one that made her decide to say goodbye?

He took a bite of his bagel and brushed the crumbs from his fingers. It wasn't as good as the bagels she'd introduced him to that year she lived in New York, but it was crunchy and buttery and good enough. He took his laptop out of his messenger bag and opened the first book in his pile, a historical overview of the bridges of Paris. But no matter how hard he tried, it was impossible to focus on the words. He sat back in his chair, his arms folded over his chest. This was crazy, he told himself. He was supposed to be working, not thinking of Tanya. Although he knew the two were related. In fact, he'd come to realize this week that he'd chosen to research locks and bridges specifically so he might understand what had happened as he waited on the Brooklyn Bridge, the twilight approaching and the twinkling lights on the buildings across the river just starting to be visible.

It was so cold on that bridge, he remembered. The wind was brisk and sharp, and his hair whipped around as he stood on the pedestrian walkway. His fleece jacket wasn't nearly warm enough, but he'd been living in Florida and didn't have proper winter gear. Ironically he'd relocated to Florida after college so they could be together near her family, just as she'd started toying with the idea of moving to New York. She'd eventually accepted a position with a nonprofit helping at-risk children, and he'd gotten into the routine of visiting her one weekend a month. But he hadn't come last month, since he'd had to make some trips to Minnesota to help his parents move into a new apartment. So it felt like forever since he'd seen her. He'd come straight from the airport to the bridge.

And now he waited, his eyes tearing from the cold, on the spot where Brooklyn bumped up against Manhattan. A historic spot, a symbolic spot. Two different neighborhoods, connecting in the middle. It made so much sense, meeting here. He waited, the minutes passing, other people walking by him. He waited some more. What was taking her so long? He'd made a reservation at her favorite Italian place at the base of the bridge on the Brooklyn side for afterward, and he didn't know how long they'd hold it. Restaurants were busy the week before Christmas. He stuffed his hands deeper into his pockets, and his left one circled the small padlock, the metal so cold it stung his fingers. Tonight he'd give her the lock. Next week she could pick out a ring. He knew she'd prefer to choose one herself. She had strong tastes, and he didn't want to make a mistake.

And then he saw her. He recognized her black wool coat and black hat with the white pom-pom, her black hair peeking out from below the hat's bottom edge. She smiled and hugged him, but when he tried to pull her closer, she pulled back. Just a touch, but he felt it. And he knew then. He knew her that well. So he went to pull the lock out of his pocket. It was small and cheap, gold in color, a trinket he'd picked up at the little toy store around the corner from his house. He thought she would think it cute, the cheaper and cheesier the better. They'd seen the locks when they went to Paris, and he'd been planning all year to propose to her with a lock like the ones they'd seen.

"Marry me," he wanted to say when he reached her. But he couldn't.

"A river flows from Eden to water the garden," she said as she looked out over the dark water, quoting her favorite verse from Genesis, the one she'd written about as a biblical studies major. Then she turned to him. "I can't do this," she said. "I can't." And she ran back toward the Manhattan end of the bridge. Should he run after her, he thought? Should he call out to her? But he didn't do either. He knew it wouldn't make a difference. She'd had one foot out the door since the day they started dating, he saw that now. That was the direction their story had been taking all along. He pulled the cheesy, cheap lock out of his pocket and looked at it, cradled in his hand. Then he threw it over the railing into the water. The tradition was to throw the key, not the lock, but he threw them both. They disappeared instantly. Nobody would ever know they were there. Except him.

> *It was a car crash,* her sister had written. *Maybe you heard. I don't know if you're still in touch with her friends. I know it's shocking. I'm still in shock, and it's been seven months. And I know what she decided all that time ago. But now I have to do what I think is right.*
>
> *His name is Henry. He's twelve...*

He heard giggling and looked up to see a group of students at a round table opposite him. He hadn't noticed them before, so they must have come in while he was deep in thought. Two girls looked over at him, and one pressed her palms toward the others.

"Guys, come on," she said to her friends. "It's a professor, he's trying to work. Sorry!" she called over to him.

"No problem," he said with a wave. He didn't want to make it seem that they'd done anything wrong. It was summer, and they had a right to hang out. Maybe he was invading their space. He was still a stranger here, and Gorson was still a mystery. He didn't know the conventions, the routines. He didn't know the unwritten rules.

Like when someone finds out she's pregnant, she's supposed to tell the father. She doesn't have to marry him. But she should let him know…

He closed up the computer and waved again to the students. He figured he should leave. But he didn't even know where to go. If he went home, he'd still be in the dark.

He grimaced. Talk about symbolism. He was definitely in the dark. He'd been in the dark for a long time.

He went back to the student center and worked for a few hours at a table in the lobby, then took out his phone to call Gull and order some dinner. That's when he noticed he'd missed a call from that morning. He didn't recognize the number, but there was a voicemail: "Hi, this is Caroline Rantzen, Maxine's friend, we met last night at the Grill? I'm calling about that art program for high school seniors. My daughter would love to be part of it, and you were so nice to offer to make a call for us. If that's still okay, we would really appreciate it. Thanks very much. Oh, and I hope your house is ready soon."

He replayed the message, and soon realized he was smiling. He remembered thinking about her, picturing her in his mind last night, as he strode home with his dinner in hand. She was pretty, that was for sure, her honey-colored curls soft and loose, the waves sort of jumbled as they spilled over her shoulders. And she'd looked cute and comfortable, so at home, wrapped in that oversized cardigan. And he'd liked her voice—that's one of the things he remembered, one of the things that appealed to him now as he heard her message again—clear like a bell and just as tuneful. He'd had no idea last night if he could help her daughter get into the program. He'd offered mostly because Maxine and Gull had been so good to him, and he wanted to help out their friend. But also because he wanted to see her again.

He called her back and she answered, which was a nice surprise. He'd gotten so used to being alone this week that he'd been expecting to reach her voicemail.

"Hey, Caroline? It's Aaron Weldon," he said. "Sure, happy to help. I'll go over there first thing in the morning and let you know what I find out."

CHAPTER NINE

Monday was free, no college visits scheduled, so Caroline let Lee sleep in. She took an early run and came home to a platter of muffins and a bowl of berries on the kitchen table, and a pot of coffee in a thermal carafe on the countertop. The aroma of Maxine's coffee, slightly sweet like cinnamon toast, filled the room, and she poured some into a mug and treated herself to a drop of cream, rather than her normal fat-free milk, from the pitcher in the refrigerator. Then she sat at the table with a muffin and some fruit, pulling one knee up toward her chin and resting her foot on the seat, the way she always used to sit in this house. The sunlight streamed in above the white café curtains, and she pushed her curls behind her ears and lifted her face toward the glow. The warm breeze kissed the curtains, ruffling them ever so slightly. She took a luxurious sip of coffee, wishing that time could stand still for a bit.

But it couldn't, and she had things to do before Lee woke. She tiptoed upstairs to take a quick shower and then brought her laptop back down with her. She fired off emails to the mayor and the town's six trustees, which she'd found on the town's website, requesting a meeting at their earliest convenience. Then she opened up a new document to type some thoughts for her meeting with Samantha Mackel, having left a voicemail for her last night to say that next Monday morning would be fine for a meeting. But how would she make her case? Her most sincere reasons for keeping the garden were hardly persuasive, because they were so small and personal. What could she say? Please save the garden because my mother started it? Because my dad loved her so much that he picked her up and twirled her on the footbridge and gave her a necklace with two linked hearts? Because my mother got so sick after spending a whole day there in the rain? She wrote down her memories of watching her mom that day on the footbridge, but then crossed them out. She didn't want to sound like a downer. And the community didn't want to go backward. They wanted to look to the future. That's exactly what they were doing in planning a library expansion.

She stared at the computer screen, thinking about the way Aunt Risa was in meetings, always direct and dispassionate. She never let long silences unnerve her because—as she'd explained in staff meetings—those silences encouraged others to rethink their positions. And she always made her position sound irrefutable, coolly ticking off the reasons all parties would win if they got on board with her. "What a cool customer," Will always said with an admiring laugh.

It had proven to be an effective business strategy, so Caroline thought she'd give it a shot. But what would be a convincing argument? *The Lily Garden adds to the beauty of the town and is an appealing place to spend some time,* she typed. But then she paused. That didn't work. The garden needed care, the footbridge was partially rotted and unstable, and the fence blocking the slope to the inlet was nonexistent. At best, people probably considered it a curious but space-wasting wilderness. She tried again: *The garden has been the setting for countless marriage proposals and weddings, as well as simple romantic strolls.* Okay, that was true. She'd have to do some research to nail down the numbers to replace "countless." Aunt Risa would never be so vague.

But the bigger problem was that this argument was backward-looking, too. She could hear Aunt Risa in her head, warning the sales team that you can't champion an idea your client perceives as obsolete. You can't ask someone to make an investment—in time, money, or effort—if the return was nonexistent. What made her mother's garden worth saving? If the reason were simply that the garden was pretty, that would hardly be convincing, as there were many pretty and romantic spots in town: the walkway along the lake, the gazebo on the green, and the trails behind the Lake Summers Resort, to name a few. Main Street itself was charming when the sun was setting lavender behind the Victorian-style buildings, especially with the new benches and streetlamps. Even the deck outside the Grill was romantic, as she'd seen on Saturday night—the young couple in the corner drinking liqueur and sharing dessert and looking like they thought they were the only two people on the planet.

On the other hand, none of these spots were as secluded, none had that sense of wildness, that connection to the colors and whims of nature, that her mother's garden did. *With a little work, the garden can be a unique, secluded, nature-infused venue for weddings, marriage proposals, and romantic strolls—even more so than it has in the past,* she typed. *And with some PR and a few well-placed ads, it could even become a draw for couples from outside the community, maybe even spurring local tourism and boosting revenue for local retailers.*

She stopped and reread the paragraph. It made her uncomfortable, using the potential of financial gain to sell her mother's garden. But she knew Aunt Risa would approve. In fact, Aunt Risa would consider this the most persuasive of her arguments.

Pushing the laptop aside, she went to refill her coffee cup, and as she did so, she noticed the most recent weekly issue of the *Lake Summers Press.* Maxine must have left it on the countertop for her to see. Its Page One headline was huge and bold: PRELIMINARY LIBRARY PLAN RELEASED. DIAGRAMS INSIDE! And when she opened the paper up to the center spread, she found a detailed sketch of the renovated library, with bullet points noting the expanded children's room, increased meeting spaces for town clubs and organizations, and a tech center with office equipment like copy machines and laminators for small businesses that couldn't afford their own.

She sat back at the table, feeling as though she were standing on train tracks trying to stop a speeding train heading her way. She'd stayed away too long, and now it seemed she was too late to save her mother's legacy.

The sound of footsteps startled her out of her thoughts, and she looked up to see Lee walking into the kitchen, her eyes squeezing shut as she yawned widely. "Hi," she said as she poured herself coffee.

"Good morning," Caroline said. "How'd you sleep?"

Lee nodded, carrying her coffee to the table. She took a muffin from the platter and brought it to her nose, then peeled away a section of the paper wrapper and took a bite.

"Oh, Lee!" Caroline said. "Do you always do that?"

"Do what?"

"Smell your food like that before you eat it? I never realized that. My mother used to do that, too! She smelled every-thing—food before she ate it, clothes from the dryer before she put them on. I can still remember how she would lift the pillowcases to her nose before she slid the pillows inside. And she was always sticking her nose into the flowers in the garden." She shook her head. "Oh, Lee, there are probably so many ways you're like her."

Lee cocked her head. "Do I look like her?"

"Maybe." She touched the side of Lee's face. "Yes, here. The bottom of your face. Your little chin. I see it now."

"Okay, stop," Lee said and squirmed away. She peeled the muffin's wrapper further and took another bite. "I wish I met her," she said when she'd finished chewing. "Everyone here knew her except me."

Caroline folded her arms on the table. "I know what you mean. I didn't even get to know her that well…" She paused. "But you know what?" she said, sitting upright. "I'm going to introduce you to her today. And myself, too. We're going to look at everything—where we lived, where we ate, the lake, the garden, all of it. Finish up and get dressed. We have a lot to see, okay?"

Lee nodded, and a little while later they were walking down Main Street. A block away from Mrs. Pearl's, they turned left on to Walnut Street and stopped in front of a clothing store called Lexy's Closet. Caroline pointed to the second floor.

"That's where we lived," she said.

Lee looked up. "You lived in a *store?*"

"No, silly. It was above the store. A lot of these shops have apartments on the second floor. See?" She pointed to a narrow door between the clothing shop and a market, with the number 111 written across the glass. "We lived at 111A Walnut Street. It had an A because the front door was around the back. Come, I'll show you."

They walked down an alley to the back of the building and came upon the entrance to a house. There was a small stone porch lined with a white railing and a blue door with a wind chime hanging down. A cloud-shaped sign with the words "FOR RENT" and a phone number was taped to a window.

"See?" Caroline said. "There was a living room and kitchen downstairs, and two little bedrooms upstairs for my parents and me. My parents' windows were the ones we saw around the front. Come on, let's try to go inside."

She went onto the porch and knocked on the door, but nobody answered. She tried the doorknob, but it didn't turn. She went to peek through a window, but the window shades had been pulled down.

Lee came up behind her. "You lived right in the middle of town? Wasn't it noisy?"

Caroline laughed. Of course Lee would question that. The only home she'd ever known was the carriage house behind Aunt Risa's sprawling Colonial with its vast lawn, the neighbors' homes barely visible. The only people she regularly saw outside were the gardener, the sprinkler guy, the mail carrier, and an occasional UPS or FedEx driver.

"I loved the noise and all the activity," she said. "There were so many people around all the time, and my mom knew everyone. The store wasn't a clothing store back then. It was an art store. Bobbie's Palette. My mom used to go there to buy clay and easels and paints and brushes, and sand for sand art. Oh, all kinds of things for the classes she would teach at the library."

"She taught kids' classes? That's so sweet."

"She wanted to be a kindergarten teacher, but she never went to college. She planned to go when I got a little older." Caroline chuckled. "A Rantzen who never went to college. Hard to believe, right? But she fell in love and ran off with my dad. I guess she loved him enough to put everything else on hold."

She felt Lee touch her elbow. "How come you never talk about him?" she asked.

"My dad?" Caroline hesitated. "I don't… I guess I was with my mom so much more. I didn't know my dad as well. But he was great. Very sweet and handsome. Very strong." That is, she thought, until her mother died. Then he wasn't strong at all. Standing next to Lee on the porch, she remembered staying at Maxine's house the night he took her mom to the hospital. She'd been in bed when she heard him come back to Maxine's, awake even though it was very late. She'd started to go see him, but then she'd heard this awful sound, this wailing sound, desperate and hopeless: *No… no… no…*

Tiptoeing to the staircase, she'd peeked between the posts of the banister. It was her dad making that noise as he sat in Maxine's armchair, hunched over with his head in his hands, and Maxine knelt beside him and stroked his back. She'd stared at her dad for a moment, frozen, hating the sound but unable to escape it. Finally, she ran back into bed, telling herself she didn't really see what she'd seen, she didn't really hear what she'd heard. Telling herself that if she went back to sleep quickly, she'd wake to find it never happened.

"Anyway, when it was an art store, it was owned by this very nice couple—a woman named Bobbie and her husband. I wonder if it even looks the same. Let's go in."

They retraced their steps down the alley, and she led Lee into the clothing store. A young woman with a high brown ponytail and a sleeveless peach-colored dress came to greet them. "Can I help you?" she said.

Caroline introduced herself and Lee. "We just came in to look," she said. "I used to live in this building when I was a kid. In the apartment on the second floor, with the entrance in the back. I brought my daughter here so I could show her around."

The woman's eyes widened. "You... wait, you lived around back? But that's where the woman who made the Lily Garden lived."

Caroline nodded. "That was my mother."

"Get out!" the woman said. "I got married in that garden! Seven years this past June. It had been raining that week, but that morning the sun came out and the flowers were all glistening and smelling so good. Oh my God, it was the best day! I look at those pictures all the time. My husband grew up here, that's how we knew about it. And we liked it so much here that we decided to stay and open our own shop.

"Anyway, it's nice to meet you, I'm Lexy Stone," she said. "And I have to say, I'm so sad they're tearing the garden down. Not that I often say that out loud, because many of my customers want that whole area redone. But not me, boy."

Caroline smiled, cheered by the young woman's energy and enthusiasm. It was so good to hear yet again how much her mother's hard work had meant to people. "I'm sorry, too," she said. "I've been trying to explain to my daughter a little bit about my mom. We're going to the garden next. And I was hoping to show her where we used to live. Do you know if there's a way we could get inside back there?"

"I think you need to contact the broker," Lexy said. "When we moved here, it was a preschool, but that moved into the elementary school last spring. But there's no second floor there, you know. The building was reconfigured, and the second floor is now part of our store. It's a really pretty space, go have a look."

Caroline thanked her and went to the back of the sales floor, where an L-shaped staircase led to what had once been the second floor of her home. She crossed the open space, thinking how strange it was to see racks of dresses and pantsuits where her parents slept, and a display of sweaters and scarves where her own bed used to be. The bathroom had been turned into a stockroom, and a corner of her bedroom had been made into a fitting room. She tried not to dwell on the thought of people pulling clothes off hangers and trying them on, thrusting a hip this way or turning a shoulder that way, in the place where her bookshelf and wooden dresser had been.

But the strangest change of all was the golden-brown wood floor, flawless and polished and shiny. It had been so old when she'd lived there, scratched and darkened by her family and the families that lived there before hers. Parents and children who had walked on them dozens of times a day, their feet sometimes in slippers, sometimes bare and still sandy from the lake, and sometimes in boots that should have been left outside to dry. Gone was the scratch she made when she pulled her desk chair to the center of her bedroom to build a tent with her bedsheets, as well as the deep gouge from when her dad dropped the second-hand writing desk he'd bought for her mom for her birthday and carried upstairs by himself. Her mom had loved the desk—but Caroline suspected she'd loved the gouge as much.

She looked at Lee, who was standing by one of the racks in the center of the floor, browsing the clothes. "Oh my God, so pretty," Lee said, pulling out a light-blue blouse and slim black skirt. "This would be so good for the Alvindale thing. I owe myself a present for working so hard at the textiles board this summer." She held the pieces to her body. "What do you think?"

"It's very pretty," Caroline said. "Try it on."

"Oh, God, Mom, this is weird for you, isn't it?" Lee said. "I'm sorry, let's go—"

"No, it's fine," Caroline told her. "It's nice that you've found an outfit in this very place." She nodded so Lee would go ahead, and then went to sit on a folding chair near the wall, close to where her bed once had been. "We'll be okay," her dad often said when he kissed her goodnight during the first weeks after her mom had died. "We'll be just fine, Sweet Caroline." And yet there she was, confused and sleepy, when Jackie brought her back to his house on the morning of her eighth birthday. Gull closed up the Grill early that night—there weren't many people out anyway, since it was the dead of winter and super cold—and he cooked her chicken riggies with extra sauce, just the way she liked them. Maxine set a table right in the middle of the restaurant and sat her at the head, and gave her a cardboard "Birthday Princess" crown. The riggies were delicious, paired with garlic bread dripping with warm butter, and Mrs. Pearl's shredded-coconut cake showed up on the table for dessert, as though nothing was off.

"Don't you worry," Maxine had said after Caroline blew out the candles and opened her present, a stack of three popular music CDs that Maxine must have run out that afternoon to buy. "We'll have a second celebration when your dad is back."

But Caroline knew there'd never be a second birthday dinner. She didn't know how—she just knew it. And a few days later she'd

learned that her dad had been found dead at a distant construction site where he'd been doing some work on the side. After
that, more of her things showed up at Maxine's house—her pink
blanket, her stand-up mirror, her princess alarm clock, all of her
winter clothes, and the spring ones too. And soon she was eating
grilled sandwiches at the Grill as she did her school assignments,
and drinking hot chocolate with whipped cream and chocolate
shavings on top, and everyone at school was jealous of her, as
they'd always been of Jackie and Ben.

*

Lee bought the outfit, and they stopped by a few more shops
and then decided on lunch at Lonny's Fine Foods—a misnomer
since, as Caroline explained, the only thing Lonny served, fine
or otherwise, was hot dogs. "This place has changed," she said, as
she led Lee up to the deck, with its stylish aluminum tables and
chairs. "They never had outdoor seating. And twenty varieties of
hot dogs?" she added, looking at the whiteboard menu. "When
I lived here, there were two choices: with or without mustard."

Lee rolled her eyes. "I can't believe how people eat here. I
would get the worst stomachaches if I ate like this every day."

"Even Gull's food?"

"Well, not most of his food. Not when he makes stuff just for
us. But Mom, come on, have you seen that menu? Fried cheese?
Hot and spicy nachos? And there's a thing called Garbage Plate.
Garbage Plate!"

Caroline laughed and raised her palms as if to say, It is what it
is. Like chicken riggies, garbage plates were a regional specialty.
They varied slightly from restaurant to restaurant, with Gull's
version sporting a mishmash of home fries and macaroni salad
as a base, with two bun-less cheeseburgers, a heaping of raw
onions, and plenty of hot sauce on top. Yes, it sounded awful,
but it tasted great. And the thought of it was comforting now,

even as Lee made fun of it. Gull's food, served in the restaurant or in Maxine's kitchen, had always soothed her and made her feel safe. What would the comfort markers of Lee's childhood be? Spreadsheets? Sales reports? Fancy canapés at Aunt Risa's famous holiday parties? Coffee in a mug with the Rantzen logo?

They went with a tropical choice for lunch, hot dogs topped with mango salsa, and they agreed it was delicious.

And then it was time to see the garden.

They left Lonny's deck, and Caroline led Lee back along Main Street and over to Oak. After the garbage plate discussion, she didn't know if Lee would see the garden as beautiful, let alone magical. How would she feel if Lee was thoroughly unimpressed? There would be no going back once Lee was there.

They went behind the library building and started on the dirt path, past the late-summer bloomers Caroline had seen yesterday. Soon they came to the footbridge and walked up the planks until they were in the center, the rocky area beneath them. That's when Caroline saw the garden the way Lee no doubt saw it: not lush and vibrant, but messy. Not alive and enticingly wild, but scrubby and sad. The footbridge felt more shaky and unstable than it had yesterday. The absence of a fence made the deep slope feel threatening.

They leaned gently on the railing and looked down toward the inlet, just as two women in running clothes came onto the footbridge from the opposite direction. "Wow. That's nuts," one of them said.

"I know, right?" the other agreed. "I don't even let Connor come out here when he goes to the library after school. I tell him, 'Only use the front door, don't go to the back.' I swear, this hill is so steep. If a kid came out here alone and tripped, he'd fly down to the water."

"And no one would even hear if he called for help," the first one said. "When is the renovation starting, anyway?"

"Not soon enough," the other one answered, and they both nodded in greeting to Caroline and Lee, and continued toward the end of the footbridge.

Caroline waited until they were gone, and then looked toward the water again, feeling foolish. She'd been telling Lee for the last couple of days how wonderful the garden was, how much love had gone into its creation and care—and here were two women who couldn't wait for it to be destroyed. And the saddest thing of all was that she thought Lee would see the women's point. Lee was a reasonable person just like Aunt Risa, and these women had reason on their side.

She felt Lee's eyes on her. "Are you okay, Mom?" she said.

Caroline straightened up. "Of course. It's fine. I'm fine."

"Don't worry about them, they're idiots," Lee said. Caroline hated having Lee try to comfort her. That wasn't the way it was supposed to be. Her own mother had always been strong. Even in the days before she died, the days when she was feeling sick, she'd never made Caroline think she was weak or diminished.

"They're wrong, Mom," Lee said.

Caroline shook her head. "No, they're worried about their kids," she said. "I can understand that. I just never saw this place as dangerous."

"It's not," Lee said. "It's those women. They're crazy moms, like the ones at my school who go complaining to the principal if their kid doesn't get an A+ on a paper. They're overprotective. They need to get a life. I hate moms like that. I'm glad I don't have one."

Caroline wrapped her arm around Lee's shoulders. "Come on, let's keep going," she said. "There's still more I want to show you."

They walked off the footbridge and through the rest of the garden, and then went through the back entrance into the library, Caroline pointing out the corner where she used to sit with her friends, purportedly to study but mostly to watch for cute boys.

They emerged out the front and were turning onto Main Street when Caroline felt Lee take her arm.

"Mom, look," she said. "I love the garden, and I see why you love it. And I want you to save it. And I want to help if I can.

"And also, I want to go to the art program you guys were talking about," she said. "Did you find out if that professor can get me in?"

"I called him, and he said he'd find out. But Lee, I don't want you to do this because you feel sorry for me."

"I'm not," she said. "Jackie said Gorson's a great school, and this would be a good program for me. And Maxine said it's only a few hours, so I don't know why I was resisting it. Maybe seeing the garden made me think about it differently. I love to draw. I think it would be fun to be in a college art studio. Maybe even meet some real art professors."

Caroline looked at Lee, then smiled and leaned over so their heads touched. "I am so lucky," she said. "I have the most amazing daughter."

"It's not that big a deal," Lee said. "Don't make this all dramatic, or I'm going to change my mind."

"Okay," Caroline said. "I won't." But she gave Lee's shoulders another squeeze anyway, feeling glad about how things were changing. Ever since the two of them left on this trip, Caroline had felt a wall between them. But now, finally, after this day together in her beautiful hometown, it seemed the wall was beginning to crack.

Lee pointed up the hill at the Smoothie Dudes shop. "I saw a sign before about new fall flavors," she said. "Want to go?"

"Actually, I think I'm more in the mood for coffee," Caroline said, pointing at Mrs. Pearl's across the street. "Why don't you go get yourself a smoothie? I'll stop in here and we can meet back at the house."

Lee nodded and jogged ahead, and Caroline started toward the café. Some couples were sitting at round metal tables in front of the entrance. And there was a man in a Miami Open cap at a table set apart from the others, his hand wrapped around a coffee cup.

It was Aaron.

She breathed in sharply. She hadn't seen him since that night at the Grill, although she'd talked to him yesterday when he called to say he'd be happy to see if he could get Lee into the Gorson art program. And both times, he'd seemed so friendly, almost happy-go-lucky. She'd enjoyed the way he'd joked with Gull, and she'd appreciated how he'd offered her his phone number and then promised to head over to the admissions office to check things out for Lee. But now she saw a different side to him. He looked concerned—no, more like sorrowful—as he rotated his coffee cup on the table, his chin down, his lips a straight line.

She thought about approaching him, just saying hello, but she didn't want to bother him. He looked like he wanted to be alone. The problem was that she had to walk by his table to get to the café's entrance. She tried to move quickly, staying as far from him as she could, but still, he looked up when she passed.

"Caroline, hi," he said, standing. "Aaron," he added, pointing to himself, as though he thought she might not remember who he was.

"Of course. Aaron, hi," she said, suddenly feeling guilty for having invaded his privacy by watching him without his knowledge. "I'm sorry, I didn't mean to interrupt…"

"No, it's fine. I was going to call you tonight," he said. "I have good news. Your daughter has a spot in the program if she wants it."

"Really?" Caroline said. "Oh, that's great. I'm very grateful."

He shook his head. "I can't take any credit. There was a cancellation just as I showed up at admissions. Right spot, right time. The introductory session is Thursday morning at eleven."

"This is such a coincidence, we were talking about it a moment ago," Caroline said. "Lee just left to get a smoothie." She pointed up the hill.

The Lily Garden   113

"And you didn't want one?" he said.

"I was more in the mood for coffee."

"Well, hey, would you like to sit and—" He looked at his phone. "Actually, no, I've got to get going. I'm supposed to be meeting with my landlord right now."

"Oh?" Caroline said, trying not to show her disappointment. She would have liked to sit with him. In fact, she was surprised at how much she would have liked that. "That sounds promising. Think she'll have good news?"

"I hope so," he said with a grin. "That's what I'm going to find out. Otherwise, I'd be glad to… you know. Stay."

"Oh, no, sure, it's fine. I'm meeting Lee back at Maxine's anyway," Caroline said. "I'm sorry she's not here so she could thank you herself."

"Too bad. I would have liked to meet her, too," he said. "But… but hey, why don't the two of you stop by my office on Thursday around ten thirty?" he said. "Not that I need the thanks, but I can tell her what I know about the program and walk you over to the first session."

"Okay. Sure," Caroline said. She was tickled that he wanted to see her again.

"Good. I'll text you over my office address. Along with the registration materials."

"I'll look for it," she said. "Thanks again. And good luck with the house."

"See you Thursday," he said with a wave, and she watched him toss his coffee cup in a trash can and start in the direction of the lake. Then she turned to go into Mrs. Pearl's, struck by how sad he'd looked a little while ago, when he was by himself, and how he'd changed so drastically when she showed up. She wasn't used to that. She had spent so much time around people like her aunt and even Will, who were used to saying exactly what they were thinking and having staff around to make sure whatever was on their minds got addressed. It was sweet, generous, that he had put aside his concerns to greet her and tell her about Lee's enrollment.

Still, it stayed with her, too, as she stood in line for her coffee: how alone he'd looked. She knew that no matter how sad she might feel in the coming days as she immersed herself in old memories, she had Lee and Maxine and even Gull and Jackie to prop her up and help her through. She thought how hard it must be for Aaron, to be sad and still pretty much a stranger in town. She wondered what was troubling him, and if he had anyone to talk to.

And if there was anything she could do to help.

CHAPTER TEN

The next day Caroline and Lee visited two more schools that were on their agenda, and Wednesday they spent at the lake. Sitting on the blanket with her knees gathered beneath her chin, Caroline watched her daughter, clad in a tasteful navy-blue bikini, wade in up to her waist and make a graceful surface dive into the water. Lee was so bold. Not that swimming in a lake took a whole lot of courage, but it was Lee's attitude, the way she owned whatever situation she was in, that Caroline found so remarkable. Caroline hadn't been at all like that growing up. She'd never have taken off her shorts and marched into the water the way Lee just did. She'd have proceeded slowly, waiting until she was sure nobody was looking, maybe keeping a towel around her waist until she'd reached the water's edge. She'd never asked questions—not about why her mother got so sick so fast, or why Maxine was so willing to give her up to Aunt Risa. She supposed she didn't want to be a bother. Or maybe she was scared of the answers.

But her mother had been bold like Lee, Caroline thought, as she took off her t-shirt and felt the sun warm the triangle of skin that her V-neck swimsuit exposed. Her mother had left a home of privilege and set off on an adventure with a man who had no money to speak of, simply because she loved him. And she'd lived exactly as she wanted to, setting up her house, making friends like Maxine, teaching children's art classes, and showing her daughter by example what mattered in life. She'd tended the garden anew each spring, knowing all the while that no matter how hard she worked, it would all be gone by late fall. "You have to act like everything you do is forever, Caroline," she'd said one early-April day as she surveyed the winter-tossed landscape, then squatted and let handfuls of dirt flow between her fingers. "You have to believe that everything you care about will last and last. Because that's the only way you can truly give your heart." Caroline wished she could love the way her mother did, completely and without fear of the future. She didn't know if she had it in her. All she knew was that she'd never loved her husband, Glenn, the way her mom had loved her dad. And she could never love Will that way, either. Was the problem with these two men? Or was the flaw in her?

And what about Lee, she thought as she watched her daughter swim to the yellow buoy in the distance with measured, efficient strokes? She couldn't remember a time when Lee looked the way her mother had that day in the rain, smiling with total abandon, her chin and cheeks muddy and her hair plastered to her head and the inside of her fingernails caked with dirt. Had Lee ever truly been thoroughly and deliciously filthy? Not that Caroline wanted Lee to be entirely like her mother. She certainly didn't want Lee to run away and get married at nineteen and have a baby a year later. And yet, was the only alternative the one Lee had grown up with—always having a bunch of safety nets below her? Would her daughter ever throw her head back and twirl in the rain, in the arms of her one true love?

Would *she?*

Was either of them capable of it?

Maybe she and her daughter weren't as different as she thought. Maybe they both spent way too much time wanting to play it safe. Caroline had never before fully understood how her mom had up and left the security of her home and family to move to Lake Summers. Why take such a risk? But sitting here now, with the breeze from the lake whispering along her shoulders and remembering how much her parents had adored each other, her mother's decision to run away with her dad didn't seem like much of a risk at all.

*

On Thursday after breakfast, Caroline sent another email and left a voice message for the mayor, reiterating her desire to talk to him about the garden. Then she and Lee took off for Gorson College. She could hardly believe how much she was looking forward to seeing Aaron. And she was especially happy to be going to his office. She wanted to get to know him more, see all the sides to him. They barely knew each other—they'd only talked three times, twice in person and once on the phone—and yet she found herself often thinking of him. She liked how he'd greeted her when she stopped by his table at Mrs. Pearl's, how truly pleased he'd seemed to see her. And she liked how he looked, his almost contradictory features—his slight frame but strong build, his firm jaw but gentle gaze and crinkly eyes. He was equal parts dashing and down-to-earth, and she found it a delightful blend.

It was a short but pretty drive over rolling hills, the roads intersecting acres of farmland, the green fields stretching end-lessly behind wooden fences with cows or horses visible in the distance, and she turned her attention to her daughter. Lee had filled out the registration materials last night, and Caroline had been glad to see that the fee was reasonable and refundable in the event of an early withdrawal. She promised Lee that if she didn't like how today went, she could pull out, no questions asked. From the driver's seat, she glanced at her daughter, sitting cross-legged in the passenger seat, working on her mock business plan for Alvindale. It would be good for Lee to do something more artistic, for a change.

They reached the school, which was gorgeous, as Jackie had said. Willow trees lined the driveway leading up the hill, their branches forming a canopy overhead. A small pond sat in the middle of a grassy field beyond the willows, drenched in sunshine. The buildings had cool stone façades, with pitched roofs and romantic casement windows, and there was a chapel with a tall steeple and gilded dome halfway up the hill. An expansive building—possibly the library—was on the right, with a rooftop veranda that no doubt had a glorious view of the mountains. The trees it revealed in the distance would have a whisper of gold and orange, Caroline thought. A hint of the chorus of color that would burst onto the landscape in a few short weeks.

They parked in the visitors' lot, and Lee found a campus map on her phone that highlighted the way to the history building. It was a three-story structure that dated back to 1870, according to a plaque near the door, and Caroline marveled at the thought of students and professors from so long ago walking through the halls. Inside, they went up a central staircase to the third floor, then followed the signs to the faculty offices. They reached Room 343, and Caroline knocked on the door.

A moment later Aaron opened it, and Caroline was struck again by how friendly and down-to-earth he looked. He was dressed similarly to the way she'd seen him before, this time in a dark-green t-shirt paired with jeans, gray sneakers, and a gray Gorson hoodie. But now she could see features that she hadn't noticed earlier: his dark, close-cropped hair, which had been hidden the other times by his Miami Open cap, and the tiny cleft in his square chin, which the dim light at the Grill had obscured. She noticed again how his broad grin caused the skin outside his eyes to wrinkle, this time behind black-framed glasses; and she thought the lines curving almost down to his cheekbones gave him an appealing air of vulnerability. He was an important guy, someone with stature, according to Maxine. Yet he seemed so unpretentious.

"Caroline, nice to see you again. Lee, nice to meet you," he said and reached out to shake her hand. "Sorry the door was closed, I didn't realize it was ten thirty already. Mornings really fly around here. Please come on in."

He stepped back from the door, then jogged to the sofa on the other side of the office and picked up a tennis racquet, a sweatshirt, and some socks that were lying on the cushion.

"Sorry for the mess," he said with an embarrassed laugh as he put the clothing into the bottom drawer of his desk and laid the racquet on top of it. He took off his glasses and put them on the racquet. "As I mentioned to your mom the other night, Lee, my house isn't ready yet. So I've been spending a lot of time here. Too much, actually," he added as he picked up an empty cardboard hot dog cradle from the windowsill.

"You're still not in your house?" Caroline asked. She liked how he had directly addressed Lee. After all, she was the one they were there for. "I thought everything would be set by now," she added.

"Well, things got better, and then they got bad again," he said. "Two days ago they found a leak in the kitchen pipes and had to turn the water off. I can spend the nights without electricity and appliances, but a person needs running water."

"Oh, no! Where've you been sleeping?" Caroline said.

"You're looking at it," he said, pointing to the sofa. "More comfortable than you'd think."

"You slept on the couch?" Lee said.

"I would try to get a hotel room or Airbnb, but I keep expecting the house to be ready the next day." He shrugged. "Anyway, it's fine. The locker rooms at the campus gym are amazing. Nicer than any bathroom I've ever seen. Great water pressure in the showers."

Caroline smiled and noticed that Lee did, too. She was glad her daughter also found something charming and unexpected about a college professor describing his personal-care routine.

Aaron looked down, evidently remembering that he was still holding a hot dog cradle. "From Lonny's," he said. "Have you been there?"

Caroline nodded. "On Tuesday," she said. "And I used to go there when I was a kid, too. Although he's expanded his menu a lot since then."

"Oh, that's right, you lived here," he said. "But I bet you didn't know they make breakfast hot dogs. You learn these things when you don't have a kitchen. I ran over and grabbed one early this morning when I stopped by the house to see if there was any more progress. Yesterday I had a breakfast smoothie at the Smoothie Dudes. Have you been there? Those guys, Stan and Trey—they really know their way around a piece of fruit."

He tossed the cradle into the trash, then half sat on his desk. "Well, enough about me and my tale of woe," he said. "Lee, let me tell you what I learned about this program you're signed up for. As I mentioned to your mom, this morning's just a ninety-minute introduction. But over the weekend and into next week, they have a lot of seminars and workshops, and you can choose which ones to go to. And there's a mixer Saturday night, where you can meet some Gorson students who've been taking classes this summer. The art studios are open to you, too, if you want to work independently. They opened one of the dorms for kids who are in from out of town, but I figured you'd prefer staying with your mom at Maxine's."

He looked at his phone. "We might as well head on down there," he said. "You can meet some of the admissions staff and get a good seat before it begins." He stood, knocking the coffee mug on his desk over—fortunately it was empty—and then reached for a badge and a folder with the Gorson logo that were on his chair.

"Okay, so it's in the auditorium in the admissions building, which is to the right of the library, I think," he said as he handed her the materials and they left the office. "I'm still learning my way around the campus, so I'll have to stop and get my bearings once we get outside…"

Lee smiled and held up her phone. "I have the app," she said.

"Boy, could I have used you last week," he said. "You're lucky you're good with maps. Any chance I could keep you on retainer?"

Lee laughed, and Caroline did, too.

They left the building and started down the hill. "So, where were you teaching before?" Caroline asked.

"Florida," he told her. "A small city school called Pine Beach College. Although I grew up in Minnesota. Where's home for you two?"

"Chicago," Caroline answered.

"I knew I recognized a couple of fellow Midwesterners. Do you live in the city?"

"No, about a half hour north."

"Oh, nice. I mean, it sounds nice," he said. "Not that I've ever been outside the city. But I do like Chicago."

Caroline nodded. She could tell that Aaron was the kind of person who didn't seem to worry about every little word he said, and that put her at ease. He fit in so well with the Lake Summers vibe. Back home, everyone was always intense, so even funny mistakes became calamities. Once Uncle Rich sent a message to a client saying that a salesperson "named Nancy Sanders" would stop by—except he typed a *k* instead of an *m,* so the sentence read, "naked Nancy Sanders." Caroline, who'd been cc'd on the memo, laughed out loud as she read it—but when she went down the hall to point it out to Uncle Rich, he became apoplectic. "Get it back!" he'd screamed at his assistant. "Get it back, now!"

They reached the building and found the auditorium. Aaron offered to introduce Lee to the admissions officer leading the session, but Lee told him she'd be fine and could make her way alone from here. She walked down to the stage and caught the attention of the man on stage. They spoke for a few minutes, and then she took a seat in the front row. Caroline was proud of how composed and independent Lee was. And yet, she also felt unsettled because she knew Lee hadn't learned to behave that way from her. It was Aunt Risa who had taught her how to carry herself in professional situations. Caroline couldn't even think right now of a positive characteristic or talent that she had passed on to Lee; not one commendable trait that she could point to and say, "There it is. That's my daughter."

Lee looked at them, and Caroline mouthed that she'd meet her in this spot when the program was over.

"Glad she got us here," Aaron said. "I'd never have been able to show my face to Maxine or Gull again if I had gotten us lost on campus and she never made it to the session."

"But you got her enrolled in the program," Caroline said. "I really appreciate that."

"It wasn't any magic, believe me," he said. "Meanwhile, you have an hour and a half now to wait. Can I buy you a cup of coffee? There's an outdoor café on the roof of the library."

"I'd love that," she said. "If you're sure you have the time."

"I can use the distraction," he said. "My work is at a standstill at the moment. Serious writer's block—or researcher's block. Hopefully, another coffee will give it a jump-start." He walked a few steps forward, then stopped and looked around. "Now here's the real test," he said. "Can I find the library without your daughter? I'm no good with maps, so my phone won't help. I'm more the kind of guy who operates on instinct. I think we go out this way and then turn left… mind if we wing it?"

"Not at all," Caroline said.

They started back up the hill, the path curving around a small bend, until they came to the large building she'd noticed when they arrived. She'd been right, it was the library, and coming from this direction, they were able to walk right onto the rooftop veranda. The hill had been challenging, and she liked that he wasn't too proud to acknowledge it. She laughed as he raised his fists in victory when they stepped onto the veranda's flat slate surface.

The seating area was empty, so they chose a table near the railing. "Sorry, the coffee here doesn't hold a candle to Mrs. Pearl's," he said. "Or Gull's, for that matter. It tastes a little better iced, but still. Is there anything else you'd like?"

"Iced coffee would be great," she said and reached for her bag to get her wallet.

"No, please." He held up his hand. "This is on me. Faculty discount. Ten cents off a beverage. Gotta love being an academic. Cushy life, I know."

He went into the building, and Caroline took a seat. She removed her sweater, her arms now bare in her sleeveless black top. The sky was blue and stretched forever, while a few nearly translucent strips of cloud added contrast. The hint of chill in the air felt refreshing on her neck and shoulders.

He came back holding two cups of iced coffee, with napkins, straws, cups of creamer, and packets of sugar wedged between his forearm and his chest. He put the cups down and then spread everything else out. "Just one more thing," he said and jogged back in, emerging with a large cardboard bowl with whipped cream and shaved chocolate peeking out over the top.

"Sorry, I know it's not even lunchtime, but I couldn't resist," he said, as he put the treat in the middle of the table, then handed her a smaller bowl and a spoon. "I hope you like chocolate-chip ice cream. There's a dairy farm down the road, and there's nothing fresher in the world. I don't think a day has gone by that I haven't had some."

"Of course, Bill's Dairy," she said. "Is that still there? I haven't thought about that place in so long." She remembered how she and the boys would beg Maxine to take them there after school. Bill's chocolate ice-cream cake in the shape of a turkey was a staple each year on Thanksgiving.

"You know it?" he asked.

She nodded. "The Ice Creamery in town gets its ice cream from them. But it was always so special, to go to the dairy. We loved standing on the railing—Maxine's boys and me. Looking at the cows while we ate."

He took some ice cream, holding the bowl steady as the side of his spoon sliced through the whipped cream and chocolate. "So you grew up near them?"

"Actually, I lived with them," she said. "My parents died when I was young, and it was a few years before my aunt came to get me. Maxine was a second mother to me."

"I'm sorry you lost your parents," he said. He was still for a moment. Then he put the spoonful of ice cream into his bowl and went back for more. "Please have some," he said. "I can't eat this all by myself."

She smiled and dug in.

"So when was the last time you were back?" he asked.

"Not since I was twelve."

"You left when you were twelve and you haven't been back since?"

She nodded. "It sounds surprising, I know. I don't know how it happened. Except that we have a long history in Chicago, my family, and a business that keeps us all very busy. My mom was the outlier, leaving to come here." She tasted the ice cream, letting the cold sweetness melt into nothing in her mouth.

"How about you?" she said. "How do you like it here?"

"I like it a lot," he said. "The people are great. But it's very different from where I was before. The quiet. How spread out everything is. The nights."

"The nights?"

"Yeah. It gets pretty dark in this area at night. Lots of time to spend in your own head. Although maybe that has more to do with my living situation than anything else. No electricity and all. I sure will be glad to finally get my lights on."

"Don't knock the nights," she said. "They're one of the best parts of living here. Especially when the days get short. We used to take these long walks by the lake, my parents and me, after the summer had ended and the town was quiet. It was so dark on those moonless nights that you had to bring a flashlight, even when it was six o'clock. And you could hear the water in the lake but couldn't see it at all."

"And you liked that?" he said, his eyebrows raised, his tone teasing.

"I did," she said. "Sometimes when it got really cold, we'd go down to the lake with thick fleece blankets and a thermos of hot cocoa. And we'd sit wrapped up in the blankets and drink the cocoa, and sing. Just sit together and sing. Show tunes, Christmas carols, nursery rhymes, everything. My mom loved to sing, and I thought she had the most beautiful voice, although I remember my dad laughing and my mom punching his arm, so I guess it wasn't as beautiful as I thought. But I felt so safe and cozy under that blanket next to my mom and dad."

Caroline dipped her spoon into the bowl again, the ice cream now melting and mingling with the whipped cream and chocolate. She had never shared that memory before. She didn't know why she had now. It just happened—the way he looked at her so closely as he listened made her want to talk. Still, she hadn't meant for the conversation to get so personal. She took a breath and changed the subject.

"Well, the good thing is that you arrived in time for the Moonlight Carnival," she said. "Have you heard about that?"

"A little," he said. "A block party, right?"

"Way more than a party," she told him. "It's a whole extravaganza. It started years ago when people decided they wanted a way to celebrate the end of summer, and not let it be such a downer when the town was emptying out. So they created this crazy event. They close up Main Street, and there are rides and carnival games, and tons of food. It's always the last Saturday in August. And it starts in the early evening and lasts until sunrise."

"Sounds like it's not to be missed," he said. "Will you still be in town for it?"

She nodded. "I wasn't even thinking of the Moonlight Carnival when I planned this trip, but luckily the dates worked out. Lee has another one of these high-school programs the following week at Alvindale, and then she starts her senior year. So we'll close out August with a bang here and get back to real life after that."

"Wow, another college program," he said. "You've got quite a daughter. You and her dad must be very proud."

"Her dad?" She shook her head. "No, her dad's not around. He died when she was a baby."

"I'm sorry," he said. "I figured he was back in Chicago."

"It's okay," she said. "It happened a long time ago. It's been just the two of us for so many years. I'm going to miss her so much when she leaves for college." She put her chin in her hand. "Do you have kids?"

He paused. "No," he said. "No. No," he repeated, his gaze on the table.

There was a lull in the conversation, and Caroline sipped more coffee. She felt she had made a mistake, asking that question. She wanted to apologize, as he did about Glenn, but feared that would make things worse.

He lifted his head. "So, tell me about the garden," he said. "The one that Maxine mentioned the other night."

"My mother's garden," she said, touched that he had remembered about it. "She built and tended it for years, and it was beautiful. And it's about to be destroyed, if you haven't heard."

"That's what Maxine said. Why's that? I'm not up that much yet on local news."

She told him about the complaints and the library expansion. "I actually had a whole different trip with Lee planned. But then Maxine sent me the article, and I had to come back and fight for it. It's so beautiful, or at least it used to be, with a footbridge that overlooks the inlet. People used to get engaged there all the time, sometimes married."

"What do you know?" he said. "I might need to take a look at that. It's my research—the connection between romance and bodies of water. The historical context, the cultural implications. Why water is the place where people promise to love, seal their love…" He sighed and rolled his eyes. "It sounds kind of fuzzy when I try to explain it. Mostly I'm just trying to make connections and see where it leads. And see if I can eventually invent a thesis interesting enough to keep my job here. Although probably not."

She looked at him, and she found herself wondering if he was talking at least a bit about his own life. Maxine had said he wasn't married, and she wondered now if he had ever been married. Or in love. It had sounded for a moment as though he were remembering something personal, before he poked fun at himself. And she was sorry he had poked fun. She had a lot of affection for love stories that involved water.

"I don't think it sounds ridiculous," she said. "I love how that sounds. And honestly, it rings true to me. One of my favorite memories is of watching my mom and dad on that footbridge in the rain. My dad picked up my mom and twirled her around, and I could hear the inlet below, and it was so romantic. I think the rain and the rushing water is what made it that way."

She suddenly realized how much time was passing, and picked up her phone. "Oh, look," she said. "Almost twelve fifteen. I guess I should be getting back for Lee."

He nodded. "Last chance," he said, and they both took a final spoonful of ice cream before he threw away their trash. Then he surveyed the landscape. "Okay, so now we have to find our way back," he said. "I swear, my year here is going to be up by the time I know my way around this campus."

They left the veranda. "Any chance you'll be sleeping in a real bed tonight?" she asked.

"I hope so," he said. "But at some point it'll be done. She's trying her best, my landlord. I can't be mad at her. And actually, I'm getting kind of attached to that office couch."

"Are you always this easygoing?" she said.

"No, I'm really a monster," he told her. "I think this place has changed me. I think the mountains are a good influence on me. My students in Florida found me terrifying."

She laughed. "Somehow I find that very hard to believe."

They headed back down the hill, finding their way to the admissions building without any trouble. "I'll leave you here," he said when they reached the door. "I'm sure Lee will want to talk to you alone. But she can call me if she has questions about the mixer on Saturday night, or about anything else. And you can, too. Or I'll see you at the Grill. I'm sure I'll be picking up more meals there."

"Thanks, Aaron," she said. "For the program and the coffee and ice cream."

"I had a nice time," he said.

"Good luck with your house. I hope you can move in soon."

"Thanks. I'll let you know. I'll stop by the Grill and let you know."

She waved and lingered at the doorway for a few moments, watching him start up the hill again. It was funny—she'd told Aaron a lot about her parents today, in the short time they had. About the lake and the hot cocoa and the singing. About the footbridge and the rain. If he wanted stories about love and water, she had plenty. But one story she couldn't tell was how her parents had met. No one had ever told her about it. Maybe no one knew.

And suddenly she found herself wondering how her mother felt the first time she met her dad. If her mom couldn't wait to see him again.

Because that was how she felt right now.

CHAPTER ELEVEN

"Let's start with the big stuff," Jackie said. "Sofa, recliner, bed, table."

It was late that afternoon, and Aaron was in the garage with Jackie and Stan, strategizing how to move his furniture into the house. They were all dressed for exertion, in t-shirts and gym shorts, with Stan sporting a blue bandana tied around his head that kept his bushy brown hair in check. Mrs. Sobel had texted Aaron a few hours ago to say the house was finally ready, and word had spread around town. Jackie had called, offering to help with the move, and when he stopped by the Smoothie Dudes to pick up a couple of jumbo-sized smoothies on his way over, Stan had decided to help out as well, leaving Trey to handle the store.

"Bet you're happy to settle in," Jackie said as he picked up the end of Aaron's tan sofa.

"Even happier to sleep on a bed again," Aaron said as he lifted the other end and Stan took the middle.

"Where you been sleeping anyway?" Jackie said.

Aaron answered as they shuffled across the driveway and toward the front step, the screen door propped open with a ceramic planter from Mrs. Sobel's garden. Stan and Jackie were both big guys and super strong, and Aaron couldn't believe how the sofa was dipping on his side. He took a deep breath and heaved it higher. He needed to get back to the college gym this week—and not just to take a shower.

They maneuvered their way to the living room. "Where do you want it? Across from the fireplace?" Jackie asked.

"Sure," Aaron said, and they moved it into position and set it down. He stood and arched his back as he surveyed the first floor. It was a nice place, just as it had seemed in the pictures he'd seen when he started searching online. Small, but plenty of room for one. The living room was spacious enough for everything he had—his couch, the leather recliner his brother had given him, a couple of lamp tables, and his TV, which would fit nicely on the wall above the fireplace. The back window had a glimpse of the lake that was especially pretty right now, as the sun headed downward, glowing golden above the water.

They returned to the garage and picked up his bed. Tanya had found it at a second-hand store, and they'd refinished it with a cherry stain when she lived with him in Florida. She'd left it with him when she moved to New York because her place was way too small for it. Still, she'd loved that bed, and he always expected her to come back for it. He never considered getting rid of it, even after he moved out of the house they'd shared and into an apartment. He was sure he'd hear from her again, if only to arrange to come get it. He held onto that bed so he'd have it when she called.

The three of them carried it upstairs. "Slowly, slowly," Jackie directed as he angled the headboard section and pulled it up the narrow stairway, and Aaron and Stan pushed from below. "Which bedroom, left or right?" he asked.

"Left," Aaron answered, and they shuffled in that direction. He figured he'd use the second bedroom as an office. Both had large windows, which he liked, although he could only hope they were good enough for a cold winter. And, of course, that Mrs. Sobel had put in a decent heating system. He wasn't worried about the lack of air conditioning, even though it was still August. The enormous birch trees, thin and taller than any tree he'd ever seen before, provided plenty of shade for the bedrooms, and the lake breeze would most certainly keep things cool at night.

They returned to the garage and came back with the recliner and then the round dining table, which Aaron had decided to put near the living room window since the house didn't have a formal dining room. It used to be his parents', and like all their furniture, it was formal and ornate, with a pedestal base and intricately carved claw feet. He'd never thought about the style before—it was a table, and it did its job. But now, as the house began to fill up, he noticed what a strange mash-up of furniture he had: the basic furniture store sofa, the half-broken recliner, the vintage table, the thrift store bed. He looked at Jackie and Stan as they lowered the table into place. They were both probably close to his age, thirty-nine. Maybe Jackie was a little older, maybe Stan a little younger. He didn't know what kind of furniture they had, but somehow he was sure their homes looked like grown-ups lived there. Unlike this place, which had the feel of an off-campus apartment.

I'm not asking you for anything, the email had said. *You've probably been settled for a while, maybe even with a family. I just wanted to give you the chance...*

They continued with the mattress, the bedroom bureau, the TV, and then the desk for the second bedroom. "That's all of the heavy stuff," Aaron said. "Only some chairs and lamp tables left, smaller stuff. If you need to go, I can handle the rest."

"Nah, let's get this done," Stan said. "Trey's not expecting me back till later."

"I'm in no rush," Jackie said. "Beth's at the lake with some friends and my mom's got the girls."

"Okay, great. Thanks," Aaron said, and they headed back to the garage. He wondered what it was like to be Jackie or Stan, to always be able to reel off where the people you cared about were and when they'd be expecting you. Caroline had been like that, too—the way she'd checked her phone, sensing it was coming time to go meet Lee. Even when they were talking and sharing the ice cream, he knew she always had Lee in the back of her mind. He'd never had that with anyone, not even Tanya. She'd hated when he tried to pin her down, even about simple things—what time they could meet for dinner, or whether they should plan to see a movie that weekend. She always said the best thing about their relationship was how they respected each other's independence. How few tedious demands they made on each other. He said he agreed, but only because he loved her. He didn't want to give her reason to leave…

"Break time," Stan said after they'd brought in the chairs for the table, and he went to the back patio where he'd left the cardboard tray with their smoothies. Meanwhile, Aaron brought in the box with his toaster and coffee maker, and other kitchen gadgets.

"Nice job Mavis did here," Jackie said as he followed Aaron into the kitchen and looked around. "Quality appliances, nice wood floor. Big stainless sink. Nice island, you can throw a few stools around it if you want. And you even got yourself a little wine fridge."

Aaron nodded. It was an interesting touch, the built-in wine refrigerator near the dishwasher. Unexpected, but kind of appropriate for a small town where everyone knew everyone and people came together a lot. It would be nice to stop by the wine store in town and stock it. Maybe even have some company once in a while.

Stan came in with the smoothies, and Jackie grabbed one and took a sip. He squeezed his eyes shut and shuddered. "Yowza!" he said. "That'll put hair on your chest."

"What, too sour?" Stan said. "Too sweet?"

"Too… I don't even know how to describe it," Jackie said. "Like a blowtorch. Another two sips and I could have charged upstairs with the bed on my back. Man, you could send a guy to Mars on this."

"Come on, it can't be that bad," Stan said and drank his about a quarter down. "It's fine. Don't be a wimp. Your wife drinks these all the time, I might add. Your kiddo does, too."

"*Lola* drinks this? You have to be kidding me."

"Drinks it up and asks for seconds."

"What's in it?" Aaron said, picking his up and studying it. It was the color of a ripe Florida orange.

"Nothing crazy," Stan said. "It's our Late-Summer Citrus Blend. Just a little motor oil for thickness. And some turpentine for a kick."

"I don't know you guys that well, but I'm assuming that's a joke," Aaron said and took a sip. It was sour for sure, but still pretty tasty.

"So who's the brains behind this one, anyway?" Jackie said. "It's got to be you. Trey's way more subtle."

"Actually, Bella invented this," Stan said. "She's got a feel for this stuff."

"Bella's back in town?" Jackie asked.

"Yeah, got in last night."

"How old is she now?"

"Nine. Almost ten."

"That old? Crazy. How did that happen?"

"Got me. Goes by in a flash."

"Who's Bella?" Aaron asked.

"Trey's daughter," Stan said. "She lives with her mom in D.C., but we get her the beginning and end of summer and the week after Christmas."

"So Trey's got a kid," Aaron said. He was surprised, although there was no reason to be. It was one of those things—you don't have kids, you assume others don't either. But then you get proven wrong. You never knew who was a parent.

Stan nodded. "She keeps us on our toes, always trying new things. Last year it was ballet, now she wants to learn tennis."

"Ah, great sport," Aaron said. "I played all through school when I was a kid. Still do." He pointed to the racquet resting atop his two large suitcases in the corner of the living room.

"We bought her new shoes and a tennis racquet for her birthday," Stan said. "Man, kids are expensive. I don't know how you're doing it, Jackie—two here and two on the way."

"Yep, a quartet by the winter," Jackie said. "I know, it's madness. But it's great, having kids. Putting something good out in the world, right? Although when you go to a restaurant and your kid flings her spaghetti on the floor and the waiter slips on it and drops a tray of glasses, then it doesn't quite feel like you've done the world a favor. But you guys get the idea."

"You got kids, Aaron?" Stan asked.

"Um… no," Aaron said. He felt them both looking at him, reacting to that strange "um." "I mean, I have a niece and nephew. My brother's kids."

Jackie put down his smoothie. "Okay, men, the end is in sight," he said. "Let's do it and be done."

They went back out for the side tables, lamps, and a few area rugs. "So I hear Caroline brought Lee to Gorson today," Jackie said.

Aaron nodded. He was glad Jackie had brought that up. He was hoping they'd talk about Caroline. Her openness and her understated passion—the way she'd spoken about Lee, her mother, and the garden—was so appealing. It felt good that she had trusted him with all that. He admired that she wanted to save her mother's garden. And there was something, too, about the way she looked. Her wavy golden-brown hair that she had pulled back into a ponytail, kind of messy but kind of controlled too. And how she had scaled that hill today without getting the slightest bit breathless. Her pretty, tanned shoulders.

"Heard you got them in at the last minute," Jackie said.

"Not that big a deal," he told him. "I just reached out to ask."

"My mom would be awfully happy to get Lee here. It would mean Caroline would be back a lot, too."

"Yeah, well, sounds like she has her heart set on Alvindale. Not sure Gorson can compete with that."

They went back out for the final boxes with dishes and other kitchen and bedroom items. "So, Bella going to be here for the Moonlight Carnival?" Jackie asked Stan. "Aaron, you heard about that?"

"Yeah, Caroline was telling me."

"She wouldn't miss it," Stan said. "You guys staying?"

"Sure, we'll be heading back to Buffalo after."

"Any idea who the Midnight Couple is?" Stan asked.

"No idea," Jackie said. "No announcement yet, far as I know."

"What's the Midnight Couple?" Aaron asked.

"It's a couple that gets engaged at midnight during the carnival and promises to get married before Thanksgiving," Jackie said. "Otherwise, the town will be in for a brutal winter. At least that's the story. So one couple always steps up. We did our part, Beth and me. I asked her to marry me at midnight at the Moonlight Carnival night six years ago. And we got married on the first of October. And Stan and Trey were the couple last year."

He put the last box on the kitchen counter and then went to sit on a chair, sending his legs sprawling. "Okay, I am officially exhausted," he said. "You got a nice home, my friend. I know you may be here only for a year but I wish you a ton of happiness." He pulled himself up again. "Come on, Stan old man. Let's get going while I still have a drop of energy left."

"Hey, wait," Aaron said. "Can't I buy you guys some hot dogs and beers at Lonny's? For doing all this?"

"Gonna have to take a rain check," Jackie said. "There's the last Thursday concert of the summer on the green tonight. The last one's always the biggest, with dancing, fireworks." He looked at Stan. "You guys setting up a kiosk?"

Stan nodded. "So don't screw with me. Is the Citrus Blend okay? Or should we go with one of our regular flavors for wusses like you?"

"It's fine," Jackie said. "I have tender taste buds."

Aaron followed them to the door. "Look, you guys, thanks," he said. "I owe you a dinner at Lonny's."

"And don't think we won't remember," Stan said.

"Why don't you meet us tonight?" Jackie said. "My whole family will be there. Gull's in charge of food, you know we'll have plenty. Gonna be a good time."

Aaron thought for a moment, then shook his head. "Thanks anyway," Aaron said. "But I have a lot to do, unpacking and all. But thanks anyway. And thanks again for all the help."

They nodded and headed down the street. Aaron went back into the house and made a couple of adjustments, moving the throw rug in front of the sofa, plugging in the table lamps. It was nice of Jackie to invite him to the concert, but he didn't feel like he belonged. It was a family get-together. Besides, he needed to unpack the kitchen stuff, and his clothes too. Classes would be starting soon. He needed to get the house organized now, while he still had time.

In the kitchen, he pulled a strip of packing tape off of one of the boxes. He was sorry it hadn't worked out, to go over to Lonny's with Stan and Jackie. It would have been fun, to hang out with those guys. It hadn't occurred to him that they wouldn't be able to. Back in Florida, he was always around a lot of single guys just like him—grad students, faculty members. He hadn't known a whole lot of family men.

He put the dishes in the dishwasher—they'd been wrapped in newspaper, so were pretty smudgy—and then continued with glasses and utensils until the dishwasher was full. He'd have to stop somewhere tomorrow and get some detergent and other household supplies. He went upstairs to unpack a few more boxes with assorted things—some shoes, clothes, towels, and sheets—and then stopped and looked at his phone. Seven o'clock. Earlier than he'd been eating this week, but he was hungry. And tired and sweaty. And hot dogs still sounded pretty good to him, even if he'd be alone.

He took a quick shower, grateful the water was working, and then locked up the house and headed out, watching the sun lower, large and golden, over the lake. It was a pretty night to be out. He arrived at Lonny's, where a sign on the door said the place would be closing at eight due to the concert but would reopen again after the fireworks. Not surprisingly, the deck was empty. He went to the takeout window and ordered a beer and a couple of old-fashioneds, with mustard and sauerkraut. The counter guy brought him his tray and he carried it to the nearest table.

The town certainly had its own rhythm, he thought as he took the first bite. Tonight was not the night to go to Lonny's, and everybody knew it except him. He was still an outsider. But he wouldn't be for long, he told himself. Pretty soon he would know where to go and what to do, just like everyone else. And there was a lot coming up, even as the summer came to a close and the town emptied out. There was the Moonlight Carnival and then all the fall events Mrs. Sobel had listed when he'd first called about the house: the Halloween celebration, where kids painted scary scenes on merchants' windows; the scarecrow festival, where families made scarecrows on the green out of old clothes and bales of hay, and then sold them as a fundraiser for the hospital; and the holiday express, where firefighters paraded their firetrucks all over town, tossing candy canes to kids waiting along the route.

"It's a great place to raise a family," she'd said. "Or to live alone," she'd added hastily, as though she remembered he was moving by himself. "That works, too. It all works. Just a very wonderful town." He'd thought she sounded sorry for him.

He finished up and walked down off the deck and back onto Main Street. The sound of instruments filled the air, and even though he hadn't planned to go, his feet started moving in the direction of the green. As he approached, he could see that a makeshift stage lit by floodlights had been set up at one end, and the large grassy area in front of it was starting to fill with blankets and lawn chairs and people. There were huge speakers and microphones around the perimeter of the stage, and in the center, a few guitarists, a saxophonist, and a pianist were warming up. A drummer was twirling his drumsticks between his fingers.

He looked across the lawn, and he spotted Maxine's whole clan. She was unpacking sandwiches from a cooler, while Gull was ladling pasta from a pot into bowls. Jackie helped his pregnant wife into a lawn chair, then picked up his baby from her stroller and put her onto his shoulders. On an adjacent blanket, he saw Caroline and Lee, Caroline sitting with her legs outstretched and Lee sitting cross-legged. Maxine stroked Lee's shoulder to get her attention and handed her a sandwich. Over by the stage, he saw a table with the Smoothie Dudes logo. Behind it were Stan and Trey with a girl who had to be Bella. She finished filling a cup from the metal vat and showed it to her dad, and he put his arm around her shoulders.

And suddenly Aaron wanted to know this world, this world of parents and children. It was a world so foreign to him. His own parents had always encouraged his brother and him to strike out alone, to follow their own pursuits, no matter how quirky they were or how far away they led from the company of others. Their family had moved often in and around Minnesota when he was growing up; his parents, both college professors, always wanted to explore different academic settings. But people here were so different. This was a world where people stayed, like Maxine and Gull, or came back, like Jackie and Caroline, bringing spouses and children with them. He wanted to know how that felt, to be responsible to others, responsible to family. Responsible to children. Did he have what it would take to be part of that world?

He didn't know. But Caroline belonged in that world. She was completely devoted to Lee, to helping her find her future, especially now that college was only a year away. *It's been just the two of us for so many years,* she'd said. *I'm going to miss her so much.* He wanted to know how that felt, to raise a kid, to see a kid grow up. To have that much love to give a kid. He wanted to know how she'd found the strength to do it. And what she did when it got hard. How she'd done it so well. And what he could learn from her.

Continuing along Main Street, he took out his phone. He still had her number from when she'd called the other day. He started to call, then changed his mind, because he didn't want it to ring while she was at the concert. He'd send a text instead. It was better for him, too. That way, if she wasn't interested, he wouldn't have to figure out a clever way to get off the phone.

Hey, just wanted to see how Lee liked it today, he typed. *I hope she had a good time. And if she's going to the mixer Saturday, I was wondering if you might want to show me your mom's garden. And maybe afterward, we can grab some dinner.*

He finished typing then put his phone away. He didn't want to interrupt her right now. He'd send it later, when the concert would be over.

And he'd wait at home for her reply.

CHAPTER TWELVE

When the concert and the fireworks ended, Caroline helped load Gull's truck with lawn chairs, blankets, and picnic paraphernalia, and then waved as Maxine and Gull drove off, Gull having decided to reopen the Grill for a few hours for concertgoers in need of a drink or late-night snack. Lee went to join Jackie and his family to wait in line for smoothies, and Caroline decided to walk back by herself. The evening was beautiful and the moon almost full, and shining white against the inky sky. Almost perfection, she thought. Almost.

She was glad to have some alone time to think about the day. She'd been sorry to say goodbye to Aaron when they reached the admissions building and she went inside to meet Lee. She'd enjoyed their conversation, how her explanation about the garden had led them to the subject of bridges and water and love. It was nice to know that someone else not only cared about these things but was studying and writing about the way they were linked. No one back home thought like Aaron did. No one had these kinds of conversations with her. Leaning against the wall to wait for the auditorium doors to open, she remembered how closely he'd listened, too, when she described those winter nights with her parents. He was a stranger, and yet she'd felt he wanted very much to get to know her.

She'd felt a tug on her arm, and realized that the auditorium had emptied and Lee was right next to her.

"Hello-oo!" Lee said. "What's up with you? Daydreaming?"

Caroline laughed and waved her off. "Sorry, just zoning out. So how was it?"

"It was good," Lee said, her tone noncommittal. "Fine. The people were nice, the curriculum pretty normal for these kinds of schools. That professor guy was right, what's his name, Adam—"

"Aaron."

"Yeah, Aaron—the art studios are amazing. They took us there for a look. It's wild how nice they are, big and clean, and all these different materials and media. And I can use them anytime while the program is going on."

"That's exciting," Caroline said.

"And they do have a lot of events going on," Lee added, holding out a folder with the Gorson logo. "Workshops and projects and private conferences with teachers if you want. And there's that mixer on Saturday with upperclassmen. That sounds fun. I guess."

They reached the car. "So, what do you think?" Caroline said. "You want to keep going?"

Lee gave her a look. "I know *you* want me to."

"Not if you don't want to," she said. "I'm glad you gave it a try. But this is your vacation. I don't want you to spend your time doing something you hate."

"I don't hate it," Lee said. "I like Alvindale better. As a school."

"I understand that."

"I mean, I don't want to study art. I already know that. I have a whole plan worked out with Meems."

"But you can still change your mind, lots of times if you want—"

"I don't want to change my mind."

"That's fine, too."

"Mom, why are you confusing me?"

"I'm not. I'm just—"

But Lee was already in the car, and she slammed her door. Caroline got behind the wheel, and they drove home in silence, with no decision about Gorson one way or the other. Caroline knew this wasn't simply a choice about how to spend the next few days. Lee clearly saw the Gorson program as a threat to her autonomy, as well as a huge betrayal of Aunt Risa. She loved being the golden girl, Rantzen Enterprises' chosen one, and felt indebted to her great-aunt for putting her in that position. But Caroline couldn't help thinking she also was drawn to the art program at Gorson, and the opportunity it represented. She was sure Lee was lashing out because she was scared she'd fall in love with the program, and she wouldn't know how to face Aunt Risa after that. If she didn't care so much about art, she could attend for fun, as Jackie said. She was getting worked up because she cared.

They stopped at a supermarket on the way back to town to pick up some groceries to restock the refrigerator, and then made their way back to Maxine's house. Lee fixed herself a sandwich and went out onto the porch, and Caroline went upstairs to change into running clothes, still too full after the ice cream to eat anything more than a peach and some grapes. She took a nice run to the lake and back, then showered and helped Maxine pack the ice chest with food to bring to the green for the final summer concert. Lee came back from her own run a little while later and came down to play with Jackie's girls until it was time to leave.

Walking home by herself now under the glow of the moon, she felt her phone buzz in the pocket of her skirt. She took it out, and when she saw it was from Aaron, she stopped to read it. She felt herself smile at the message, and pressed a fist to her mouth so no one would see her looking so goofy, beaming into her phone. He was asking her out. She knew it must have been hard for him to reach out like that. He was friendly and funny, but he didn't strike her as overly confident, the kind of guy who went out with women a lot. She read his message again. She wanted to say yes. But Lee still hadn't decided what she planned to do Saturday night. And she also felt guilty, remembering all the times she'd refused to go out with Will, telling him she wouldn't date while Lee was still living at home. She thought she'd meant it. And yet, here she was, hoping Lee would go to the mixer, so she could spend an entire evening with Aaron.

She reached the Grill and went inside. A few tables were occupied, with couples and a few families sipping drinks or having dessert or comfort food, nachos or chicken wings with blue cheese dip. There was a server working the floor, while Gull and Maxine were speaking to each other near the bar. Maxine smiled when she saw her.

"Lee beat you home," she said. "Jackie just brought her back."

"Oh. Did she say anything? About Gorson, or anything?"

Maxine shook her head. "No, just thanked us and went to the house. Why? Is anything wrong?" She patted the chair next to her, and Gull poured hot water into two mugs and slid over two tea bags. Then he went into the kitchen.

Caroline sat down and took a sip of tea. It was exactly the position she'd been in so many times when she was young—maybe not as late at night, but certainly in the same spot—talking to Maxine about whatever was on her mind. Homework. Friends. She hadn't even realized how much she'd missed these heart-to-hearts.

"I don't know if she's going back to Gorson on Saturday evening. We had a disagreement this morning."

"Well, she is seventeen," Maxine said. "I think that's normal for mothers and teenage daughters."

Caroline looked down at the bar. "And... and Aaron texted me while we were at the concert. He asked if I'd like to show him around the garden and have dinner on Saturday. If I needed something to do on Saturday while Lee was busy."

Maxine smiled. "I'm sure he didn't say it like that—if you needed something to do."

"No, he didn't," Caroline said. "It sounded like he wants to see me."

"Well, that's lovely," Maxine said. "He's such a sweet guy." She tugged on a piece of Caroline's hair that had fallen toward her face. "You feeling guilty about it?"

Caroline nodded. "A little."

"Does this have anything to do with the young man you mentioned to me? Will, I think, right? The one who doesn't know you're in Lake Summers? The one you told you couldn't date while Lee still lived at home?"

Caroline sighed. "I thought I meant that," she said. "I thought taking care of Lee was all I wanted. I'm not looking to fall for anyone. I never expected to."

"And you think you're falling for Aaron?"

"I don't know. I don't even know what that feels like. I mean, I've only just met him. And I've never fallen for anyone before."

She shook her head. "I never felt this way about Glenn. I mean, we were comfortable together, the marriage made sense. And a piece of me has always expected that eventually I'd give in and be with Will, and we'd be comfortable, too. But this feeling I have for Aaron—wanting to be with him and talk to him, thinking so much about his smile and his eyes, the way they light up when he's talking to me—it's so unlike me to be like this."

"But if you didn't love Glenn, honey, why did you marry him?" Maxine said. "Why would you even consider being with Will, when you don't feel that spark?"

"Because it's… easy. It's what everyone back home thinks I should do. Anything else would be rocking the boat."

"So? Rock the boat! You only go around once in this life, why not get what you want, what you deserve? Think of your mom. She put love before everything."

"And look what it got her."

"But she was happy here. You don't stop bad things from happening by refusing to love. Yes, sometimes it's hard to follow your heart. Sometimes it causes problems or even rifts. But you do it anyway because it's worth it."

Caroline looked at Maxine. "I don't want to feel attracted to Aaron. It's too complicated. I'm not comfortable feeling this way."

"It might not be comfortable, but it's how you feel. Honey, don't make more of this than it is. Spend the evening with Aaron. He's a historian, and he'll be interested in the garden, and maybe he'll have some ideas about how to save it. That was the thing about your mom, she took life as it came. She planted those flowers every year, not giving even one thought to what bad things could happen, if there'd be too much rain, or not enough, if the winter had been too warm or too cold. She just… gardened."

She got up to help a server pass out some dishes, and Caroline finished her tea and went to the house. Upstairs, Lee was sitting up in bed with her legs crossed under the covers, the Gorson folder on her lap and the Alvindale one by her side.

"Okay, Mom," she said. "Just listen. I like Gorson, okay? It's an interesting place. I like drawing and painting a lot, and I'm not going to lie, I did find those art studios amazing. Do I want to go there for school? I don't know. But I will keep going to the art program. I want to go to the mixer on Saturday night, and then I want to do some of the seminars and use the studios. I want to see what happens. But that's it. I don't want to see any other colleges while we're here."

"Not even Boston University?" Caroline said. "I thought you wanted to see that one."

"No, not even that one," she said. "My head is spinning from all these tours, I can't even keep the schools straight anymore. I don't want to hear any more admissions stats or follow any more tour guides. You said it was up to me, and this is what I want to do. I want to throw myself into the Gorson program and just enjoy it like Jackie said. Okay?"

Caroline sat down next to her on the bed. She thought about what Maxine had said—how her mother had never wasted time worrying about different scenarios; she'd just gardened. That was exactly what Lee wanted to do, what Lee was telling her right now. She didn't want to think about this school or that school. She wanted to make the most of what was right in front of her.

"I'm sick of all those tours, too," she said. "And I agree completely. Just enjoy those art studios and do what you like. That's exactly what I want, too."

*

So instead of heading out to the tour they'd scheduled for Friday morning, Caroline suggested they do some shopping. She'd seen in the Gorson brochure that there were two upcoming parties—the mixer tomorrow night and a reception next weekend when the program wrapped up—and she thought Lee might want a new outfit to wear. The one she'd bought for the Alvindale program was way too businesslike. They invited Maxine, who didn't need to be at the restaurant until the afternoon, and went back to the clothing store they'd visited earlier in the week, the one around front from her old house. The owner, Lexy, was happy to see them and showed them all her newest items. Lee ended up choosing a cute navy-blue romper and a white eyelet dress, and Maxine bought a red A-line dress with a button-down front and full skirt, which looked beautiful on her. She said it would be fun this year to wear something new for Moonlight Carnival.

Caroline ended up buying herself a dress, too—a sleeveless, V-neck sundress in a blue-floral print, with a sash belt. She thought she might wear it on Saturday evening. She'd told Lee before they went to sleep last night that she was thinking of seeing Aaron while the mixer was going on, and Lee said she was glad Caroline had plans. Caroline responded to Aaron's text: *That would be nice,* she'd said. *I'd like that.*

As they were leaving the store, Caroline asked Lexy if the apartment in the back had been rented yet. She was hoping someone might be there who could let her look around. But Lexy told her she hadn't seen anyone there lately.

They went back to the house to drop the packages off and have a quick lunch, and then Caroline and Lee decided to go to the lake. They found two sand chairs in Maxine's garage that folded up into backpacks for walking, and they stopped at Mrs. Pearl's along the way for coffee and a bag of mini muffins for snacking. Although it turned out to be too cool for swimming, they enjoyed their coffee as they gazed at the water. Then Caroline emailed the mayor again. She'd heard back from three trustees, who told her that they couldn't do anything for her, that Mayor Young was the person she had to speak to. One advised her that he was out of town this week, but he always checked his messages, so she should keep trying.

She finished the email, then looked over at Lee, who had taken out her sketchpad and pencils and was working on a black-and-white sketch of two seagulls gliding above the water. She was glad at how easy things felt between them today. She imagined that if her mom hadn't died, they might have spent an afternoon like this when she was seventeen. Maybe she'd have been working on drawings of her own, maybe considering going to Gorson herself. Maybe her mom would have been writing lesson plans, having finished her college degree and begun teaching at Lake Summers Elementary. She watched Lee use the side of her pencil to shade in the water lapping the shore. It was such a relief that she and Lee were now on the same page. The trip to Lake Summers she'd planned so abruptly was working out.

Later, when they got back to the house and Lee went upstairs to change, Caroline's phone rang. It was Aunt Risa. "I'll be outside," she called up to Lee and went to sit on the front doorstep.

"Well, hello," Aunt Risa said. "We were getting worried that we haven't heard from you. Everything okay?"

"We're fine, Aunt Risa," Caroline said. "I'm sorry I didn't call. We've been busy."

"I'll bet. No problem. So how's it going? How was Boston?"

"Actually, we never made it to Boston."

"What are you talking about? You flew in there last Saturday."

"No," she said, feeling her heart race. She told herself to calm down. She wasn't a misbehaving child; she was a grown woman, and Lee was her daughter. But who was she kidding? Even in the office, people knew to be scared of Aunt Risa's reactions if they lowered the price on an item or promised quick shipping or offered a client any perk that she wasn't expecting.

"We're in Lake Summers," she said.

"You're where?"

"We went to Lake Summers. And we're staying with Maxine. You remember her, right?"

"What? What do you mean? Why on earth are you there?"

"Because I read an article that they were going to demolish the garden my mom built here. I don't know if you even know about the garden, but it's important to me, and I have to try to stop them."

"But what about Lee? What about Boston University and all the schools you wanted her to visit?"

"We saw some, and we canceled some."

"I knew she wasn't interested in the colleges you were proposing. I knew it was a waste of time. But I wish you would have told me. It's strange, not knowing where the two of you are."

"Lee *is* interested in a school here," Caroline said. "It's a small and very well-respected liberal arts school called Gorson College. She's enrolled in a program for high-school kids and is considering it as an alternative."

"But she's going to Alvindale. Your uncle and I have done a lot to ensure she gets in."

"But she's still young, and she has a right to change her mind."

"This doesn't make sense, Caroline. I'm talking about her future. I don't know what silly ideas she has in her head, but this has to stop. Can I talk to her, please?"

"She's not with me right now," Caroline said. "And I'd prefer you not talk to her at all. At least not until we get home."

"What is wrong with you, Caroline? Where is this coming from?"

"This is coming from a place of wanting her to make her own choices. And of feeling bad that I never did. That I was taken from here when I didn't want to go." She listened to herself, shocked at what she was saying. She hadn't expected to go down this road. But it infuriated her, how Aunt Risa felt entitled to control Lee's life. She braced herself for her aunt's response.

"Taken? I didn't take anything from you!" she said.

"You took *everything*," Caroline told her. "You even took away my last name—my dad's name, Howard. Caroline Howard. You made me Caroline Rantzen."

"We did that for you—so you'd feel part of the family. So you wouldn't have to explain to the kids at school why you had a different last name from us. Oh, Caroline, this is ridiculous. You had to come back with me. You couldn't stay there. That woman couldn't have raised you. You weren't her family."

"What?" Caroline said, shocked at Aunt Risa's outrageous claim. She felt her hands start to tremble. For so many years, she had wanted to have this talk, to challenge her aunt's decision to take her from the place she'd known as home, from the people who had made her feel safe and helped her through the awful sadness of losing both of her parents. She was shocked, too, by her own boldness, a boldness she'd never believed was inside her. But more than that, she was proud of herself for finally speaking up.

"She was my mother's best friend," Caroline said, remembering the night before she left, how sad she and Maxine were as they packed up the last of her things, including the box of Gull's chocolate-chip brownies. Maxine wanted to keep her—Caroline was as sure of that as she'd ever been of anything. Aunt Risa had to have bullied her or threatened her to get her to give in so easily. "You were out of the country, you didn't even know about me," she said. "Maxine loved me and would have been happy to keep me."

"She wasn't going to raise you," Aunt Risa snapped. "Just ask her. She said you belonged with family."

"She meant *she* was my family."

"She said you belonged with your mother's family. Ask her, if you don't believe me. She'll tell you that she agreed you needed to come home with me."

Caroline felt her back stiffen, as though she could physically block Aunt Risa from saying anything more. She'd never known her aunt to be a liar, but this all took place a long time ago, and she was sure her aunt was remembering the conversation as she wanted to remember it, not as it happened. "You're wrong," said. "Maxine never would have said that."

"Then ask her. Just ask her."

"I don't need to ask her. I know she wanted me to stay with her. I would never insult her by bringing this up. I'd never ask her if she ever told you it was fine for you to take me. I'd never do that to her, I'd never—"

Caroline stopped and put her hand over her mouth. What was she doing, getting so worked up, letting Aunt Risa manipulate her like this? Because that's what her aunt was doing, trying to turn Caroline against Maxine, so she'd bring Lee right home. And it wasn't going to work. She hadn't meant to get into a fight about *this*. The conversation wasn't supposed to be about her.

"Lee has a right to decide her own future," she said. "And that's what she's doing right now. She has talents and interests she should have explored long before now. And if you care about her at all, you'll step aside for now and let me take care of my daughter."

Aunt Risa paused. "I'm your family, Caroline," she said, her voice cracking. "I've only wanted the best for both of you."

Caroline caught her breath. She'd never heard or seen Aunt Risa cry before. And she felt bad about it. Yes, she was angry, but she wasn't the kind of person who brought others to tears.

"I don't mean to hurt you, Aunt Risa," she said. "It's my fault that it's come to this. I've been too passive about Lee for way too long. We'll be home next Sunday, okay? And then we can have a family dinner and talk."

"Caroline, listen to me," said Aunt Risa, her voice sounding clipped again. "I'm going to tell you this once more, for your own good. You don't know the whole story. You're angry because you don't understand. And you're taking it out on Lee, and she will pay the price."

"No, she's not paying any price—she's getting the benefit of learning her own mind," she said. "I appreciate all you did for me, Aunt Risa, I really do. And I appreciate all you've done for Lee. But there's a limit to what a person owes their family. When it interferes with what you owe yourself, then you have to put an end to it."

"But she can't turn her back on Alvindale. We've worked very hard to strengthen her application."

"I know."

"And we worked very hard to build this business, Caroline. You never were interested, I understand that. But we've made an investment in Lee."

"You didn't make an investment in her," Caroline said. "You helped raise her. She's a person, not an asset."

"You are misinterpreting me…"

"We'll be home next week. We'll talk then. Goodbye, Aunt Risa," she said.

She hung up the phone, her breath so ragged, it was difficult to breathe. And yet she felt empowered. She had stood up for herself and her daughter. Maxine would be proud of her. Her mother would be, too.

She went back inside to see what Lee wanted to do for dinner. The only question was whether her new-found boldness would be as strong and long-lasting as her mother's. Or whether it would diminish as the summer wound down and September approached.

CHAPTER THIRTEEN

She turned onto Oak Street and saw Aaron waiting for her in front of the library building. They had arranged to meet there at six o'clock, after Caroline had dropped Lee off at the mixer and gone back home to change. Maxine had told her not to worry about the time, that Jackie would pick Lee up later. "Have fun," she'd said. "Just relax and enjoy." It was exactly what she wanted to do. The evening was warm, and she'd worn the blue-floral dress she'd bought yesterday. It was summery and feminine, and fit her mood exactly. She twisted her hair into a loose knot at the back of her head. She'd always loved the feeling of a warm breeze on her shoulders and the back of her neck.

She slowed her pace and took a moment to drink in his appearance. He was wearing a white button-down shirt with a navy-blue check pattern, with tan chinos and dark shoes. The outfit was significantly less casual than what he'd worn to his office, and she was flattered that he had dressed up for the evening. He was looking down, his shoulders a little hunched and one hand stroking his chin. It was kind of a nervous posture, which drew her to him even more. She liked that he could be vulnerable—a quality she never encountered back home. She decided that Maxine was right—she was going to put all other thoughts aside tonight and just be with Aaron.

He straightened up when he saw her and put his hands in his pockets as he walked over to meet her. "Hey," he said. "You look lovely."

"Thank you," she said. "You look nice, too."

They strolled toward the back of the building. "So Lee decided she liked old Gorson?" Aaron asked.

"She did," Caroline said. "She wants to explore the school. So we're not looking at any other colleges this week. Gorson is second only to Alvindale right now."

"What do you know? I bet that's not a common lineup."

She laughed. "I'm glad she decided to give it a shot," she said. "I like Gorson. It's the kind of school I wish I had gone to."

"Where did you go?"

"Where else? Alvindale. It's kind of the family institution."

"Smart runs in the family."

"Well… I don't know. Mostly we're just big believers in toeing the line. That's usually the best way to keep the peace at home." She shrugged off the thought, reminding herself that she didn't want any negativity affecting her evening. "Anyway, here we are. Ready to see the garden?"

"I am. Show me the way."

She led him along the side of the building and to the back lawn, and they continued to the dirt path and the flowers. At this time of day, the colors were so vivid—the orange lilies, the yellow-and-white daisies, the deep-red dahlias. The sun was low in the sky, the earth was dappled by flecks of light where the sun broke through branches of nearby trees.

"It's beautiful," he told her.

She smiled at him. "It is, isn't it? I know it's hard to understand. I mean, I worry that most people who come here simply see some pretty flowers. That's the problem with trying to make a case for it. Nobody sees what I see when I stand in this spot."

"So tell me," he said. "What do you see?"

She took a few steps closer to the lilies and reached out her hand, letting an orange petal settle on her fingertips. "I see coming out here on a chilly April day with my mother and looking at nothing but dirt and dead grass. And I see my mom's green wheelbarrow, loaded with seeds and tools and gardening gloves, and a couple of wide-brimmed hats. And I see her absolute certainty that everything in front of us was ours to transform. And we'd imagine how beautiful the lilies would be when they came up—they were my dad's favorite because that was her name. And then we'd scatter the zinnia seeds and cosmos seeds or whatever else struck her fancy. She wasn't a very disciplined gardener. She wanted a wild tangle of shapes and colors."

"Your mom's name was Lily?" he asked.

"That's why they called it the Lily Garden," she said. "My dad loved that she had a flower name. They gave me a flower name, too."

"Caroline?"

"Sweet Caroline," she said. "Have you ever seen it? It's an amazing plant—strong and hardy, a little exotic, with these huge pink flowers, the size of a dinner plate." She lifted her hands to show the diameter. "She used to plant them every year."

"What about Lee?" he said. "That's not a flower name, is it?"

"It is," she told him. "Liana. A strong, tropical vine. I loved naming her after a plant that was forever climbing higher."

She walked ahead to where some lavender flowers—asters maybe?—were in bloom. "I understand people want a bigger library," she said. "That's a great thing. I would want that, my mother would have, too. But there are other ways they can do it. This garden also is a part of the community. There was a lot of love here. And promises and dreams. And not just my family's. A lot of engagements and weddings took place here. A lot of family stories got their start here."

"Then you need to tell people," he said.

"I'm trying," she said. "But I waited too long. I should have come back a long time ago."

"You're back when it counts."

"No, I'm late. Maxine says there have been murmurings about this for a few years. I don't know why I never checked up on this. Why I didn't pay attention.

"Anyway, let me show you the footbridge," she said. "That's the thing you're most interested in, I think."

She led him on to the end of the path, where the footbridge crossed the rocky dip. They stepped onto the planks, and knowing he was walking on them for the first time, she was aware of how rickety they were. They reached the center, and they both leaned on the railing in the direction of the inlet. The lowering sun sent ripples of gold on the water. The breeze pushed back the strands of hair that had come loose from her bun and were lightly brushing her face.

"I really liked hearing about your research," she said.

He chuckled. "I'm not sure there's a whole lot there," he said. "I've been in academia a while. There's a fine line between profound wisdom and long-winded gobbledygook."

"It's not gobbledygook," she said. "One of the last times my parents were together, they were twirling around on this bridge in the rain. I watched them. And I knew that was love. I was only seven and I knew. And sometimes I tell myself it was all for the best, the way it ended. Because where else is there to go, once you've twirled around on a footbridge in the rain with the one you love? How does it get better than that?"

She felt him looking at her, as she looked out toward the inlet. "How did your parents die?" he asked quietly.

"My mom died of pneumonia. And a few months later, my dad died in a construction accident. He was a builder and he was working extra hours to make money. He fell off a beam and broke his neck. Nobody found him until the next day."

Aaron sighed. "Wow, Caroline," he said. "That's a lot to go through as a little kid. And I'm so sorry. But look how far you've come from then, look what you've done. Lee's amazing, and it's all because of you."

"No, it's not because of me."

"No, it is. It is." Holding onto the railing, he leaned his body back, as though he were trying to distance himself from some scientific phenomenon to gain perspective. "I see how you talk to each other," he said. "How devoted you are to her." He moved in closer again and turned to her, laying his forearm on the railing. "And about it being for the best that it was the end of your parents' story—I don't agree at all. They had a lot to live for. They had a daughter to raise. And a granddaughter to meet… Nobody would ever choose to miss that. If they had the choice."

She looked down. Of course, he was right. There was plenty ahead for her parents after that day. There was plenty for them to try to stick around for. They should have had more foresight, they should have been more responsible. Her mom wasn't feeling well that week, and she shouldn't have been outside in the rain. Her dad should have brought her home immediately, instead of twirling her around. And he shouldn't have been working a dangerous job by himself. But they were young and they weren't thinking about what could happen.

"Although I understand what you're saying," he added. "There's no denying the power of a love like that. You lose control, and you can't think about anything but being with that person. I don't know what else could be like that. Unless, maybe… having a kid…"

She stayed quiet, letting his words linger in the twilight. What was he telling her? That he had had a love, an all-consuming love? That he had lost it? She had no idea how hard that must be. She'd never felt what her parents had, being so in love with each other, and now she wondered which of the two of them had it worse: Aaron, because he'd once been in love and now was alone; or her, because she had never known that kind of love at all. But he was right, she did have Lee. And she loved her more than anything. She didn't know how she was going to bear it when Lee left next year. She didn't even want to think about how heartbreaking that would be.

She breathed in and ran her fingertips over her cheeks. The mood had gotten way too serious. It felt wrong because, as Aaron had said, they didn't know each other yet. Tonight was supposed to be fun. "See down there," she said, leaning forward and pointing toward the underside of the bridge. "There used to be this hook under the bridge, and my dad hung a bucket there, and that's where he would leave little presents for us to discover while we were gardening."

He raised his eyebrows. "Under this bridge?"

"Sometimes it was candy, or a treat from Mrs. Pearl's, a little note to say hi or a coloring book. I would stand on this bridge, watching my mom as she balanced on the rocks to go underneath. It was like that fairy tale with the troll. I'd jump up and down and she'd call up, 'Who's tripping over my bridge?'"

He grinned. "Let me get this straight," he said. "Your dad *rappelled* to the underside of the bridge to hide things—"

"Come on," she said. "It's a tiny footbridge, he did not rappel—"

"—and your mom did the same thing to find them? While you were jumping on top of her? They couldn't just *hand* each other stuff?"

She laughed and nudged him with her shoulder. "It wasn't all that dramatic. It was fun. I loved hearing my mom's voice coming up through the planks. I only wished she'd let me go under the bridge, too."

"She wouldn't let you under there, huh?"

"She said I had to wait until I was older."

"Well, you're older now," he said. "Okay, let's do it."

"What?"

"Show me where your dad hid the presents."

"You want to go under the bridge and see the hook?"

"Sure. Why not? I like games, too. Just because I have the title 'professor' in front of my name, it doesn't mean I'm a total wimp."

"No, no. I don't think that's a good idea," she said. "The bridge was a lot more secure back then. And I don't know what's under there now. I'm sure nobody's been there in forever. There could be rats, or something even more disgusting. Toxic mold, animal carcasses…"

But even as she was talking, he was already heading back toward the path, and she smiled as she followed him, charmed at how playful he was. They stepped off the last plank, and she started to ask if he was sure he wanted to do this, but she never got the question out. He turned to face her, and suddenly she was aware of him so close to her—how irresistible his smile was, how good he smelled, how sweet the creases extending from his eyes as he looked at her so attentively. She didn't care about the bridge or the rocks anymore. All she wanted to do was kiss him. She felt him put his hands on her shoulders, and she raised her chin and closed her eyes. But the rocks beneath her were loose and uneven, and before she knew it, her left foot was sliding behind her. She threw her body forward and grabbed his shirt, and that made him start to fall, too. They both began moving their feet as though they were treading water, trying to get some traction as they grasped each other's forearms. Finally, they made it back up to flat ground.

"I guess that wasn't my best idea," he said. "How did your parents do it?"

"I don't know. Maybe they had better shoes," she said, and they let go of each other's forearms. Caroline still wanted to kiss him. But it wasn't going to happen. Not now. The moment had been fragile, and now it was gone.

"I'm getting hungry. Are you?" he asked.

She nodded. "Let's go eat."

They agreed on Italian food, and he led her to a little place he'd discovered near his house, with a tiny terrace, the tables bedecked with candles and red-checked tablecloths. They ordered a margherita pizza and an arugula salad to share, along with a bottle of Chianti. The waiter came with the wine, and Aaron invited her to do the tasting. It was delicious, fruity and tart, and she nodded for the waiter to fill their glasses.

"To your mother's garden," Aaron said, holding his up. "And to your success in saving it."

Caroline smiled, and they clinked glasses and sipped.

"So you raised Lee all by yourself?" he asked.

She nodded. "Her dad died when she was a baby."

"Was that hard? Being on your own like that?"

She thought for a moment. "I hardly remember it any other way. But my aunt and uncle helped me. I was only twenty-two when she was born. The two of us sort of grew up together."

"What was he like? Your husband?"

She ran her fingertips along the base of her wineglass. "He was a good man. Very kind. Very smart. Honestly, it was so long ago, it feels almost like a dream when I try to think about him. We met at one of my aunt's cocktail parties, and we got engaged a few months after. We'd only been married two years when he died. He was forty-three. A congenital heart condition that was never diagnosed."

"Forty-three?"

She nodded. "That's why I was attracted to him. He was so… established in his life. He had a house and a job, and he knew who he was and what he wanted. That's what I needed back then. Someone who was older and made me feel safe. Settled."

She looked down, embarrassed at how unromantic her marriage sounded. Embarrassed that she couldn't say she'd been in love with her husband. As she'd told Maxine, she still felt bad about that. Glenn was a good person. He'd deserved a life with someone who really loved him.

The waiter returned with their food, placing the pizza on a pedestal tray in the middle of the table. Aaron used the metal spatula hanging from the side to serve them each a slice and then passed her the salad bowl.

He took a bite of pizza and then raised the slice. "How does it compare to Chicago?" he said.

"Nothing compares to Chicago pizza," she said. Then she took a bite. "But this is actually pretty good."

She scooped some salad onto her plate. "So, tell me about you," she said. "Who were you before you became Lake Summers' newest year-round resident?"

"Not all that much to tell," he said. "I grew up in Minnesota, like I told you the other day. My parents were both college professors, no surprise. My brother is a teacher, too. Well, now he's superintendent, living in Pennsylvania. Happily married, two kids."

"And you?" she asked. "Have you ever been married?"

He looked away for a moment. Then he turned back to her. "Almost," he said.

"Almost?"

He chuckled. "Well, almost in my mind. Not in her mind. Not even close. She's the reason I moved to Florida. I went there to be with her."

"Oh," she said. "So you were really in love."

"I was crazy in love." He shrugged and gave a small laugh, as though aware he was showing his vulnerability.

She rested her chin in her hand. "What was that like?"

"It was the best feeling in the world, at first," he said. "I wanted to be with her all the time. But we weren't the greatest match.

She was chaotic and driven, and all I wanted was to be the one to bring her home. But she liked being the way she was. She was never at home when she was with me. I wish I had realized that sooner. It would have made things…" He shook his head. "It would have made things a whole lot simpler."

He put down his slice and looked at his plate. "You know, there was this thing… she studied biblical literature in college, and there was this verse she always repeated: 'A river flows from Eden to water the garden.' Well, I never knew what that meant, except that I thought it was nice, a river out of Eden. But I came across the verse the other day when I was working. Turns out that the one river in the verse eventually separates into four different ones. So I guess she was always telling me she wouldn't stay."

She looked at him, wanting to know more—where this woman was now, whatever happened to her. But he rotated the tray, studying the pizza and taking another slice. She could tell he wanted to change the subject.

"It must be exciting, Lee going into her senior year," he said.

"It is," she said. "Senior year is a big deal. Prom. Graduation. I'm excited for her. But it's hard, getting ready to say goodbye."

"She'll always be your daughter."

"Of course she will. But it's going to be different. I mean, I'm not going anywhere, but she is. Like she's supposed to."

She took a sip of wine. "The thing is, you have a kid, and it feels like she's going to be young forever. And she's going to school and learning to swim, and playing softball, having dance recitals, and it's all so busy you don't even see how fast time is going. And then all of a sudden she's in high school, and then she has her driver's license and then one day she's seventeen and has one foot out the door. And you have absolutely no idea how it happened." She smiled. "Sometimes I wonder if I'm so attached to this garden because it's the one thing I can hold onto. Maybe it's just my silly way of dealing with Lee growing up."

"No, no, don't think like that," he said. "The garden isn't only about you and Lee. It's like you told me—it's about history and tradition and family. These are important things for a town to recognize. Don't minimize what you're trying to do."

"Okay, then," she said with a firm nod of her head, and they went back to their food.

A little while later, they finished up and left the restaurant's patio. Main Street was quiet, the domes of the streetlights glowing, throwing down faint shadows. They approached Oak Street and the library, where they had started their evening.

"So how does the garden look in the dark, with just the moonlight?" he said.

"I don't remember, but I think it's probably amazing," she said.

They retraced their steps from before, along the side of the library and around to the back. Although the streetlights from Main Street were visible, the path was still dark, and Caroline took out her phone and put on the flashlight. Her shoes sank slightly into the soft dirt. They reached the footbridge and went up to the apex, looking toward the inlet, their hands on the railing. The sky was dotted with stars alongside the half-moon. The water gurgled.

Aaron put a hand on hers. "Caroline," he said. "Sweet Caroline."

She smiled and looked down. This seemed so irresponsible, what they were doing. She was leaving town in a week. But she knew how much she was drawn to him, and she could tell he felt the same, and that was all she cared about. She rotated her hand and interlaced her fingers with his. They stayed that way for a few moments, feeling the breeze, listening to the water below. Then he brought her arms around his waist and wrapped his arms around her, on top of hers. She moved in closer, leaning her head toward him, and she felt his kiss on her forehead, his lips cool and pliable. She lifted her chin and found his mouth and felt his lips press into hers. And she let herself feel that pure sensation, his lips on hers, her body against his chest, his smell rich like sandalwood.

She'd never had such a lovely kiss before.

And for a few moments, she let herself believe the night would never end.

❦

CHAPTER FOURTEEN

The next morning, Caroline woke to the sound of voices downstairs and the smell of fresh coffee. She stretched luxuriously at the thought that another Sunday family breakfast was in the works. Lifting her head, she looked at the clock on her night table. Nine thirty. Much later than she normally woke up, even on a weekend, but she wasn't surprised—she had fallen asleep so quickly and slept so deeply that it felt as though she'd laid her cheek on the pillow only a moment ago. Smiling, she draped an arm above her head. She'd had such a wonderful evening with Aaron. She'd let herself lose track of time, which she never did. Their first moments on the footbridge, then dinner, then returning to the bridge for that amazing kiss—it wasn't so much that time had flown, but more that it had stopped mattering. And it had felt so good, for the first time in her life, to feel she had all the time in the world.

With mixed feelings, she pushed off the covers, sorry to end her reverie but eager to help with breakfast. In the bed next to her, Lee was still sound asleep. They hadn't had a chance to talk yet, since she'd arrived home after Lee went to bed last night. So she didn't know if Lee had enjoyed the mixer or not. She was curious, but decided to let Lee sleep in until breakfast was ready, and they could catch up afterward. Moving quietly, she took a quick shower and then slipped into her favorite slate-blue sundress and pulled her hair back into a ponytail. She closed the bedroom door behind her and went to the staircase, excited to tell Maxine what a good time she'd had and how grateful she was that Maxine had encouraged her to go.

But she didn't get a chance. No sooner had she come down to see Maxine and Lola setting the table, and Beth putting the baby into her high chair, than the front door opened and Jackie walked in. Aaron was alongside him.

"Look who I bumped into at Mrs. Pearl's," Jackie said, clapping Aaron on the back. "I told him this family values academics too much to let him get by without a big, home-cooked breakfast every now and then."

Gull appeared in the doorway to the kitchen, an apron around his waist and a spatula in his hand. "I thought we got rid of this freeloader already."

"Oh, you be quiet!" Maxine scolded him as she waved a dish towel in his direction. "Aaron, we are delighted to have you. Jackie, go get another folding chair, the oatmeal is ready, and Gull is finishing up the pancakes and bacon."

Jackie went to the hall closet, and Aaron stepped over to Caroline, as she stood on the bottom step. He smiled. "Good morning," he said quietly, and the greeting seemed an affirmation that all was different this morning. Things had changed between them last night.

"Good morning," she answered, feeling her cheeks warm. She knew her smile was probably a mile wide, but she couldn't contain it. She was very happy to see him again so soon. He was wearing jeans and a forest-green shirt with the sleeves rolled up, and she thought he looked boyish and handsome at the same time. And he had on a large silver watch, and she wondered how he'd gotten it and if someone had given it to him and why he'd decided to wear it today. He had a light layer of stubble on his jaw, and she wondered if today was special or he always looked this way on the weekends, and she realized she liked him both ways equally. And she noticed that his build was kind of muscular even though he was thin, and she wondered if tennis was responsible for that and how often he played and what made him like it. There was so much about him she wanted to know.

"Sleep well?" he asked, brushing her forearm lightly.

"I slept great," she said. She loved the feel of his fingers on her skin. "You?"

"Yep. Me too," he said, and she smiled again, because she knew that all this talk about sleeping was code for how glad they both were to be together again.

"Everything's on the table," Maxine called out.

"I'm just going to get Lee," Caroline said, and Aaron went into the kitchen. She started up the stairs, but then saw that Lee was already standing on the top landing. "Oh hi, honey," she said. "I'm glad you're awake. I wanted to let you sleep, but everyone's here for breakfast."

Lee walked downstairs methodically, her lips pressed together.

"And you'll never guess who's here," Caroline said. "Jackie ran into Aaron in town and invited him over—"

"I saw," Lee said, her words clipped. She passed Caroline and went into the kitchen.

Caroline watched her, puzzled. Why would she be in a bad mood? Was she angry at having been woken up? Or did she have a bad time last night, and was she frustrated that she couldn't talk about it right now, with so many people around? Caroline knew that both of those reasons were possible. Had Lee seen her and Aaron standing close to one another, talking privately? Had she seen him stroke her arm? Was she upset about it?

She sighed and followed Lee into the kitchen. Maxine put Caroline in between Aaron and Lee on one side of the table, opposite Jackie, Beth, and their children. She and Gull were at either end. Caroline poured the coffee and then took her seat.

"So, Lee," Aaron said as he put his napkin on his lap. "How did it go last night?"

"Yeah, tell us," Jackie said, as he scooped up a pancake and put it on Lola's plate, then poured some syrup over it. "How's this school Aaron keeps touting? Does it measure up? Or is he full of baloney?"

"It's okay," Lee said stiffly, her chin down as she stirred her coffee.

The table was silent for a moment, as clearly no one had expected that tone. It was so different from the way Lee had been last weekend at breakfast, so different from how she'd behaved all week. Even the children were quiet.

"Anything else?" Caroline said, hoping to convey that no matter what was bothering her, her attitude wasn't acceptable. "Can you elaborate?"

"It was fine," Lee said. "I have nothing to else to say." She took a bite, still looking down.

There was silence again. Then Maxine piped up. "A woman of few words," she said. "I think 'fine' is a perfectly apt description. If Lee wants to say anything else, she will."

"So, how's the new house, Aaron?" Beth said. Aaron answered that he liked it but was a little concerned about whether the windows would be thick enough for the winter, and before long, the conversation moved to the cost of heating oil and who around the table had the best snow-shoveling technique. Caroline was grateful to Beth for steering the conversation in another direction, and to everyone else for leaving Lee alone. She looked at Aaron briefly with an apologetic smile, and he shook his head slightly, as if to tell her not to worry, he knew how teenagers could be. Then she turned the other way and watched Lee eat her pancakes, her eyes focused downward as she poured syrup and then cut into them with the edge of her fork. She was anxious to get Lee alone.

When the meal was over, Caroline offered to clean up. Maxine thanked her and took off for the restaurant with Gull, and Aaron whispered he'd call her as he brought his plate to the sink. Jackie and his family filtered out, and soon it was just Caroline loading the dishwasher and Lee clearing the table.

"So now Aaron's a part of this family?" Lee said with a sneer as she put the empty pancake platter on the countertop.

"No, of course not," Caroline said. "He was a guest for breakfast."

"What, are they trying to push you two together now? You and Aaron?"

"Lee! Jackie invited him because they're friends!"

"I don't understand this family," she said. "Why do they keep pulling more people in? Don't they like each other enough?"

"What are you talking about?"

"I'm just saying, why are they pulling us into their family? Don't they realize we have our own family? We're not looking for another one?"

Caroline closed the dishwasher door and leaned her back against the countertop, her arms folded across her chest. "What's the matter, Lee?" she said. "Are you angry because I had dinner last night with Aaron? Because you said you were okay with that. And I'm sorry I got home after you went to sleep, if that's what you're angry about. I'm sorry we didn't get a chance to talk last night."

Lee shrugged and went back for the coffee cups still on the table. "No, it's not that."

"Then what is it? You didn't like the people last night? It's fine if you didn't like it—"

"No, it's not that either."

"Then what is it?"

"It's just that…" Lee picked up a spoon and stirred it around in one of the used coffee cups. "It's just that I feel like I don't know who I am anymore."

"Oh, Lee, that's so normal," Caroline said. "It's a scary time, going into your senior year of high school. Everybody your age feels a little lost—"

"No, Mom, that's not it," she said. "It's that I'm around all these unfamiliar people, so many of them. It's different for me than for you because you grew up here. I'm not going to lie, everyone's very nice, Maxine's so nice, I'm not trying to be mean…" She looked up at Caroline. "It's just enough, Mom. I need to get back to myself again. I want to go home. Two weeks is too much here. Can we change our reservations and go home tomorrow?"

"Tomorrow?" Caroline said. "But honey, I haven't even done anything about the garden yet. I'm supposed to meet the newspaper editor tomorrow. I can't drop that now—"

"Fine," Lee said. "It was a stupid idea. I don't mean to take you away from what you're doing about the garden. I'm sorry, okay? Forget I said anything." She flung the spoon into the sink. It made a dull clatter against the stainless-steel surface as she left the kitchen.

Caroline walked to the doorway and watched her head upstairs, then heard the bedroom door shut. This wasn't the Lee she knew at all. Angry and pouty, even rude at the breakfast table. Sounding so anxious. She knew it was true, what she'd said about senior year. No matter how confident Lee normally felt, the future was coming fast, and being far from her home was probably adding to the stress of it. But she couldn't leave now. The garden was too important. And, she had to admit, Aaron was becoming important to her, too. She didn't know what could happen between the two of them, but she knew she wasn't ready to shut it all down after one evening together. She would simply have to be more sensitive to Lee. Maybe not be part of so many family activities with Maxine and the gang. Maybe not have Jackie share in the driving to take Lee to the upcoming week's activities. Definitely spend more with Lee alone, and filter in time with Aaron only when Lee was busy.

She went upstairs and knocked on the bedroom door, then opened it up. Lee was lying face down on her bed.

She sat down next to her on the bed. "Hey, I'm sorry you're feeling this way," she said. "I know it doesn't look like it, but it's hard for me here, too, trying to figure out how I fit in. So I can imagine how you're feeling. I never meant to make you feel like you didn't know who you were anymore."

Lee sat up and scooted herself back against the headboard "I'm sorry, too, Mom," she said. "I didn't mean to be like that today, and to say those things. But we've been here a long time. Okay, I know it's only a week, and there's only one more week to go. But it feels like a long time to me. It's got nothing to do with the people here, they're great. But I miss my life. My own life."

Caroline patted her leg. "You know what?" she said. "How about if we take a day trip together? McCauley Mountain isn't too far, and there are some great hiking trails there. We'll pack up some water and snacks, and get in the car and go. We can even pack some clothes and find an Airbnb somewhere. We can make a whole little side trip of it, as long as I get back in time for my meeting tomorrow."

Lee shook her head. "No, Mom, that's not what I want," she said. "I need some alone time, some independence, okay? Some Lee time." She got up and walked to the dresser, where the Gorson folder lay, and she took out one of the pages. "I've been looking this agenda over, and there are a couple of interesting workshops this afternoon, and the studios are open. But I want to pick what I do, and I want to decide on my own, whenever I'm ready to do it. I don't want everyone here all involved in where I'm going and what I'm doing and how I like it, okay? Just let me do my own thing, okay?"

Caroline nodded. "Of course. Whatever you want."

"And I want to drive myself over there. I drive all the time at home, and I'm a good driver. And you're not even using the car. I know you want to stay here for the rest of the week liked we planned, and that's the only way I can do it. Everyone else in the program is either staying on campus or getting there on their own."

"But Lee, you can't drive a rental car. You're too young. It's illegal."

"Then I'll get a ride like I do at home."

"But this isn't home. You don't know the area."

"Mom, the campus is fifteen minutes away. Everyone was using apps. You should have seen all the cars lined up the other night. If I'm going to be in this program, then I have to do it my way."

Caroline ran her fingers through her hair. "Okay, if that's the way you want it. You do your thing and I'll do mine. And we'll meet up when we can. Just let me know when you leave and when you'll be back. And always have your phone on, okay?"

She started back to finish the dishes, looking over her shoulder when she got to the doorway. Lee had picked up the Gorson page from the dresser and was reading through it. She closed the door and went downstairs. Lee was right; she was seventeen and very independent at home. She went her own way all the time, organizing her own schedule and checking in from time to time to say who she was with and when she'd be home. She must have been embarrassed last night, Caroline thought, getting picked up by Jackie when all the other kids left the mixer on their own. She realized there was no harm in letting Lee have a little more autonomy. They were only here one more week.

That afternoon, she waved goodbye as Lee took off for the campus. It turned out there was no need for Lee to order a car after all—when Maxine heard the plan, she said she'd gladly lend Lee her car whenever she wanted it. She wasn't planning any big excursions this week, she said; maybe just to the big grocery store on Route 27 to stock up on some staples, and to the bank in Lyons Hill with Gull on Wednesday regarding some matter involving the owner of the Grill. But she always could use Gull's car, if Lee had hers.

With Lee off to Gorson, Caroline took her laptop to the porch to continue to prepare for her meeting at the *Lake Summers*

Press the next day. She reviewed the paragraphs she'd written last week about why the town would benefit from an investment in the garden. She then went on to search the newspaper's and the town's online archives for backup documentation. Happily, the garden had been photographed for the paper and mentioned in articles over and over again through the years. She counted one hundred seventy-five wedding ceremonies, and sixty-five marriage vow renewals that had taken place on the footbridge, as well as a whopping two hundred and six marriage proposals as of five years ago when the paper published an article for Valentine's Day called "First Comes Love," which reported results of a town-wide survey of marriage trends.

She took screenshots of the articles and saved the picture files, and then did a Google search of landscaper websites and gardening forums to come up with a reasonable estimation of what it would take to maintain the garden on an annual basis. She also called some home improvement stores in the area to get a cost estimate for repairing or rebuilding, if necessary, the footbridge. Within a couple of hours, she had everything she needed—facts, figures, pictures, and a persuasive business-based argument that would have earned Aunt Risa's approval.

All she needed to do was make her case.

CHAPTER FIFTEEN

The next morning, Lee took off for Gorson again, and Caroline, armed with a folder containing all the pictures and articles she'd found and printed out, and all the numbers she had gathered, went to the small Victorian house on Main Street where the *Lake Summers Press* had its office. She was wearing the smart blue blouse and white, dressy capri pants she'd brought from home, hoping for just this kind of opportunity. Samantha Mackel, a serious-looking woman with large, tortoiseshell-framed glasses and long dark hair twisted into a messy bun on top of her head, brought her into the conference room, evidently once the dining room before the house was converted.

"Mind if I record this and possibly quote you?" Samantha said as they sat across from each other around the small circular table.

"Not at all," Caroline answered, and she waited until Samantha had switched on her recorder before spreading out the photos and articles in her folder and reeling off her statistics about weddings, proposals, and costs to bring the garden and footbridge to peak condition and keep them that way.

"The garden has the potential to once again be a destination for couples and a beautiful venue for small community events," she said. "While the library expansion is certainly worthwhile, it shouldn't be done at the garden's expense. Sure, the garden will require a minimum investment in repair and maintenance, but this can be offset by charging a nominal fee to rent it for weddings or other events. With good word-of-mouth and possibly a small amount of advertising, the income can even rise. And the community will benefit, as visitors enjoy our town, maybe stay at the Lake Summers Resort, maybe shop in our stores and patronize our restaurants…"

She paused, watching Samantha lean back in her chair, her arms folded across her chest and her gaze cold.

"I get the feeling this isn't what you wanted to hear," Caroline said.

Samantha shook her head. "Caroline, you're not going to convince me to write a follow-up article about this whole debate by suggesting that the little plot of land behind the library will bring a ton of tourists here and transform our shops into gold-mines. It doesn't add up—and more important, it's not even what this community is about. Nobody wants to expand the library to increase tourism. We're expanding the library to reflect this town's love of learning and community and reading, some of our most cherished values. I can't tell the public there's a new angle here when your argument is, frankly, flimsy. It isn't newsworthy."

She sat up and clasped her hands on the table. "Look, I can do a spread using some pictures from our archives, maybe in conjunction with a piece on the next stage of the expansion. And you can write a letter, if you'd like. I'd be happy to publish that. But when I agreed to this meeting on the phone last week, it was because Gull said you had a fresh and viable argument to make. And I don't see that at all. I'm sorry."

Caroline nodded slightly and gathered the photos and articles from Samantha's desk, her head down. She put her materials back into her folder and slowly got up, feeling as though she were fighting against the movement of her legs. She didn't want to stand and she didn't want to leave, because that would mean she was accepting defeat. That unlike Aunt Risa, she wasn't good enough to make a convincing case for change. Sure, the newspaper wasn't the last word on this decision; but considering that she couldn't even schedule a meeting with the mayor, it was her best hope.

She lifted her head and looked at Samantha. "Thank you for your time," she said softly and picked the folder up. She couldn't understand how she had gotten things so wrong. Her mother had created a garden from nothing, and the whole town had loved it. By comparison, what she was trying to do should have been easy. She didn't have to create anything—she only had to remind everyone of what her mother had done, and why. How had she failed where her mother had triumphed?

She turned to leave, when suddenly the answer came to her. She'd failed because she'd been listening in her head to Aunt Risa. Her mother was the person she should have been following, should have been emulating, all along. Her mother had the right idea.

Turning back, she put the folder down and leaned forward, pressed her fingertips against the table.

"Yes, I understand that this town is built on values like reading and learning," she said. "But what about love? That's a value, too. And that's the value that drew my mother to this town when she knew nobody except my father. She was in love with him, and she fell in love with the town, and that's why she made the garden. It was a leap of faith because she'd never started a garden before and didn't know if she could keep it going year after year, no matter how cold the winter was, no matter how rainy the spring. And the community fell in love with it, the same way they fell in love with my mother. And the colors and scents and the new flowers year after year—that was my mother's story, and the story of this town that became her home."

She took a deep breath. Samantha's eyebrows were raised and her hands were less tightly clenched. She decided to go on. She had more to say. "And you don't have to look at the numbers," she continued. "You can listen to the stories, which I've been hearing after only one week back. There's Maxine's daughter-in-law, Beth, who talks about how her love for her husband soared when he brought her to the garden, and how his memories of his childhood helped show her a new, wonderful side of him. And here they are, six years later, so happy, with two little girls and twins on the way—that's the legacy of my mother's garden.

"And there's this teacher, Nick something, who I met at the Grill," she said. "He told me about going to the garden on the tenth anniversary of 9-11 and hearing his uncle's name read, and how much that meant to him. And how he goes back there to remember his uncle. And Lexy, the cute young owner of Lexy's Closet on Walnut Street—she got married in that garden seven years ago. She and her husband moved here because of it. She says she looks at the pictures from that day all the time.

"So you see?" she said, looking straight at Samantha. "Something very important will be lost if this town loses the garden. It's about what the garden gives to people, how connected it makes them feel to this town, to their families, to their lives even. This is about values, too. It's about what makes this town... what it is."

She stopped, her arms trembling and her breath jagged, waiting for a response. No matter what happened, she was glad she'd had her say. She was glad she'd spoken for her mother, and at least some of the people whose lives her mother had touched. If the answer was no—no coverage, no article—then at least she'd given it her best shot.

Samantha rubbed her hands together, her elbows on the table. "So tell me," she said. "Why am I now just hearing about all this?"

"I don't know," Caroline said. "Maxine and Gull went to all the town meetings and tried to save the garden. They told me that. And as for everyone else... I guess they thought their stories were too personal. Or too insignificant to bring up at a town meeting. It's not each individual story that matters so much as all of them together. Seeing what they mean as a whole."

"And you were the one who needed to gather them. The secret sauce," Samantha said. "You know, things might have gone very differently if you had shown up earlier in support of your mother. Much earlier. Where were you?"

Caroline took in a breath as she tried to formulate a response. Then she let it out as she lifted her hands in surrender. "I know, I should have come back long ago," she said. "It was just… complicated for me to return. And I never realized how far things had gotten. It wasn't until I saw your recent article that said the demolition was just weeks away—then I knew I had to come back, no matter how late it was."

Samantha shook her head. "You know, this is a story I would have liked to run last spring when it would have been newsworthy, part of the discussion about that land. But now, anything I run would read like a postmortem."

Caroline started to sink back in her chair. Then she changed her mind and lifted herself up taller.

"No, it doesn't have to be a postmortem," she said. "The outcome is still uncertain. I want people to have all the information. I want them to understand their decision. And even though it's late, you have to agree that it's not *too* late. No ground has been broken. No bulldozers or cement mixers have shown up. There's still time."

Samantha pressed the fingertips of one hand against her mouth. Then she pulled it away, the palm facing up. "I honestly don't know what to do," she said. "If I listen to you, I'll be opening up a can of worms and getting a lot of town officials angry with me. This is a community newspaper—yes, we cover controversies, but we don't like to be the ones that start them. On the other hand, the town hasn't yet heard this train of thought. So this is a new aspect…"

She paused. "If I do run a piece, I'm going to have to write it today. This afternoon. It has to be in tomorrow's paper. It can't wait until next week…" She sighed. "I'm going to have to think this through," she said. "Will you leave me your folder?"

"Of course," Caroline said, sliding it her way.

"Okay, then." She stood. "It was nice to meet you, Caroline. I appreciate your passion. I'm glad you stopped by."

Caroline thanked her again and walked out of the building. She could hardly believe what had happened. She'd never before made such a heartfelt plea, certainly not to someone she'd just met. But she'd felt that she had to speak up, or she'd never be able to live with herself. She knew she'd said exactly what her mother would have wanted her to. And she was proud of herself for being true to her mother's memory. Of course, she would have liked to stay there longer and argue her case over and over again, until she got a commitment from Samantha to write an article. But Samantha had given her a hearing and then made it clear that her time was up.

Now all she could do was to go back home and wait to see what would happen.

*

She was up and at the Grill at 9 a.m. the next morning, drinking coffee alongside Lee and counting down the minutes until she would know what her outburst yesterday had yielded. Maxine and Gull were behind the bar, stacking dishes and glasses and looking very busy, although Caroline could tell they were anxious, too. Yes, an outburst—that's what she considered it now, after replaying the conversation with Samantha in her mind all last evening. A raw expression of emotion that came from her core, a response to a need, visceral and overpowering, to make one last stab. She still didn't know how she felt about being so candid. A part of her didn't recognize the person who'd been standing in front of Samantha yesterday. But a bigger part felt proud that she hadn't lost her nerve at the last moment. There was no doubt that her phone call with Aunt Risa had emboldened her. She'd spoken up for Lee because she no longer could stand Aunt Risa pressuring

Lee to conform to her desires. And while Samantha Mackel was no Aunt Risa, Caroline had again felt she was speaking up for someone she loved who couldn't speak up for herself.

She finished her coffee and was about to get more when Jackie came running into the restaurant, a stack of newspapers in his hands. "Holy cow, Caroline!" he said. "You're not just in the paper! You're on the front page!"

He put the issues on the table, and everyone came running over. There was a picture of the garden, with the flowers looking breathtaking against the trees with the blue sky beyond and the footbridge in the background. Atop the photo was a big, bold headline—A DAUGHTER'S STORY, A TOWN'S TREASURE.

Caroline skimmed the copy on the first page, then opened to the jump page inside, which was even more wonderful. The story continued for paragraphs and paragraphs, with Samantha interspersing the text with photos from the archives. There was even a sidebar with quotes from Nick Peters and Lexy Stone. Samantha evidently had tracked them both down and interviewed them after Caroline left yesterday. Overall, the article told a story of the garden in words and pictures, starting from the 1980s and ending just a few months ago, with the town's board vote. Hairstyles changed, fashions changed, and even people's expressions varied, depending on the occasion. But what was constant was the garden and the footbridge: a gorgeous backdrop, steadfast and strong, reliable and historic.

"Oh, God, this is unbelievable, Mom," Lee said. "Look what you did!"

Caroline reached out and hugged her, feeling tears starting to form. She wasn't the only one crying over the article; Maxine was, too, and even Gull's eyes were looking watery.

Jackie squeezed her shoulder. "Okay, okay, no time for tears!" he said. "This is just the beginning! Come on, everyone! We've got to make sure the whole town knows!"

Caroline and Lee followed him outside and down Main Street, and they bought up copies from the market and the pharmacy. Then they split up to hand them out at retailers and eateries throughout the town. Caroline wanted everyone to see the story as soon as possible, instead of waiting until it arrived in their mail later that day or even tomorrow. It was amazing, how enthusiastic the shopkeepers and their customers were. "Well, look at that, I'm famous!" Lexy said as she looked the article over. "It was an honor to be interviewed, truly. I'm all for the library expansion, but they can find a different place for it, can't they?"

A couple of hours later, Caroline made her way back to the house. Maxine's car wasn't in the driveway, and Caroline assumed Lee had taken off for Gorson again. She stood for a moment in the empty spot where Maxine usually parked. It was good that Lee was taking advantage of the Gorson program, she told herself. And it was good that she felt more independent, now that she was driving herself to and from the campus. But Caroline also felt a little hurt. She'd thought Lee had spent the last few hours handing out newspapers, as she had. She hadn't realized Lee had abandoned that project so soon.

She turned away from the house and climbed the stairs to the Grill, which had a nice lunch crowd for this late in the summer. Maxine was carrying a couple of steaming plates to a table, but when she saw Caroline, she gestured to a server to take them from her and rushed right over. "Look at this!" she said, pointing to a sheet of paper that was tacked to the wall near the register, the lines filled with signatures. "Some customers started a petition to revoke the library expansion plan. It's filling up fast—this is already our second page!"

Just then Gull came from the kitchen, holding out the restaurant's landline phone. "Caroline, you're going to want to take this," he said.

She took the phone and put it to her ear.

"Hey, it's the woman of the hour," the voice on the other end said. "Sorry to reach you this way, but I have the Grill on my speed dial. Well, guess what, Ms. Rantzen? You have my attention. This is Mayor Young. We need to talk. How's Thursday?"

CHAPTER SIXTEEN

"Think of it like you're shaking hands," Aaron said, lifting his racquet to demonstrate, his fingers grasping the grip firmly but still giving the neck a little wiggle room. "How do you do, Mr. Handle? Nice day for a little tennis." He held the racquet head to his ear. "What's that you say? Smashing? Net-tacular? Bouncer-ific?"

Bella lolled her tongue and rolled her eyes as if to say, "Are you kidding me?" But Aaron could tell it was good-natured, so he laughed and spun the grip in his hand. "Okay, okay, I'll stop with the dumb jokes," he said. "Now, let me see you try. Good, good. Now show me a swing."

They were at the tennis court behind Lake Summers High School. It was a hot day, the sun beating down on the court. Aaron brought the bill of his cap lower to block the glare and then leaned over, his hands grasping his knees, to watch her. Bella pulled the racquet back, then swung it forward and across her body, the head ultimately landing in just the right place, on a diagonal extending from her opposite shoulder.

"Good," he repeated. "Nice. But you'll get a little more speed and a little topspin, too, if you drop your wrist"—he reached over the net to position her with her back to him, then covered her hand with his own to guide her swing—"and push through before you go up. Okay? Now take a couple of practice strokes."

She turned back around and brushed some loose blond wisps away from her eyes. Then she took a deep breath. "Drop my wrist," she mumbled, repeating Aaron's directions. "Push through… and… up!" she said as she slowly moved the racquet forward, her eyes glued on her working hand.

"Yes!" he said, covering over her hand to guide her once more. "Just keep it smooth, don't freeze out in front. And not so high at the finish," he added, tugging the head of the racquet toward the sky. "Not all the way up here. Just nice and comfortable, over the shoulder. Nice and easy. Take a few more practice swings, and then we'll have a rally."

He stood back again and watched, glad that he'd remembered Bella had taken up tennis when he'd stopped by the smoothie shop yesterday before heading to campus. Trey had introduced them, and when he found out Bella had brought her racquet but didn't have anyone to play with, he'd offered to give her some pointers. Now that his house was livable and he had electricity, wi-fi, and kitchen appliances, he didn't feel compelled to go to campus every day. He'd be there soon enough when classes started in two weeks—and for now, he liked being in town when he wasn't working. It was interesting, eye-opening, getting to know the people.

Now Bella bit her lip again and nodded to herself, then readjusted her grip on the racquet. She looked just like Trey—thin and fair-skinned, with the same narrow nose, the blue eyes that dipped downward at the edges. And she behaved like him, too. He'd seen Trey do that same thing, bite his lip and nod slightly a few times, before taking an industrial-sized tub of frozen yogurt or sherbet out of the walk-in freezer and bringing it to the counter. He wondered how that felt, to have a kid with the same looks and the same habits as you had. Did Trey see the similarities? Or did he need others to point them out to him? Neil, his brother, was always saying that his daughter was becoming the spitting image of his wife, but his wife didn't see it at all. He wondered when a kid would begin to pick up his parents' habits. Would he have to be watching those habits from the day he was born? Or could it be inborn, part of his genes? Did it happen when he started to try new things—run or swim or hit a tennis ball for the first time? Might a kid be like you if he never saw you until he was almost a teenager?

Bella took another few swings, each one getting better—less stilted and more connected. Then they started to hit back and forth, and soon they had worked up a nice tempo, Bella sending the shots over the net consistently in a smooth, rainbow-shaped arc. She seemed to be having fun, Aaron thought. As was he. And it came as a surprise, that he was enjoying himself, since he'd felt reluctant as he stopped by the recreation booth near the tennis courts to borrow the standing basket. What did he know about nine-year-old kids, he'd thought as he waited for Trey to bring Bella over? Thinking now about Stan and Trey and Jackie and Caroline—his contemporaries here in Lake Summers—he realized that he'd never really grown up the way they had. He'd kept a student's mindset while they'd been building normal adult lives, having children, and making those children their priority. It was as though he'd stopped moving on when Tanya left him on the Brooklyn Bridge, and he'd been running in place ever since. As though he believed he could wait for a while, and then get on with his life when she returned to him. Yes, he'd had birthdays—he'd seen thirty and thirty-five, and forty was on the horizon. He'd advanced in numbers. But not in any other way.

And that's why he'd felt so bad when Clara came to his office on his first day on campus, and he'd stood there in his t-shirt and sneakers, feeling her contempt. She was right to be contemptuous. She'd seen it. He was a kid.

"How am I doing?" Bella asked.

"What? Oh, amazing," he said. "Really nice. Good rhythm."

"Can I get some water? My dad likes me to drink water when it's hot."

"Yeah, sure. Of course. You don't have to ask. Go get some water, sure. Then we'll try some backhands, you're definitely ready."

She bent down to put her racquet on the ground, then skipped to the bench at the side of the court, where she'd left the red-capped water bottle she'd taken from Trey's hand when she'd kissed him goodbye. He should have told her to get water long ago. It was a hot day, the sun was strong. Could she get dehydrated? Would that be serious? It must be if Trey was always telling her to drink water. And now that he thought of it, his brother did that, too—always bringing extra water bottles when he took his kids for a hike or a bike ride. How did parents know to do that, to always have water handy? How did parents pick up those things? How did they know so much—what their kids could and couldn't do? When he was leaving the smoothie shop yesterday, he'd seen Lee getting into Maxine's car and driving off on her own. Of course, Lee would have a driver's license, he thought. But still, how did Caroline know it was okay for Lee to drive? She didn't know the area, and it wasn't her car, and she was still a kid. How had Caroline decided that was okay? How did she know Lee was ready to take herself to campus. How did she *know?*

Bella came back to the court, tightened her ponytail, and picked up her racquet again, and they rallied on. He'd never taught tennis before, but it wasn't that hard. After a few tries, he found he was able to aim the ball where he wanted, ensuring it would land at the right point and bounce at the right height to connect with the sweet spot of Bella's racquet. He watched her grow relaxed and confident, sending the ball back to him with more speed and more power. Quickly their hour was up, and the next pair of players were sitting at the fence door, waiting to start.

"Looks like it's time to take it in," he said. "We can do this again if you want, while you're in town. Just a few more lessons, and you'll be ready for the U.S. Open."

She rolled her eyes. "Yeah, right," she said, and then ran to the bench to put her racquet into its case and grab her water bottle. They made their way back to Main Street, as she asked him when he came to Lake Summers and what his job was, and then told him she might go to college or might not because she intended to be a movie star by the time she was eighteen.

"Either that, or I'll be in a band," she said as they approached the smoothie shop. Stan was on the patio bringing four large drinks to a group at a table underneath a bright-orange umbrella.

"Hi, Stan!" she called.

"Hey, Jingle Bells!" he called back. "Your dad's inside. He's been waiting for you to start the Bella-licious Special!"

"Finally!" she said, and Aaron followed her in. "Hi, Dad!" she said, walking behind the counter to give him a hug.

"Hey, there, Bella-ba-della," he said, wiping his hands on a towel.

"Oh my God," she said. "Why is everyone always making fun of my name? Stan calls me Jingle Bells, you're all Bella-ba-della…"

"I know, I know, I'm sorry," Trey said. "You're too old for that. What are you, like thirty now?"

She rolled her eyes, her arms still around his waist.

"Too old for this?" he said and tickled her under her arm.

"No, Dad, stop! No tickling!" she said. She started to walk away, then ran back and tickled his waist.

"Hey, you!" he said as she ran back around the counter. "I'll get you for that."

She giggled and then leaned on the countertop, stretching her arms forward to the opposite edge. "Stan said you're ready for us to invent my smoothie."

"Yeah, but not until you get out of those sweaty clothes and take a shower."

"Oh, come on. I'm not that sweaty."

"Go on, now. The sooner you go, the sooner you'll get back. What do you say to Aaron?"

"Thanks for the lesson, Aaron!" she called as she left the store.

"You were great," Aaron said and watched her leave. "She can go to your place by herself?" he asked.

"Sure," Trey said. "It's just around the corner."

"But she's by herself."

"But she's nine. If she has a problem, she'll give me a call."

"She has a phone?"

"Of course she has a phone."

"Kids that age have phones?"

"Of course they do. Boy, Aaron, someone's got to get you a kid. Stat."

"Hmm," Aaron said, looking down.

Trey wiped the counter with a rag. "Hey, did Stan tell you? We're inventing a smoothie to celebrate Caroline's garden. We want to get it done for the carnival on Saturday. We never invented anything this quickly."

"She'll be happy," he said.

"We're trying to give it a real garden aspect. Lots of greens. I threw in some pumpkin and some beets, too. And we'll finish it with some edible flowers. I made a little batch this morning—want a sample to give us some feedback?"

"I think I'll wait," Aaron said.

"I don't blame you. It needs work. But we'll finish it up before the weekend. Can I get you anything? Even just some ice water?"

The door opened, and a couple of teenage boys walked in. "No, I'm fine. Take care of your customers," Aaron said.

"Hey, thanks for the lesson. She had a good time. I can tell. I really appreciate it."

"She's a great kid, Trey," he said. "Happy to do it again while she's here."

He gave a wave and left the store for home. He was going to campus this afternoon for a meeting with Clara to discuss the two freshman courses and the junior seminar he was teaching this fall. And he wanted to finish unpacking. His clothes weren't completely out of the suitcases yet, and there were some final boxes in the kitchen to go through. He wasn't even sure what was in them. He'd packed up so fast, he didn't even remember what he'd decided to take and what to leave behind. It had turned out to be good that he still had two months to go on his lease, he'd thought as he locked the door of his Florida apartment, waved to the guys in the moving truck, and got in his car for the ride north. Not that he liked the idea of paying double rent, but he was glad to know he could go back for the rest of his stuff. It had made it seem less reckless, the way he'd reversed his decision so suddenly. The way he'd called Samuel, his old mentor, after he'd turned down the position and asked if it was still available. "Yes, of course," Samuel had said. "Glad you changed your mind."

He didn't know it wasn't that Aaron had decided he wanted the job; no, he'd decided he needed to get away.

He continued down Main Street, thinking about Caroline—all the decisions she'd made, all she'd navigated on her own. He admired her. She'd shaped a whole other human being. But it wasn't just about guiding Lee's life, setting limits, and making choices. She adored Lee. He'd watched them yesterday walking together out of the Grill. Caroline had her arm around Lee, and Lee was looking up at her and talking, and then she gave her mom a big, impromptu hug. He thought about what Caroline had said the other night at dinner, how raising a child goes by in a snap.

He wondered now about Tanya. Had she felt the same inclination, to give everything she had for her child? Did she have it in her to be that way?

Passing the market, he thought about running in for a sandwich for lunch, and then noticed a newspaper displayed in the rack outside the entrance. It was this week's edition of the *Lake Summers Press*—and a color photo of Caroline's garden was splashed across the front. He grabbed the top copy and was paging through the issue to find the article when he heard a voice from next to him. "So exciting, isn't it? She got the story, just like she wanted."

He looked up to see Maxine pointing at the paper. Gull was beside her.

"It's amazing," Aaron said. "She met with the editor Monday, right? I had no idea they'd print an article so soon."

"It came out yesterday," Maxine said. "I guess you don't have a subscription yet. Most people got their copies already, and I can tell you, it's creating quite a buzz. We have a petition up at the restaurant to save the garden with six pages of signatures already."

"Wow," he said, finding the spread. "Look at this. She must be thrilled. Is she around, do you know? I'd like to say congratulations."

"As a matter of fact she's holding down the fort for us for a little while—Gull and I have a matter at the bank to take care of," Maxine said. "Why don't you go up there? Lee is at Gorson, so Caroline's by herself. I know she'd love to hear that you saw the article."

"Think I will," Aaron said, and he waved as the two of them walked on. He went into the store to pay for the newspaper, then came back out and crossed over to the Grill, glad for a reason to see Caroline. He wanted to hear if she'd heard back from the mayor yet, now that the newspaper article was out, and what she was going to do next. But he wanted more than that, too. He wanted to see her again, to take her out again, even. To see her dark eyes glow in the evening again and her hair ruffle on her shoulders in the breeze.

She was behind the bar, putting some bottles of beer on a tray when she saw him. She pushed the tray toward a server on the floor and then wiped her hands on her apron and came over to him.

"Hey," he said, holding up the paper. "Congratulations. You did it! Your beautiful garden, right here on page one."

She nodded and smiled, her eyes wide. "Thanks—well, I didn't do anything yet, except give the editor some reasons to run this."

"That's huge," Aaron said. "And I hear there's a petition too. I'll put my name down. Got a pen?"

She slid a pen toward him and pointed to a clipboard on the end of the bar. He walked over and lifted the pages, then signed on the first empty line. "Look at this, seven pages now," he said, sitting down on a stool. "I'm impressed."

"I know, crazy, right?" she said. "I never knew people would feel so strongly."

"Did you hear from the mayor yet?"

"He called yesterday. I have a meeting tomorrow."

"No kidding," he said. "That's great. I'm happy for you." He hesitated, wanting to give her a hug but not sure how to manage it with the bar in between them. Finally he lifted his arms and was relieved when she reached for him in return. It was a quick hug, but as they moved apart, they found each other's hands and linked their fingers together on the bar.

"I wanted to call you last night and tell you everything, but I took Lee out to a movie and then we got ice cream and it got so late," she said. "I was going to call you in a little bit. There's just always a lot of people around, and Lee too…"

"It's okay," he said. "I know you have a lot going on. I'm just glad for you." He looked around. Even though there weren't many people in the restaurant, it felt crowded to him. He lowered his voice. "Any chance we can get together tonight?"

She leaned closer toward him. "Lee will be back for dinner, and I want to be here for her," she said. "But I have some time this afternoon after Maxine and Gull get back. Maybe we can take a walk by the lake?"

He shook his head. "I have a meeting on campus and I have to do some prep for it. Tomorrow night?"

"No, I think Lee will be home tomorrow night."

"And you don't want to leave her for a little bit?"

"I can't. She's feeling a little shaky about all the changes in her life right now. I brought her here for a mother–daughter vacation, and I can't just walk out on her. She was kind of upset when I got back so late the other night," she said. "It's hard for me to see you unless she has other plans."

"No, I understand, I get it," he said. "When are you leaving?"

"Monday morning," she said. "Can we see each other Friday night? Actually, I don't even know if that would work. But there's a reception and goodbye dinner at Gorson on Saturday night that I think Lee wants to go to. Can we maybe spend time together then? Your first Moonlight Carnival, it'll be fun…"

"Sure, don't worry," he said. "Sure. We'll work it out. I should go…" He saw her look down, and he lifted her chin with his hand. "Hey. What's wrong?"

"I don't know. I feel so torn. It's been so easy, Lee and me. I've never been in this kind of situation before. I never realized how complicated it could get…"

"Don't worry, don't be upset. It'll work out. Let me know how it goes with the mayor," He started to leave, then turned back.

"Hey, Caroline," he asked.

She looked up.

"You're not going to understand why I'm asking you this… I'll explain it one day… but just answer me this. If you'd had a choice when your aunt showed up… if you had the choice to stay here and live the life you had, would you have done that? Even if your aunt, your actual family, was there in Chicago, would you have preferred to stay here? Just stay here in Lake Summers with Maxine?"

She thought about it for a minute. "I don't know how to answer that," she said. "I mean, I'm glad my aunt came to get me. Because that's the only way I would have ever had Lee…"

"I know, I know," he said. "But what if you didn't know all that? What if it was just the option of never even knowing you had an aunt, of just staying here when you were… twelve, right? Just living here with Maxine and her sons. Would you have chosen that?"

"Just thinking how I felt when I was twelve?" she said. He nodded. "Well, of course I'd want to stay with Maxine. I loved it here. I would have given anything to stay here. This was my family, Maxine and Gull and Jackie and Ben. This was the family I'd have chosen. If I'd had the choice."

He ran his tongue along the inside of his teeth and nodded. "Okay," he said.

"Why do I have the feeling that's not the answer you wanted?" she asked.

"No, no, nothing like that," he said. "It was just theoretical. Anyway, it's nothing. I'm going to go. I'll see you, okay? On Saturday, if not before."

He wanted to reach over and kiss her, but it felt way too public to do that right now. The kiss had worked the other night, in the garden, in the moonlight. But that had been like fastening a lovers' lock to a bridge. Something only for the moment.

He left the restaurant and walked down the stairs. She had been honest, and he understood what she'd said. Of course she'd have wanted to stay with Maxine, her mother's best friend, the person she knew and loved. Of course she hadn't wanted anything to change.

He headed back home. He knew what he had to do. He had to email Tanya's sister. And tell her not to change a thing. It was best for the kid to keep things the same.

CHAPTER SEVENTEEN

The next morning, Caroline finished her run and came back to get ready for her meeting with Mayor Young. She decided to wear a black-and-white checked skirt and a white sleeveless blouse, and her favorite leather sandals—tan with a wide band across the toes and low, stacked heel. The weather had turned humid, so she decided she'd pull her hair back into a loose braid. Overall, it was a good look for the purpose: casual and approachable but still neat and sophisticated.

She gathered the documents she wanted to show him—the *Lake Summers Press* article, the old photos she had brought to Samantha Mackel's office, and Maxine and Gull's petition. She knew winning the mayor over wasn't going to be easy. While there were now ten pages of signatures in support of the garden, she'd seen some people at the Grill yesterday refuse to even look at the petition, and had overheard one heated discussion between a couple about to sign it and a woman trying to talk them out of it. She suspected the mayor had heard from plenty of people like the two women she and Lee had run into on the footbridge—people who were anxious for the expansion to get underway. So she planned to bolster her case with printouts of pictures Jackie and Beth had taken on their phones in the last two days, showing store owners and customers holding the newspaper and giving a thumbs-up to the camera. Jackie had even gotten a video of Stan, Trey, and Bella combining ingredients for what they'd dubbed the Luscious Lily Libation. It still smelled a little too much like freshly mowed grass, and Jackie had been scared to taste it, but the guys had promised they'd have the recipe perfected for the carnival.

She checked her appearance in the mirror one last time and then grabbed her bag off the chair. On the desk was the Gorson brochure, with the event Lee was planning to attend today circled: a mountain sketch meet-up. The students were to assemble on the library's rooftop veranda and find a spot where they considered the view most evocative and dramatic. She headed downstairs. She hoped she'd eventually get to see some of the work Lee had been doing.

Lee wasn't in the kitchen when she got downstairs, so she went into the restaurant. There she found her daughter working at a table, her Gorson folder open and her sketchbook out, a partially eaten plate of Gull's blueberry pancakes next to her, a pat of butter melting on top and syrup dripping down the sides.

"Yum," Caroline said. "Decided on a hot breakfast today, huh?"

Lee closed the folder and put it on top of the sketchbook. "I went downstairs when you were out for your run and Maxine said Gull had fresh blueberries this morning. She said if I wanted, he'd whip me up some blueberry pancakes before he got ready to open the restaurant."

"So, what are you working on right now? Can I see?"

"Nope," Lee said. "Not ready for outside eyes yet."

"What is it?"

"Um..." Lee looked at her pancakes. "A food scene."

"A food scene? And you're sketching your breakfast?"

"Why not? It looks kind of pretty, doesn't it? With the syrup dripping down the sides and making a puddle, and the bite taken out of it..."

"Well, you're the artist, not me. Here, I'll make it even more interesting," she said as she grabbed Lee's fork and tore off a nibble for herself.

"Thanks, Mom. Much better. Appreciate it. Now give me back my fork, please?"

Caroline handed it over. "I think the mountain sketch today is going to turn out to be a fog sketch. Not too nice out. Would they cancel the workshop if it rains?"

"Well, if they cancel, we'll be busy anyway. We're supposed to start hanging our work for the closing reception on Saturday night."

"Wow, it's almost over. That went fast, right?"

"Yeah."

"And you've enjoyed it?"

"Yeah."

"Great. Okay, cutie. I'm going to get some coffee and then I'm off. Wish me luck!"

"Good luck, Mom," Lee said. "You'll do great."

Caroline kissed the top of her head and walked behind the bar to pour herself some coffee. She loved how Maxine's house and the Grill had become home for her again, and were becoming like home to Lee. She leaned against the bar and breathed in the aroma, seeing herself here permanently. If Lee ended up at Gorson, it could work. She could find a little house and Lee could live with her and commute to school, or live in the dorms and still have a bedroom in the house for school breaks. She'd love having Maxine and Gull so close, seeing Jackie and his growing family for the holidays. And she'd love finally watching Lee following her own heart—trying new adventures, taking risks, and making her own decisions about how she wanted to live her life. For too long, Caroline had stood by silently and watched her daughter find satisfaction from earning Aunt Risa's approval. But now things were different. She felt good about helping her daughter embrace her own talents and drive. She was finally the mother Lee had always needed. The kind of mother her own mother was and would have continued to be.

And if Lee went to Gorson, that would also open the door for her to be with Aaron. Of course, the logistics were a little tricky, as Lee still had her senior year to finish up in Chicago, and Aaron's position at Gorson was only for one year. But they could maybe figure out a way to stay close. And they could maybe fall in love. She'd spent so many years thinking she couldn't love, but she wondered now if she simply had never found the right person. And if Aaron might prove to be the person she'd been looking for all along.

She left the restaurant and walked down Main Street, and a few minutes later arrived at Village Hall. She checked in at the front desk and was directed upstairs to a conference room, where she spread the petitions and her pictures out on the oval table. Mayor Young, a tall man with a ring of white hair, came in and introduced himself. They sat down next to each other, and she proceeded to tell the story she'd told to Samantha Mackel.

"The garden embodies what this town is all about," she concluded. "Community and family. And love. My mother created an array of colors and shapes and fragrances, and she always made sure that when one variety came to the end of its blooming season, another variety was right there to take its place. It was wild and untamed on purpose. There's no other place in town like it—the green and the lake are beautiful, but they're open spaces, and my mother's garden was always meant to be more intimate, a place you could go to be by yourself or with the person you love. And that's what people have done, for more than thirty years. That's what the article in the paper showed. I understand there's a need to expand the library, but surely there's another way. The footbridge can be repaired, and we can add a very nice wooden fence, same as we used to have. I know the library plans are moving ahead, but there has to be a way you can revise them to keep this beautiful spot."

The mayor leaned forward and clasped his hands on the table. "Ms. Rantzen," he said, and from this tone, she suspected that good news wouldn't be coming her way. "I know the garden well. And I knew your mother, too. My daughters were in her art classes. One of them got engaged in the garden. My parents renewed their vows on that footbridge. My mother still has the picture from that day on the breakfront in her dining room."

"So you know," Caroline said, relaxing. "You know what I'm talking about."

"I do," he said. "That garden is a part of my own family's history. I completely understand. And if you had started this effort even a year ago, I might have been on your side. But it's too late now. Our town doesn't work fast, but once the wheels get moving, they don't stop for anything. We're weeks from the start of construction. The plans for the expansion are signed off. With all due respect, Ms. Rantzen—you're too late."

Caroline felt her breath stick in her chest. Of course, he was right. "I didn't know," she said. "I didn't realize a year ago how serious all this was. But other people spoke up. Maxine and Gull from the Grill, they went to the town meetings."

"But they're not family. It would have made a difference if Lily's daughter had been there."

"But I'm here now."

"But it's over." He lifted and then dropped his shoulders as if to show there was no other deduction possible. "It's not a situation you can gloss over now with memories and feel-good stories. There are serious issues with that patch of land behind the library. That slope to the inlet gets more dangerous with every passing year. We consulted with an engineer and found out we'd need to even out the slope with tiered terraces or steps to make it acceptable. But that's too expensive. We didn't even have someone committed to maintaining the garden the way your mother did, or even volunteering to oversee the landscaper's work. But there were plenty of people advocating for the library plan. At that point it was inevitable."

He reached into a folder in front of him on the desk and pulled out two colored drawings, which he pushed her way and rotated so she could see them. The first was of the inlet, looking down from the footbridge. But instead of a muddy slope, there were three tiers of broad, grassy terraces breaking up the hill, with a stone staircase leading from one tier to the next; and a wide paved walkway near the inlet, with a waist-high stone wall that would prevent anyone from falling in. The second drawing showed the same view looking upward from the inlet toward the library building, picturing the tiered terraces, the footbridge, and the dirt path leading from either side of the footbridge into the garden's depths. In the corner of each drawing was a date. *June 1987.*

"These are beautiful," Caroline said. "What are they?"

"They're renderings of a proposed redesign of the land behind the library," he said. He paused, then added, "Your mother drew them."

"My mother?"

"She was quite an artist. And she had so much imagination. She thought the whole area would be called Library Commons. And the path down by the water, Library Walk. She imagined kids sitting on the lawn and reading books, and adults having book talks out there. I found these drawings in a file in the storage room when I took office and started cleaning out all the files. There was a document with notes from the meeting she had with the town board back then to present her ideas."

"She proposed all this? Back then?"

He nodded. "The issues with that slope aren't new. They've always been there. And she had a plan. Who knows what would have been if she'd been around to fight for this."

"But I don't understand," Caroline said. "You found this. It's here. Why can't we continue with what she started?"

"I tried. Believe me, I tried. I brought these out a few years ago when the board first began to think about redoing the back.

But it's an incredibly ambitious design. And then we had that teenager fall down the slope and break his arm, and everyone had a knee-jerk reaction. They didn't want to think about the slope anymore, they wanted the whole issue to disappear. And there was an ongoing move to build a new children's room in the library anyway. It all came together after that.

"The town doesn't have the money to build what your mother envisioned," he said. "Not now and probably not even when your mom drew these." He put the drawings back in the folder and pushed them her way. "I want you to have them," he said. "They're not doing anyone any good in the storage closet. Maybe they'll be a nice memory for you. And help ease the disappointment."

She grasped the folder in her hands. "No, I'm not going to walk away now," she said. "These drawings only make me want to fight harder. It's not even just about the garden anymore. It's about the whole beautiful space that could have been."

He smiled. "Now you sound like her," he said.

She tilted her head. "You knew her that well? To remember what she sounded like?"

He nodded. "We used to talk when I came to pick up my girls from her class. You were running around with them. We let you three look at the books and we sat at the little kids' tables there, and we talked. She had a way about her, your mother, I'm sure you know that. Everybody was a friend. So we would talk about our lives, our dreams. I wanted back then to get into serious politics. She was planning to go back to school and get her degree. I think she missed her family back in Chicago. She was always talking about how much she wanted this town to be a great home for you and your dad."

Caroline opened the folder and looked at the pictures again— the tiers of green bordered by flowering bushes, the romantic stone stairway down the center with flower beds on either side. "It's like I'm letting her down all over again," she said, mostly to herself. Then she looked back at the mayor. "I'm leaving on Monday. Why did you wait so long to meet with me and show me these? I could have made a difference, if I had more time."

"Caroline, you couldn't have made any difference," he said. "I wasn't even going to show them to anyone. But when I saw the newspaper article, I realized they belonged to you."

"And that's it? Isn't there anything I can do now?"

He breathed out slowly. "Yes," he said. "There is something you can do. Something I think she'd want you to do, too."

"And that is?"

"Caroline," he said. "I want you to go public in support of the library expansion and the demolition of the garden."

She sat upright. Was he crazy? Hadn't he been listening to her at all? "What?" she said. "No! No, I'm not going to do that. Why would I do that? I have the support of the newspaper, and I have all these signatures on a petition. And now that I have these drawings… and they only go to show that there are other options. The garden does not need to be destroyed."

"No, it does. And you're the one to do it. Don't you see? If we open up the debate again, there's sure to be a backlash. People worked hard to get this library project through, to get the plan developed. And when you go back to Chicago, you'll be leaving a mess in your wake. Your mother loved this town, and she'd never want that to happen. Look, I'd love to see this whole thing built. I'm the one who found these drawings and brought them to the board. But it's too expensive and we're too deep into the library project."

"You don't know what you're asking me," she said. "My daughter is here—she's watching what I do. You're not just asking me to accept defeat. You're asking me to say I was wrong in the first place."

"I'm asking you to put this back in the past, where it belongs. You can honor your mother another way. Design a plaque to hang on the library wall. Dedicate a bench downtown in her honor. But you and your family have been gone too long to do anything different. Whether you agree or not, the garden is history, and the only question is what happens here after you leave. So call the paper and tell Samantha you changed your mind.

"Let the garden go," he said.

Whether you agree or not, the garden is history. Caroline heard those words repeating in her head as she left Village Hall and headed back to Maxine's. She could either make it easier for the town to accept that verdict, or she could keep things stirred up. That was her choice, according to the mayor. He'd said her mother would have wanted her to back away, but she knew he was wrong. It was impossible to believe her mother would have wanted her to lie, to say she approved of the demolition when she didn't.

Still, the mayor was right about one thing, she thought. Her mom would never have wanted the town to be divided. She would have been horrified to know that her garden was the cause of that. But if she were in Caroline's shoes right now, her solution would have been to fight to save the garden *and* unite the town. She'd never have believed it was impossible to do both. That's just the way she was.

Reaching into her bag, she took out her phone to call Aaron. He would understand what she was feeling, and he would have an idea for her or would know what to say to make her feel better. The world she was trying to hang onto—a world of nature and love and beauty—was a world he was drawn to as well. He was writing about it. She started to look for his number, but then stopped and put her phone away. She couldn't burden him like that, especially when he had his own concerns, with a new job and a new house. She'd only just met him. This wasn't his problem; it was hers to figure out on her own. And the sad truth was, she'd spent way too many years relying on other people to direct her next steps. Big steps, like where to work and how to raise her daughter; and little steps, like how to hide a minimal spot of coffee on her dress. *I'll figure this out,* Will had said that morning of her aunt's luncheon, and then gone off to find a sweater she could wear. And yes, it was nice that he'd done it. But it was *her* stain, *her* dress, *her* problem. She should have been the one to decide what to do.

She continued along Main Street and soon found herself turning onto Walnut and then walking down the alley beside the clothing shop. She wanted to see her old home again, to remember what it was like to be safe inside with her mom and dad. She went to the back of the building and stepped up on the porch. The "FOR RENT" sign was still hanging from the knocker. She knocked and then grasped the doorknob, expecting it to resist. But somehow, miraculously, it turned. She knocked again as she opened the door slowly, in case anyone was there. But no one was. The realtor must have come to show it to someone and then neglected to lock the door. It was empty. And she was in.

She stepped into the center of the room. It was remarkable, how changed it was. Just one big space. The staircase to the bedrooms was gone, as was the wall between the living room and the kitchen. The owner of the clothing store had said the house had been used as a preschool, and she could see what a nice little preschool it must have been. There were cubbies along one wall, each one still labeled with a child's name. Rebecca. Ari. Payne. There were bookshelves along the opposite wall still filled with books, and an art corner with child-sized tables sporting trays of crayons, colored pencils, and markers. She went to the window and lifted the shade. Even on a cloudy day like this, a lot of light came in. The walls were a light yellow, and small area rugs in primary colors festooned the floor. It felt like a happy place. She could see her mom leading art classes here.

She walked back to the tables and sat on a plastic, child-sized chair. The last time she'd been here was the morning of her eighth birthday, the morning Jackie came and took her to his house. Her stuff had made its way over to her new bedroom, but she'd never come back inside here again. Although she'd dreamed of coming back. She'd dreamed of being the one to unite her family here in this house again. She'd lie in her bed at Maxine's and imagine that her mom hadn't died and her dad hadn't left; that instead, they'd been kidnapped, and she would be the heroine to find them. She would make up whole stories about the dungeon they were locked in and the clues to their whereabouts hidden around town. Finally, she'd stopped having those fantasies and embraced her new family as her own. Maxine and Gull and Jackie and Ben. But then she'd lost them too. The only good part of living with her aunt and uncle was that she knew she was settled at last. Her aunt was so strong and so unyielding. After being abandoned twice, security was a benefit.

She thought now about what Aaron had said at dinner about the woman he'd loved, the Bible verse she would repeat all the time: *A river flows from Eden to water the garden.* He'd told her it was a verse about separation, about knowing things would end. How the woman he'd loved had always seen the end of their relationship, even as she was in it. Such a different way of living, she thought, from how her mother lived. Her mother had never contemplated endings. She'd never even liked thinking about the fall, when the garden would be dead. "You have to believe that everything you care about will last and last," she'd told Caroline. "Because that's the only way you can truly give your heart."

And sitting now at the little art table, she realized that these were her two options: She could memorialize her mother with a plaque or a bench, a sign of respect for what was past; or she could live like her mother did and refuse to acknowledge defeat, even though the winds were against her, and the mayor had made a persuasive case for calling it quits.

She got up and headed back for Maxine's. The first route was the reasonable and safe one, the second route the one she longed to take. But which was the *better* one? She had no idea which route to choose. And she had only three days to decide.

CHAPTER EIGHTEEN

That night, she and Lee cooked a simple dinner of baked chicken and salad. Maxine and Gull were busy in the kitchen, as the Moonlight Carnival was now just two days away. Ben was coming tomorrow afternoon with his wife and son, and Maxine was planning a big family dinner for tomorrow night. Caroline had decided not to say anything about the mayor's demand when she got back, as everyone was still pumped up about the newspaper article and excited for the weekend. Even Lee was preoccupied with weekend plans, eating dinner quickly and then squirreling herself away in the alcove of the living room to put final touches on her drawings. The closing reception and art show for the Gorson students was Saturday evening, and she said she had several works going up on display. Caroline was sorry that the reception conflicted with the carnival, but Lee reminded her that the carnival was an all-night event.

"The reception's short," she'd said. "I'll be back in plenty of time to see this wild party for myself."

Later, while Lee was still at work in the alcove, Caroline left the house and started down the gravel driveway. It was true, what she'd told Aaron when they'd had coffee on the college veranda, how nights in Lake Summers were like nothing else in the world. The memory of snuggling with her parents by the lake and sipping Mrs. Pearl's hot cocoa came back to her now, the evening's humid air weighing heavy on her limbs and making those long-ago wintry nights feel even more distant. It was ironic, she thought, how safe and protected she'd felt those evenings despite the darkness and vastness of the lake, while tonight, with the voices from Main Street reaching her ears and the lights from the restaurant's deck shining above her, she felt so alone.

And still, she didn't want to reach out to Aaron, no matter how sweet he was, no matter how romantic Saturday evening had been. It was *her* mother's garden and *her* mother's drawings, and she needed to work through her choices herself. So she was taken aback when she turned onto Main Street to see Aaron emerging from the Grill, a paper bag in his hand. She thought about returning to the alley, but not before he saw her and waved.

"Hey," he said as he came down the steps to the sidewalk.

"Hi," she said. Though she hadn't wanted to run into him, she couldn't help but smile at how glad he looked to see her. "Eggplant parm with a brownie?" she teased.

"You know me too well." He raised the bag, and she loved his expression, the way his eyes smiled sheepishly. He lowered it down by his side. "So how did it go today with the mayor?"

She breathed in, not ready to share what had been on her mind. "I have a lot to think about. And you should go eat. I hear if you wait too long, it'll taste like rubber."

He laughed. "I'll eat while we talk," he said. "Come on, let's go sit."

She relented because he so clearly wanted to help, and she appreciated that. And maybe it would be good, she thought, to sit down and confide in someone who wasn't as close to the situation as Maxine and Lee were. They walked around to the side of the Grill and up the metal stairs. Aaron sat at a small, square table and unpacked his dinner, and Caroline offered to go into the restaurant for some wine. She thought a few sips would lessen the unease she'd been feeling all evening, so she could concentrate on figuring out what to do.

Back outside, she put the glasses on the table and sat down on the chair catty-corner to him. The wine helped her relax, and she told him about the drawings and the terraces and how Mayor Young had ended the meeting.

"He said that?" he said. "That it's your responsibility to unite the community?"

"He didn't put it that way," she said. "He told me that it was wrong to go back to Chicago and leave a mess in my wake. He basically was saying that my family doesn't live here anymore, and this isn't my battle to fight."

She paused. "And he said my mother would want me to do what he was asking. To lie, and say I no longer wanted to save the garden."

"So he doesn't just want you to back off? He wants you to advocate for the demolition?"

She nodded.

"And what do you want to do?" he said.

"I don't know," she said. "I don't know. I keep thinking about that verse, that thing your… your girlfriend would say, about the river and Eden. Maybe embracing endings is the only practical way to live. Maybe I should put an end to all this. And then there's my mother, who said you should throw your heart into everything you love."

Aaron dropped his head. "Caroline," he said. "I didn't tell you that thing with Tanya because I thought you should take it as advice. Tanya wasn't good to me. She wasn't honest. You could even say she was cruel. She left me with questions that I can never have the answers to. Never."

She looked at him, suddenly understanding. "Oh, Aaron. Did Tanya… die?"

He sighed. "It wasn't while we were together. It was years after she left. But I found out recently, and now I see there are things I'll never understand. And I have decisions to make, but it's impossible to make them. Like trying to drive home when there's a whole chunk of the road missing…"

She felt the adrenaline collect in her chest, dense and fiery. She wanted to reach out and take his hand or touch his arm, but she held herself back. This sounded serious, and it scared her. She didn't know what to make of it or what she had to offer him, what she could give him in return if he shared what was on his mind. She watched him rub the lower half of his face, spreading his fingers around his jaw and then pulling them closer around his chin. She hadn't yet seen him look so agitated. He'd usually seemed so easygoing. That was one of the things that had attracted her to him in the first place.

He sighed heavily. "Caroline," he said. "I have a son. Henry. And he's twelve. And I only found out about him two weeks ago, from Tanya's sister. Tanya never told me she was pregnant." He looked straight ahead over the railing of the deck, nodding slightly, as though confirming to himself that he'd gotten the details right and that he wanted to go on.

"I came here to Lake Summers, to Gorson, because I didn't know what to do. I still don't. How can I enter his life now, when I've missed so much? How can I shake his world up even more, when he just lost his mom? There had to be a reason Tanya didn't want me to know about him, maybe a good one. How can I go against her wishes when she's not even around to explain what she did? I say it to myself, over and over, and it doesn't even sound like it could be real. I have a son. I have… a son…"

He dropped his head, and he looked so tortured, so despairing, that Caroline felt her heart breaking. He was a nice guy, a lovely guy, and he didn't deserve to be in this position. She couldn't even imagine what that would be like, to suddenly find out she was a parent. Being Lee's mom was who she was; the two of them had been practically joined at the hip since the day Lee was born. She loved that she'd been with Lee from the beginning, she loved all the memories they had made together. And she hated that Aaron was learning about his son right now. It wasn't right and it wasn't fair. And it was killing him. She remembered now that day she'd run into him outside of Pearl's, how deep in thought he'd been before he saw her. She'd known then that something was troubling him. And she was drawn to him even more now, since she knew him and had come to care so much about him.

She grasped his hand and intertwined her fingers with his. He looked up, and then reached over from his chair and ran his hand down the length of her hair. Lowering her chin, she leaned in toward him and felt his lips on her forehead, her temple, her cheek. Then she lifted her chin, and his mouth was on hers, warm and enveloping. She touched his face, her fingertips exploring the soft bristles on his jaw, as he moved his hands to her head, holding her while he kissed her more intensely. She felt like she was floating and wanted nothing more than to continue with him, to go home with him, to spend the night with him…

And then she dropped her chin again and pulled away. This wasn't right. Lee could come out at any minute. She was only seventeen. She shouldn't have to see her mom so deeply kissing a man she'd only just met. Yes, he was a good guy and she cared about him. And that was the point—if she let herself get caught up in his life and his problems, she'd never be able to escape. She'd be caught in a situation she wasn't prepared for. And she had enough in her own life to deal with right now—Lee's future and her mother's garden, and the showdown with her aunt that was sure to come as soon as she got home. For a moment, she thought about how her mother had taken off on an adventure with her father, leaving her own family behind and settling somewhere new, all for love. Her mother was brave like that. Her mother would probably urge Caroline to be bold and to let her heart lead her wherever it took her. But she wasn't like that. Or, if she had once been like that, she'd lost her ability, because of too many years under her aunt's influence. She wasn't as bold as her mother. She could never be her mother.

"I should go in," she said. "There are things you can't do when you have a kid right here…"

He nodded. "I know," he said, and smiled, as though to tell her it was okay. And she knew he knew what she meant. It wasn't just about kissing him on the deck of the restaurant, in plain sight of anyone who happened to look. He knew she was saying that she might have to put an end to this. To them.

She stood and pointed at his sandwich. "You didn't eat anything. Now it's going to taste like tires." She tried to laugh, remembering what Gull had said when he handed Aaron his sandwich the night she'd first met him. But nothing was funny right now. "I can get you a fresh one," she offered.

He shook his head as he stood. "No need. It'll be great anyway." He wrapped it back up.

"I'll see you Saturday? At the Moonlight Carnival?" she said.

"Sure," he said. "I hear it's a ton of fun."

She watched him go down the deck stairs. She didn't know what was going to happen on Saturday night. She didn't want to leave him, to say goodbye and take off with Lee on Monday morning. But she didn't think she could be with him, knowing what she now knew. She wished she could have stopped time on Saturday night. On the footbridge. Because things had been so good that night.

Life was so much less complicated in Chicago, she thought as she brought the wine glasses back to the restaurant.

Maybe it actually was a good thing that she was going back on Monday.

CHAPTER NINETEEN

Ben arrived Friday morning with his wife, Lori, and four-year-old daughter, Ava, showing up at the house as Caroline was coming downstairs to have coffee with Maxine. "Sweet Caroline!" he shouted, and enveloped her in a hug. She hugged him back and then stepped back to look at him. He was still short and slight, as she remembered, with light eyes and small features, but now he had a full amber beard that made him look confident, even imposing. Adulthood, she could tell, agreed with him: he was no longer the baby brother she'd grown up with, but a husband, a father, and an entrepreneur. He introduced her to his wife and daughter, and Maxine was bringing them to his old bedroom to unpack when they heard Gull calling "Maxie!" from the driveway.

They went outside to see Gull with his arm around a tall young man with a crew cut, who was holding the hand of a young boy. "Look who nearly gave his old man a heart attack!" Gull said, cupping the man's neck with his palm, his voice cracking. "He told me Ella was on call, so he couldn't make it!"

"Didn't want to stay away, Dad," the man said, patting Gull on the back. "Ella's home with the other three, but Ollie and I snuck away. Wouldn't miss the carnival."

"Oh, Jess, what a wonderful surprise," Maxine said and walked over to hug him. He hugged her back with one hand and waved with the other. "Hey, Ben, Lori! How are you guys? Hey, Ava, you got big! Oh, man—is that *Caroline?*"

Caroline nodded and hugged him, and met his son. She didn't know Jess very well, because he'd lived in California with his mother growing up. But he spent every July with Gull. He was older than Maxine's boys—fifteen or sixteen when she came to live at Maxine's. She remembered him as a great guy, a natural-born leader who was planning to join the military as soon as he graduated high school. Lee came outside just then, and Maxine took her by the hand and introduced her around. Then there were discussions about unpacking, having a bite, and checking out the changes in the town since they'd all been there last. Caroline and Lee decided to pick up some sandwiches at the market for lunch and then spend the afternoon at the lake, to let everyone get settled.

Dinner that night was homey and festive. Maxine and Gull had arranged for backup help at the restaurant, so everyone sat around Maxine's table, loading their plates with ribs and barbecued chicken and pasta, and sharing family updates and fun memories from long ago. Caroline and Lee were constantly pulled into the conversation, with Ben and Jackie filling Lee in on Caroline's early crushes and her date for her first school dance when she was in sixth grade, and Lee seemed to be having a ball. Caroline watched her, aware that Lee could easily have been overwhelmed by all the new family members. But instead she was open, personable, and totally engaged in the evening. It was hard to believe that less than two weeks ago, Lee had felt rattled about meeting so many people who acted as though her mom belonged to them. But she had come to understand the complexity of Caroline's background and had found a way to embrace it. Caroline couldn't have been prouder.

Eventually, the conversation turned to the Moonlight Carnival. "So, who's the Midnight Couple this year?" Ben asked, after explaining to Caroline and Lee what that meant.

"I don't know," Maxine said. "Usually we have some hint about who's planning to propose. But I haven't heard a peep. Gull, have you heard anything?"

He shook his head. "Not a word."

"I'm not surprised," Beth said. "It's a crazy tradition."

"What?" Jackie said. "You didn't like that I asked you to marry me there on the stage?"

"It was so public," she answered. "Everyone crammed together, listening and watching our every move, and then waiting for me to say yes, and then hooting and hollering for us to kiss…"

"But by getting engaged there, you saved everyone from a brutal winter," Ben said. "You have to feel good about that."

"If we accomplished that, then it was worth it," Beth said. "Happy to do my part for the town. Oh, come on, don't pout," she said, as she leaned over and kissed Jackie's cheek. "I take it back. It was a great way to get engaged."

"Maybe it will be an unexpected couple this year," Jackie said. "Maybe like… Caroline and Aaron?"

Caroline felt the blood rush to her face.

"What?" Ben said. "Who's Aaron?"

"Nicest guy, just moved to town," Jackie said. "Rumor has it he's sweet on her."

"Oh Jackie, stop," Caroline said. "I barely know him."

"Well, I happened to stop into the Grill last night, picking up some dessert for the kids, and when I looked out onto the deck—"

"Jackie, enough!" Maxine said. "Now come on, everyone. Let's clear the table and bring out dessert. We have a busy day tomorrow."

"Sorry, Caroline," Jackie said, squeezing her shoulder as he passed behind her chair to bring some plates to the sink. "You know I just like to tease."

She raised her fists like she was going to punch, and then laughed and turned back to the table.

That's when she noticed Lee staring at her, eyebrows raised. Their eyes stayed locked for a moment, and then Lee got up to help clear dishes.

Caroline looked down at her plate. She wasn't sure what Lee's eyes were telling her, but she suspected Lee wasn't happy about the notion of her mother having some kind of romantic encounter. She was glad Lee hadn't seen her and Aaron on the deck, even if Jackie had. Lee had enough to occupy her mind right now. And besides, things were complicated with Aaron, after what he had revealed to her. She shouldn't have kissed him like that on the deck, no matter how much she'd wanted to, no matter how good it felt. She vowed to herself to be more circumspect this weekend. She and Lee were leaving town on Monday, and it didn't make sense to get any more involved.

*

Despite the thick fog that rolled in overnight, the noise kicked up early the next morning as the town began getting ready for the Moonlight Carnival. Caroline was awakened at 8 a.m. to the sound of jackhammers and buzz saws. Amazed that Lee was able to sleep through the racket, she pulled on a t-shirt and shorts and went outside to see all the preparations. The police had already begun placing yellow cones at all the intersections to avert traffic from Main Street, while store owners were putting last touches on elaborate booths and displays for the sidewalk sale. One group of volunteers was constructing a massive stage stretching across the street just below the drawbridge and setting up lights and speakers, while another group was stringing twin-kling lights up on the streetlamps and wrapping them around trees and potted plants on the sidewalk. Carnival games were being set up in the street, and a carousel was being assembled. Food vendors like Stan and Trey were setting up stations and painting signs with price lists.

Watching everyone in town come together in preparation for this evening's festivities, Caroline realized she knew what she had to do about the garden. With no way to implement the ideas in her mother's drawings, she knew she had no other choice. The town had considered the options, decided that the slope to the inlet was too dangerous, and made its decision. The mayor was right—it was unfair for her to come in at the eleventh hour and rile everyone up again with her stories, however meaningful and heartfelt. Although she hated the thought of it, she would go ahead and send Samantha Mackel a statement tomorrow saying she was sure her mom would want the library expansion to go on as planned. She knew her mom would understand. She'd have never wanted Caroline to cause trouble for the town she'd come to love so much.

She went back inside to wake Lee and fix some breakfast, and when she led Lee back outside around noon, the sun was out and the transformation of the town was complete. Outside the Grill, Jackie and Jess worked on setting up a propane-powered stovetop, while inside, Gull, Maxine, Ben, and Lori were cooking up pots of chicken riggies, and mac and cheese, and large trays of eggplant parm. The kids, under Beth's supervision, were spread out on the floor of the restaurant decorating a poster to hang on the booth, and Caroline and Lee took charge of bringing out the paper goods and stocking coolers with bottles of soda, water, and iced tea. A little while later Aaron showed up, and Jackie grabbed him to help carry the extra propane tanks out from Maxine's garage.

"Are you absolutely sure you want to go to Gorson today?" Caroline asked Lee as they pulled paper goods from the stockroom shelves. "This looks like it's going to be fun."

"I'm sure," Lee said. "It's the last event. I already told you, I want to show my work and say goodbye to other kids and everything."

"Okay." Caroline nodded. "Wow, you really worked hard this week, and made it to all those seminars. I'm very proud of you."

"It's not a big deal, Mom. It just worked out."

"Do you want me to drive you?" Caroline said. "It's going to be tricky—you have to go on the back roads, Main Street is closed off."

"Mom, come on, I can figure out how to get back into town on the back roads. You stay here and be with your family."

"Honey, you're my family," Caroline said.

"Yeah, but they're family, too. It's fine."

They went back to the stockroom. "Hey, Lee?" Caroline said. "Were you upset by what Jackie said last night about Aaron?"

"What, about his asking you to marry him?"

"Yes—did that bother you?"

"Well, is he going to?"

"Of course not," Caroline said. "Jackie was just teasing."

"Then there's nothing to think about," Lee said, and started taking plates and cups outside.

Caroline followed her, agreeing there was nothing to think about at all.

Except for the fact that she couldn't bear the thought of having to tell Aaron goodbye.

The rest of the afternoon passed quickly. Lee took off for Gorson in Maxine's car at five thirty, and by six all the set-up was done, and Caroline went into the house to take a shower and change. She picked one of her favorite flared skirts and a sleeveless top to wear, and let her hair fall in loose curls around her shoulders. Going to the dresser to get her lipstick, she noticed the Gorson agenda and took a glance to remind herself when Lee would be back. The schedule said the reception was from six to eight o'clock in the admission building lobby. And then two bolded words alongside the information caught her attention:

FAMILIES WELCOME!

She picked up the paper and brought it with her as she sat down on the bed. That was strange—Lee hadn't said anything to Caroline about coming tonight. And she didn't understand why. Lee had always been the kind of kid who was proud of her work, and she'd never want her mom not to be there if other families were going. It must have been a mistake. She looked at the time on her phone. If she hurried, she could get there by seven thirty and still have a half hour to spend with her daughter.

She grabbed her car keys and left the house, running toward the Grill's sidewalk booth to find Maxine and let her know where she was going. She had promised to help out serving food, so wanted to make sure Maxine knew she'd be there as soon as she got back. She started weaving her way through the crowd lining up for riggies. But before she could find Maxine, she spotted another familiar figure standing in front of the Grill, his back in her direction, talking to Jackie and Aaron. He was tall and well dressed, with the straightest posture Caroline had ever seen.

Even from the back, she knew it was Will.

She stared, hardly believing her eyes. But then he turned slightly to the right, and his profile confirmed it. She backed up behind the line of people, not wanting him to see her until she figured this out. What was he doing here? He hadn't even known she came to Lake Summers! But… Aunt Risa knew where she was, she thought. Aunt Risa must have sent him here.

She turned and went to her car, shooting off a quick text to Maxine to let her know she'd gone to Gorson. She didn't want to risk walking further along Main Street and having Will see her. She didn't want to talk to him now. She would go to the reception and enjoy it, and then come back and figure out what to do.

She sent Lee a quick text before she started up the car: *I didn't realize families were invited tonight. I'm on my way!*

A short time later she arrived at the school and parked at the admissions building. She felt her phone buzz and saw it was a message from Lee. *No, Mom, you don't have to come,* it said. *Just stay at the carnival.*

I'm already here, Caroline texted. *I'll see you in a minute.*

No. Mom, Lee said. *Really. Go back.*

Caroline put her phone in her bag and got out of the car. She had no idea why Lee would text that. Maybe she was self-conscious about her artwork? In that case, it was good that she was showing up, Caroline thought. Maybe Lee could use her enthusiasm and encouragement.

The reception was well underway when she reached the building, with students and parents milling around. Drawings and paintings lined the walls, and ceramic sculptures sat on display tables. Caroline looked around, but couldn't find either Lee or any of her drawings. She spotted a woman with a faculty badge and went over to speak to her.

"Hi, my daughter is Lee, do you know where she is? I can't find her anywhere."

"Lee?" the woman said. "Oh yes, I remember Lee! But she's not here."

"But she has to be. She's showing her work."

"I'm afraid not," the instructor said. "We haven't seen her since last week."

Just then Caroline's phone rang, and she brought it to her ear. "Mom?" Lee said, her voice shaky. "I'm not there. I'm at the Grill. I haven't been in the program since the mixer. I'm sorry."

Caroline froze, taking in what her daughter had just said. Then she turned away from the instructor, her shoulders rigid and her jaw stiff. "Now you listen to me," she said into the phone. "Don't you move. I'm coming right back. And you better be ready to tell me everything."

CHAPTER TWENTY

Caroline gripped the steering wheel tightly as she drove back to Lake Summers, the sky nearly dark, her headlights shooting two harsh beams into the night. She didn't know what on earth was going on, whether to be angry, scared, or something else. Nothing made sense. What did it mean, that Lee hadn't been in the program all week? What about all the days she'd taken Maxine's car and said she was going to a workshop or an art studio? Why had she lied? And what the hell had she been doing all those times that she said she was going to campus?

The drive seemed endless, but finally Caroline crossed over the Jason Drawbridge. She'd forgotten that Main Street was closed, and now she saw yellow cones and red, blinking lights directing her toward the detour. She followed the arrow, circling the side streets, which were normally quiet but tonight were lined with parked cars. It seemed the entire world had come out for the Moonlight Carnival. At last, she found a parking spot several blocks from the Grill, and she bounded out of the car and ran down the streets, the heels of her sandals tapping quickly on the asphalt.

The music grew louder—a country band was evidently playing on stage—and soon she reached Main Street. It was packed with people and vendors and game booths, and she wove among them, now on the street and now on the sidewalk, ducking under balloons and jumping onto curbstones, feeling the heat of open flames as she passed food stations. Ahead of her, Lonny's was holding a hot-dog-eating contest, and nearby she could make out the whir of smoothie blenders. The laughter and joyful shrieks seemed out of place to her as her anxiety grew. The crowd was nothing more than a roadblock, the people an obstacle between her and where she needed to go. Suddenly she remembered that morning when she and Lee left Chicago and got caught on the highway with a flat tire. She felt the same way now she had felt then—disoriented, unsafe, doubting her own decisions. This is what you get when you go outside your comfort zone, when you cross the established boundaries, she thought. A piece of her wished they'd never left Chicago. There were no surprises in Chicago. Things stayed exactly as expected.

She reached the Grill's booth, where Maxine and Gull were ladling bowls of food, while Jackie and Jess wrapped eggplant parm subs. Caroline felt her anger approaching a boiling point. How had these two weeks, which should have been so happy, gone so wrong?

She went around the restaurant and was walking toward the house when she heard someone call out "Caroline," and she felt a pull on her elbow. She turned around to see Maxine, her face red and sweaty from the heat of the cooking.

"She's in the house," Maxine told her. "She's very upset."

"*She's* upset?" Caroline said. "Do you know what's been going on?"

"I do. She told me."

"She's been lying to me this whole week. She's been taking your car and running off to who knows where. Where the hell has she been going?"

"I don't know," Maxine said. "But I know there must be a good explanation. Honey, you need to calm down. You can't go in there like this if you want her to explain—"

"Maxine, no," Caroline said.

"You'll make it worse if you go in there so angry—"

"Stop! Just… stop," she said, keeping her voice low, closing her eyes to keep her emotions in check, driving all her tension into her hands, her tense, outstretched fingers. She didn't want to say what she was about to say. But she couldn't stop herself. She was too upset.

"You don't get to tell me how to act with my daughter," she said. "You lost that right long ago. You lost that right when you abandoned me."

Caroline looked at Maxine, and suddenly she wasn't the magical substitute mother who had taken her in when she was alone. Suddenly she was a tired, old woman whose eyes were widening with shock. Turning away, Caroline threw her head back and looked up at the dark sky. She hadn't wanted to have this conversation. But now she realized it was inevitable. She'd been holding it in for almost thirty years.

"Oh, God, Maxine," she said. "I'm sorry. I shouldn't have said that. I didn't mean that."

"Is that what's been on your mind all this time?" Maxine said, her voice both firm and compassionate. "No wonder you took so long to come back. No wonder it took the demolition of the Lily Garden to bring you here."

Caroline turned back to Maxine and shook her head. "I can't do this. I can't talk about this," she said. "It's too painful. I need to go home. I need to get onto a plane and go home tomorrow. Back to my job and my aunt and my house."

"And what, marry Will? What about Aaron? Isn't that a relationship at least worth exploring?"

"You don't understand. It's safe there."

"Safe from what?"

"From people saying they love you and then leaving you…"

"Like who?"

"Like all of you. My mom, my dad, you… all of you. I tried to make it work. I tried to be okay. But every time I thought I would be okay… another person left. And now… now it's my own daughter…"

She clasped her hands and rested her forehead on top of them. She wanted to go inside and talk to Lee. Find out what her daughter had been thinking. But she had opened a door, and now she had to get through it. She knew she'd be able to deal with Lee much better if she'd dealt with all of this a long time ago.

Maxine took her elbow again and guided her to the metal steps leading up to the deck. She walked up a few steps and then lowered herself to sitting, and Caroline sat down a few steps below her.

"Your mom abandoned you?" Maxine said. "Is that what you think?"

"Of course she did," Caroline said. "She was reckless, they both were. She was sick, she'd been sick all week. She wasn't feeling well, she was tired. And she stayed out all that day in the garden anyway. And that night she got pneumonia and then she died."

"Is that what you think?" Maxine repeated. She gazed toward the street, looking as though she were deciding how best to respond. Then she turned back toward Caroline and shook her head. "No, honey," she said. "She didn't have pneumonia, Caroline. Your mom was pregnant."

Caroline studied her. "She was… pregnant?"

"They had just found out. They were so happy. You were going to have a little sister or brother. That's why he gave her the necklace. With the two intertwined hearts."

"The two hearts—that was them, my mom and dad."

"No, honey. It was you and the new baby. She had taken the pregnancy test after your dad left for work, and called him to tell him the news. That's why he came running to the garden and gave her the necklace. But the baby wasn't in the right place. It was an ectopic pregnancy, and it's very dangerous if you don't catch it early enough. And they didn't. She knew she wasn't feeling well, but she thought that was normal for the first trimester. She had a doctor's appointment coming up, but she never made it there.

The tube ruptured, and by the time they got her to the hospital, she had lost too much blood. They couldn't save her."

"Oh my God," Caroline said. "My mom was pregnant." She'd never thought it was anything other than pneumonia. She had no idea how it was she came to think her mom had pneumonia, but it was the story she'd lived with. No one knew that's what she thought. So no one knew to correct her.

"And your dad didn't mean to leave you either, honey," Maxine said. "He wasn't careless. It was an accident. And when he died, all I wanted was to give you the life they would have wanted me to."

"And you did," Caroline said. "I loved it here. And you knew that." Her voice broke. "You knew how happy I was here. You knew I didn't want to leave. My aunt didn't know me, she didn't care about me. She never wanted children, she never had any of her own. And you let her take me. You didn't even fight. You just let me go."

"Caroline, she was your aunt."

"So what? I didn't even know her. I belonged here. This was where my mom came, to be with my dad and to build a new home. And you were her best friend. You were the only family I knew." She looked down into her lap. "I tried so hard to make myself believe that my aunt had threatened you in some way to make you give me up. I said that even a few days ago when I talked to my aunt on the phone. But I guess I always suspected it wasn't true. I never heard you fight for me at all. You just…" She sighed. "You just packed up my suitcases and said goodbye."

"I didn't want to say goodbye," Maxine said. "I didn't want that at all. I cried for a month."

"So why did you? My aunt didn't want me. All she wanted was to clean things up. It was messy, that my mom ran off with my dad, and didn't go to college or follow the family path into the business. She wanted me back to have control. That's all. That's how she is."

Maxine put her hand on the banister, letting her fingers press against the cool metal. "Oh, Caroline. I know you think your mom ran off with your dad on this madcap romantic adventure. I let you think that because it made you happy. And the truth is so bad. Your grandparents thought your dad wasn't good enough for your mom, and when she insisted she wanted to marry him, they disowned her. Risa and Rich were in Hong Kong at that time, and your grandparents never told them anything. And I guess your mom felt too hurt to reach out to them herself. So Risa never knew anything about your mom. It wasn't until your grandmother died and your grandfather's health was failing that she came home and found everything out. And she tracked me down because she loved your mother and hated what happened to her. She wanted to take care of you because she felt she owed it to your mother. She wanted to raise her sister's little girl."

Caroline rubbed her forehead. It felt like too much to take in.

"Honey, your aunt may be cold and she may be flawed, but she wanted to do the right thing," Maxine said. "She wanted to make amends for what your grandparents had done, and she wanted to reunite her family. And I wasn't going to fight her on that. I'm sorry, Caroline, if you never loved your aunt, if you would have preferred to be here. And I can see that you've been mad at me for a long time. But I truly feel I did the right thing. And I think your parents would have thought so, too."

"I never knew any of this," Caroline said.

"I know," Maxine said. "And I take responsibility for that. It was a mistake not to tell you all this when you were young, even though it was all so sad. I thought you'd be better off with no story than a sad story. But I see now that you filled in the details with the wrong story. And that was far, far worse."

Caroline took in a deep breath. "I'm glad you told me all this," she said. "Now I have to figure out what to do with it. I always thought my aunt was the bad guy, and I thought I could use these two weeks to get Lee out from under her grip. But I ended up pushing Lee away from *me*. She never lied to me like this before. And I have no idea why she did, or what she's been doing with herself all week."

"Well, there's only one way to find out. She loves you. She feels horrible."

Caroline stood up. "I need to go and talk to her. I have to straighten things out."

Maxine smiled. "And what would you like us to do with your young man?"

"My what?" Caroline brought her hands to her head. "Oh my God, Will! I completely forgot about him!"

"We told him you went to get Lee, and we've been trying to keep him entertained. But I did see him talking to Aaron. I don't know what they talked about, but Aaron didn't look happy."

Caroline looked up at the sky. "What a night," she said. "Let me talk to Lee. And then I'll figure the rest of this out."

She kissed Maxine's cheek, then got up from the step and walked across the gravel driveway to Maxine's house, the sound of a 1980s pop band in the background, playing on Main Street. She found Lee upstairs in the bedroom, sitting in bed, her knees bent and her back against the wall. She'd been crying: her eyes were puffy and her nose was red.

She looked up when Caroline came in. "I know you're mad," she said, her voice thin and shaky. "And I'm sorry. But I had to do it. I didn't know what else to do."

"You had to do what?" Caroline said, folding her hands across her chest. "Lee, what is going on? You've been running around in Maxine's car all week. If you weren't at Gorson, where on earth did you go?"

"But I've been going to Gorson."

"You haven't been in the classes all week."

"But I've been going anyway. I've been working on this." She reached over to the night table and picked up a stapled packet of papers. She held it so Caroline could see the cover page:

Mock Business Plan
Alvindale University Pre-College Business Seminar

"I needed to get it done for next week, Mom," she said. "And you looked so unhappy every time I mentioned it. I needed to find time to do it. And I didn't want to hurt your feelings." She put the packet back on the night table. "I was able to use the Gorson library since I was enrolled in the program. I printed it out tonight. When you thought I was at the reception."

Caroline dropped her hands and walked toward the bed. "Why didn't you tell me? I asked you if you liked the program. I said you could withdraw if you wanted to."

"You said it, but you didn't mean it, Mom," she said. "You wanted me in that art program so badly. And I tried, I really did. I went to the introductory meeting and then to the mixer. But the kids and the teachers—they're not my people. I felt so out of place. I couldn't go back after that, Mom. Do you know what I mean? They weren't my people."

Caroline nodded. She knew exactly what Lee meant.

It was the same way she'd felt when she moved to Chicago.

"So I thought I'd tell you I went to the workshops, and you'd believe I was giving them a chance. Then I could tell you I didn't want to study art, and you'd finally listen to me. And you'd let me be… who I am."

"Oh, Lee," Caroline said, sitting down and taking her hand. "I never wanted to make you someone you weren't. I was only trying to make sure you explored all your options—"

"Come on, Mom, that's nothing but a line," she said, shaking Caroline off. "What you meant was I was letting Meems control me, like she was some evil witch. And you thought if we were far away, she wouldn't have the same power. But you never accepted the truth. It's not that I want to go into the business because she tells me to. It's because I like it. It's where I belong.

"We can be different, Mom," she said. "We can love each other and still be different."

Caroline pressed her fingers to her lips and looked away, her eyes filling. "I saw you getting all caught in the money and the status," she said. "The fancy hotel in Charleston that Meems took you to and the big internship party at the country club the night before we came here. I was worried about you. I thought you were finding the wrong things important."

"Those things were fun. And maybe I got too wrapped up in them. But you don't have to stand in front of an easel to have good values. You can make the world better in other ways, too. Meems does a lot of charity stuff, and she gives people jobs and she supports women, and the company is really diverse. And I can do even more someday.

"And it's not like I haven't been listening to you," she said. "It's not like this trip hasn't made a difference." She pointed to the packet on her night table. "I finally got an idea for my business plan. It's actually not a business, it's a nonprofit. The mission would be to solicit public and private grants and donations to promote beautiful public spaces that towns can't afford to maintain. It would support things like… my grandmother's garden."

"Oh, Lee. Oh, my wonderful Lee," Caroline said and opened her arms, and Lee sprang up into them. "I love you so much. And I love your business plan, and I love that you're taking it to Alvindale next week. I'm sorry I made you feel you had to lie. I guess I'm used to thinking I know how you feel and what's best for you. But you're not a little girl anymore."

"I love you, too," she said. "And I'm sorry I lied. I really am."

Caroline reached over to the night table and got a tissue for each of them, and they both laughed as they wiped away tears and blew their noses.

"Oh, and there's another thing, Mom," Lee said. "I was really angry when I saw how into Aaron you were. So I did something crazy. I called Will and invited him here. I thought he could make you forget about Aaron. I even thought you two might be the Midnight Couple."

"*You* brought Will here?" Caroline brought a hand to her head. "I thought it was Aunt Risa. Lee, how could you do that? Honey, I don't love Will. I never gave you any reason to think I did."

"I know, Mom. I just wanted so badly for us to go back, and for things to be the way they were. I'll go find him and tell him I was wrong and I'm sorry."

"Let me talk to him first," Caroline said. "I should have been clear with him a long time ago. And then I need to go find Aaron. And explain to him why Will came here."

"Aaron knows?"

"That's what Maxine said."

Lee took her hand. "Aaron's a really nice guy, Mom," she said.

"I know," Caroline said. "He is." She took the tissues and tossed them into the trash. "Okay, missy, it's time to head outside. I have to go find both of those guys. And meanwhile, there's still one thing you have to do before you leave Lake Summers. The most fun I ever had as a kid was helping Gull ladle chicken riggies into bowls."

She hugged Lee and they both smiled at one another.

"Come, let's go grab you a ladle."

CHAPTER TWENTY-ONE

Main Street was even busier and noisier than when Caroline had come back from Gorson. Huge spotlights were now on, lighting up the whole street, making it seem like mid-afternoon, not 10 p.m. The mood was truly carnival-like, Caroline thought: exciting and thrilling and a little daring, too. Change was in the air, fall was at the doorstep, and people were eating and laughing and dancing, moving in bursts from game to game and vendor to vendor as though they couldn't forget that their days of summer revelry were ending, and every minute was precious. Despite what she and Lee had been through, Caroline was glad she'd brought Lee here. She was glad Lee was getting to see the Moonlight Carnival. It was a good lesson to learn, the urgency of appreciating every moment, especially when that moment was drawing to a close. They were heading into their last hours here.

She walked Lee over to Gull and Maxine, and they set her up at the stovetop with a ladle and some bowls. Then she looked around until she spotted two men carrying propane tanks out from the Grill's storage shed toward the booth. She waited until the glow from a spotlight lit them up. It was Jackie and Will.

She walked in their direction. Will looked great—with a white shirt untucked over jeans, his sleeves perfectly rolled up, the folds sharp and clean. Even after hauling propane tanks, his golden-brown hair was perfectly in place. Nevertheless, he combed it with his fingers when he saw her. He stopped walking and put his hands on his waist.

Jackie took Will's propane tank, and went over to Gull, giving Caroline an encouraging smile as he passed her, as though to tell her that no matter what she did, he was on her side. She smiled back and then continued on until she was next to Will.

"Hi," he said.

"Hi, Will," she said.

"You don't seem surprised to see me."

"Well, word got around that you were here."

He laughed and reached out to hug her, and she put her arms on his shoulders and gave him a quick hug back. It felt strange, as she'd never hugged him before. They'd never had that kind of relationship.

"I've been getting to know your people here," he said. "Nice. They throw a good party."

She smiled at the phrase "your people."

"Can we talk?" he asked.

She nodded. She wanted nothing more than to go find Aaron. She wanted to let him know that if he was thinking there was anything between her and Will, he was wrong. And she wanted to let him know that whatever resistance she'd felt when he'd told her about his son, she didn't feel that way anymore. Seeing Will here had proved to her that there was something worth pursuing between her and Aaron; and finally seeing her daughter as the strong, independent young woman she was, she realized that she and Aaron should be celebrating their children, not seeing them as a reason to stay apart. But she had to clear things up with Will first. It wasn't fair to leave him wandering around the town any longer without an apology and an explanation.

They started walking on the sidewalk, away from the games and all the vendors. "So, the office was pretty quiet this week," he said. "Lot of people on vacation. Your aunt was there, of course. She's planning a fall sales trip to Milan. Oh, I went through those résumés you left on your desk. I know how much you hate looking at résumés. I made some calls. There are some interviews lined up late next week…"

She stopped. "Will," she said.

He looked at her.

"Why are you here?" she said.

"Because I missed you," he said. "And Lee called and told me you'd like me to surprise you."

He scowled. "Although I seem to be getting the message that's not the case. You keep me waiting for hours. And then you don't even look very happy when you see me…"

She touched his arm. "I'm sorry Lee called you," she said. "She shouldn't have done that, and I've talked to her about it. And I'm going to talk to her some more. But…" She paused, trying to figure out how to say what she needed to. "But did you really think it was a good idea to do what she said? Because we've never been a couple. And I haven't called you once in the last two weeks. And when you called me, I wasn't even honest about where I was. You needed my daughter to tell you where we were."

"I wasn't thinking about that," he said, walking a few steps away, his voice taking on an edge. "I was thinking that we've been dragging this on too long. And that Lee's leaving in a year for college. And I was thinking we could begin to move on with… us. Because I was thinking that's what you wanted, too. I thought we were both on the same page."

"What page is that?"

"The page of wanting to be with you and take care of you…" He turned to face her. "Does this have anything to do with the professor guy, the one Jackie was talking to? Because he looked sad when I told him who I was—"

"No, it doesn't," she said. "It has nothing to do with him. It has to do with what I want out of life now that Lee is growing up. Will, I could so easily drift into a relationship with you, just like I did with Lee's dad. And it could go somewhere, it could end in marriage, if that's what you're talking about. And it would be nice, and it would be safe, and I would have you to take care of me, like you said. And I could fool myself into believing that I loved you or that what I was feeling was as close to love as I could ever get. But I don't deserve to live like that. I deserve the kind of love my mother had. The kind of love that makes you give up everything you thought you needed... And you don't deserve a wife who doesn't feel that way about you," she said.

He looked at her. "I love you, Caroline," he said.

She gave him a sad smile.

"So I don't have a chance?"

"I'm sorry."

He put his hands in his pockets. "Well, if that's the way it is, that's the way it is. I'll be okay. I'm a big boy, I can handle it."

"I know."

"Although it's going to be plenty awkward in the office."

"We can get past that, I hope," she said.

He looked down and tapped his toe on the pavement.

"I am sorry, Will," she said. "I'm sorry you came all the way out here for nothing."

He smirked. "Not for nothing. I got to taste a new chicken dish. Think I'll go get another serving." He pivoted and started back down the street. "I'll see you back in Chicago, Caroline," he said. "Enjoy the rest of your vacation, okay?"

She smiled and watched him walk back toward the Grill. She was glad for the conversation. Finally they could both move on with their lives. He was right, he was a big boy, and he had a lot going for him. She was sure he'd find someone else to fall in love with, someone who would love him, too.

Turning her thoughts toward finding Aaron, she continued down Main Street. Where would he be? Would he have gone home, or to Lonny's? Or would he go somewhere else...

On a hunch, she continued in the direction of Mrs. Pearl's, then turned onto Oak and made her way behind the library building. The spotlights shining from Main Street were so powerful, they made it easy to find her way in the dark. She started on the dirt path until she came to the footbridge. And sure enough, there he was, leaning over the shaky railing, looking out at the inlet.

He turned as her shoes tapped on the planks. "Hey," he said.

"Hi." She went and stood next to him. "I was wondering where you went. It's your first Moonlight Carnival. You're missing all the fun."

He nodded. "Yeah, well. Maybe I'll get there a little later." He looked back at the water. "Nice guy," he said. "He came all the way from Chicago to surprise you."

"Will?" she said. "He is a nice guy. That's why it was so hard to tell him he shouldn't have come. It was a misunderstanding. I explained it to him. And then I came to find you."

He looked at her, his expression hopeful. "There's nothing between you?"

"Not at all." She turned her head toward him, her elbow on the railing and her neck in her palm. "I heard you talked to him. I don't know what he told you. But there's nothing between us. There never was."

He looked back out toward the water. "Oh, Caroline," he said. "Caroline, Caroline. Here you are, coming to clear things up, and I have no clarity to offer at all. I had no business getting involved with you. When I saw that guy show up to find you, I realized how simple he could make things for you. How easy it would be for you to be with him. It's not that way with me. I'm in the biggest mess of my life."

She nodded, looking out over the inlet. "Kids do that to you," she said. "All the time. It's a good thing," she added with a smile. "It keeps you humble."

She turned serious again. "Where's Henry now?" she asked.

"In Florida," he told her. "With Tanya's sister. She knew the truth all along. And after Tanya died, she decided the right thing to do was tell me." He clasped his hands. "She's leaving it up to me. Whether to change things or leave them as they are."

"So when are you going to meet him?" she said. He didn't answer. "Oh, Aaron. Are you thinking of staying away?"

"I think he might be better off. You said it yourself. I asked you the other day whether it would have been better if your aunt never showed up and you stayed with Maxine. And you said yes."

"But that's completely different. You're not his uncle. You're his father."

He moved his hands to the railing. "I wish I knew why she didn't tell me. I need to know why she thought it was better to raise him without me. Did she think I'd be a rotten father? Or did she think I'd try to take him away from her? There's no way I can know."

"No. There isn't."

"So how do I figure out what to do? That's why I've been killing myself with all these thoughts about bridges and love and rivers. It's not even about my research project as much as it's about her. Why did she do it?"

"I don't know," Caroline said. "But I do know one thing. It doesn't matter."

He looked at her. "What? How can you say that?"

"Because it doesn't. Don't you see? You have a kid. And he's the one that matters. I just..." She shook her head. "I just spent a half hour talking to Maxine, and the biggest lesson I learned was that kids make things up to fill in the blanks in their lives. And that can screw things up a lot. Aaron, your questions don't matter so much anymore. He's the one that needs answers. He's the one that needs to know who you are."

"But I don't know if I can do it," he said. "I don't know if I can be a father."

"You don't have a choice. You already are."

He paused for a minute, then looked at her and raised her chin with his fingers. She moved in to kiss him, but just before their lips touched, a voice sounded from the dirt path. "Mom? Mom, are you there?"

"Lee!" Caroline called. "I'm here! What's wrong?"

"Nothing's wrong," she said when she saw them. "But they're about to make the Midnight Couple announcement. And there's a rumor going around that it has something to do with Gull! And everybody's crowding around the stage!"

"Okay, we're coming, honey. We'll be right there," Caroline said. Lee turned around and took back off.

"Guess we've got to go," Aaron said, and he held her hand and led her off the bridge and toward the path.

But they never got there. The rocks at the base of the footbridge were extra slippery because of the fog that morning. And before she knew it, Caroline was slipping down the hill. She went to grab Aaron's shirt as she had last week. Except this time, all she did was pull him off balance, and suddenly they were both tumbling downward.

They came to a stop about halfway down the hill, Aaron on his back and Caroline on her stomach. She sat up and rubbed her knee. "Ouch!" she said. Aaron squeezed his eyes and arched his back. Then they looked at each other and burst out laughing.

"Oh, man," Aaron said. "Are you okay?"

"I think so," Caroline said. "Think we can make it back up?"

"I guess we'd better try," he said and reached for her hand. Then he stopped, and she saw his jaw drop.

"What's the matter?" she said. "Are you hurt?"

He shook his head. "Hey, Caroline. Where did you say your dad used to hide gifts for you and your mom?"

"He put them in a bucket and hung them under the bridge," she said. "Why?"

He pointed toward the underside of the bridge, which was visible, thanks to the spotlights on Main Street. "Look," he said. "Doesn't it look like there's a bucket hanging?"

They half walked, half crawled up the slippery hill, trying to help each other without losing their own footing. Finally, they reached the bridge, and Aaron crawled underneath and came back out holding the wire handle of a rusted metal bucket. Caroline knelt next to him so she wouldn't slip again. "Is there anything in it?" she said.

He nodded and handed the bucket to her, and she took it. Her heart was racing as she looked inside, then pulled out a small plastic bag. She opened it and took out a small greeting card, with a big pink flower on the front. Inside was a message in her dad's handwriting:

Happy eighth birthday, Sweet Caroline! I think you've old enough for this! How about some chicken riggies and coconut cake to celebrate?
Love, Daddy

Then she reached further into the bag.

Wrapped in a tissue was her mother's gold necklace with the intertwined hearts.

She held the necklace up, letting the chain dangle between her fingers. And suddenly her face was soaked with tears.

Caroline sat back and covered her face with her hands. She felt Aaron move closer and put his arms around her. They sat that way for a few moments, with Aaron holding her. Then she reached out and wrapped her arms around his neck.

And as she hugged him, she thought about how lucky Henry was about to be. To finally have Aaron, his dad, in his life.

*

They arrived back near the Grill and stood with Lee just as the mayor took the stage. He thanked the vendors, the volunteers, and the whole community for what they had done to make this year's Moonlight Carnival the best one yet.

"And now it's time for the Midnight Couple," he said. "Except we don't seem to have a Midnight Couple this year." The crowd booed good-naturedly. "But calm down, calm down," he added. "Because Gull from the Grill has an announcement that I think you're all going to find pretty interesting. Gull, come on up and take the stage."

Gull walked up and gave a big wave, then took the microphone from the mayor. "Hey, everyone," he said. "Having fun?" Everyone cheered. "Now you know me, I'm not a big one for speeches," he said. "But I'll make an exception for the news I'm about to share. The Grill is finally about to change hands. We completed the paperwork yesterday. Maxine and I are now the new owners. Come on up, Maxie, and take a bow with me!"

Maxine walked onto the stage, looking beautiful in the red dress she'd bought when they'd gone shopping last week, and she took Gull's outstretched hand while the crowd applauded and cheered. Caroline clapped as loudly as she could. Gull and Maxine worked so hard at the Grill, and it was more than time that they took it over.

Maxine started to leave the stage, but Gull pulled her back. "And seeing as it's midnight and the Moonlight Carnival," he said. "Ah, what the hell. Maxie, I love you. Will you marry me?"

Maxine stood still for a second, then threw her arms around his neck and kissed him squarely on the mouth, and the crowd went crazy. A photographer with a *Lake Summers Press* tag on a lanyard fought his way forward to snap some shots, and then Maxine called, "Let's bring the whole family up for a picture!" In a few short moments the stage was full, with Jackie, Ben, Jess, and their wives and children. Caroline saw Jackie cup his hands around his mouth and shout out in her direction.

"Caroline! Lee! You belong here, too!"

Aaron moved a few steps forward to part the audience, and Caroline took Lee's hand and led her to the stage. They found a place in between Jackie and Ben. "Squeeze together," the photographer called. "Smile, everyone!"

Caroline beamed as the photographer started shooting. She knew the only person on stage she was actually related to was Lee.

But it didn't matter. She was with family.

CHAPTER TWENTY-TWO

"Are you sure you don't mind going by yourself?" Caroline asked.

"Mom, I'll be fine. Kids much younger than me take planes by themselves all the time."

"Call me when you get to the campus, okay?"

"Yes, I will. I'll call you as soon as I'm in the dorm."

It was Monday morning, Labor Day, at 10 a.m., and Caroline was at the Adirondack Regional Airport to drop Lee off. Just as there had been last-minute changes to their travel plans coming out to Lake Summers, there were last-minute changes going back as well. Lee was flying by herself directly to the Alvindale program instead of going home with Caroline to Chicago, so they could drive together from there. And Caroline was staying in Lake Summers for a few extra days.

They continued through the ticketing area and toward the security checkpoint, Lee wheeling her suitcase alongside her. "Got your business plan?" Caroline said.

Lee patted her tote bag. "Right in here. Mom, do you think Ben really liked it?"

"He was incredibly impressed," Caroline said. "He never would have praised it like that if he didn't mean it." Lee had shown the business plan to Ben after dinner at the Grill last night, since Ben's consulting firm occasionally did pro bono consulting with small nonprofits. He'd thought Lee's plan was excellent and asked her to make sure to tell him what the Alvindale professors said about it. He hoped she'd think about moving forward with it, maybe as an independent study or thesis project while she was in college.

But Caroline couldn't wait for the official start-up to see if the Lily Garden could get some funding. Not with construction on the library expansion slated for just a few weeks from now. Instead, she had a different idea. Lee had reminded her the other night that Aunt Risa was a big believer in philanthropic projects, and Rantzen contributed a good deal of money to charitable causes. So Caroline planned to go back to Mayor Young this week and see whether he'd reconsider her mother's ideas if Rantzen Enterprises would fund it. And as for the library expansion, she had an idea about that too. It had occurred to her over the weekend that her old house on Walnut Street would make a perfect location for a satellite children's library. The first floor was spacious and got lots of natural light—and since it had been a preschool, it was already configured with tables and bookshelves. The house was just a short walk from the library. And moving all the children's books to the satellite location would free up space in the library, so no new construction would even be needed.

Assuming the mayor was willing to consider her ideas—and she had no intention of leaving his conference room until he did—she'd then talk to her aunt. Thanks to Maxine, she now understood that her Aunt Risa had loved her younger sister and been appalled that their parents had disowned her. Caroline was excited to show her aunt the drawings her mother had made of the tiered terraces and the walkway by the inlet. She thought Aunt Risa might very well want to finance the building of Library Commons and Library Walk as a way of honoring her late sister.

And at the same time, Caroline wanted to apologize to her aunt for that awful phone call they'd had. She knew it was wrong to have complained so harshly about Aunt Risa's involvement in Lee's life. Lee knew her own mind. She truly wanted to head up Rantzen Enterprises one day—and since she was seventeen and on the brink of leaving home and starting her life, she didn't need Caroline questioning her.

They arrived at the security line, and Lee hugged her mom. "I'll see you back home soon," Lee said. "Say thanks again to Maxine and Gull for everything. I had a really good time these two weeks, Mom. And yesterday was amazing."

Caroline nodded. It had been amazing. They'd all gotten up late, after staying at the Moonlight Carnival until 3 a.m. Then everyone—including Aaron—had gathered at Maxine's for Sunday breakfast, though it was more like lunch by the time everyone arrived. Afterward, Jackie had gone out to get gardening supplies as well as some carpentry tools, and they'd all gone to the garden. Even Beth—whose belly seemed to have gotten way bigger in two weeks—came along to help, as did all the kids. Gull and Jess got to work securing the planks and railings of the footbridge, while the rest of them worked on the flower beds—pulling out crabgrass, deadheading flowers, and trimming back plants that had wandered onto the dirt path. The afternoon had flown, and when they were done, the garden was lovely and the footbridge more secure. But the best part had been that everyone had wanted to participate. Caroline knew her mother would have been very happy.

She waved as Lee got through security, and then watched her head toward the gate area until she couldn't see her anymore. Last night had been bittersweet, with everyone coming to Maxine's house to have dessert and say goodbye. Jackie and his family were going back to Buffalo, and Ben and his family to New York. Jess and Gull had decided to go on a fishing trip up north to Lake Champlain for a few days, with Maxine offering to watch Jess's son, Ollie. Gull apologized for going away so soon after their engagement, and Maxine said not to worry, she had no intention of being "that kind of wife."

Then she'd given him a sideways look. "Just make sure to arrange for enough coverage in the kitchen while you're gone," she'd said. "Otherwise I'll divorce you before we're even married."

Caroline had laughed, along with Aaron, Lee, and everyone else. She loved these people so much. She would have liked to have more time with them. But at least it wouldn't be another twenty-seven years until she saw them again. Everyone—including Lee—had promised to return to Lake Summers on the weekend of October fifteenth, for Gull and Maxine's wedding. They were planning a big reception at the Grill—and assuming everything worked out as Caroline hoped, they wanted the ceremony on the footbridge.

Caroline left the airport and headed back to town. She had promised Aaron she'd cook dinner tonight, so needed to stop at the market. She had told him she'd had way too much rich food while she was here, so intended to fix a nice, light dinner—fresh fish, roasted vegetables, a big salad, and a nice bottle of Chardonnay from Aaron's fully stocked wine refrigerator. And maybe they'd take a romantic walk afterward, she thought, and then end the night with a couple of Luscious Lily Libations from the smoothie shop. Stan and Trey had ended up mixing in pineapples and mangoes with the green ingredients, so the smoothie was delicious—sweet and refreshing. It had been an unqualified hit when they introduced it Saturday night after Gull's proposal, and it was going into their regular flavor rotation.

Driving on the winding road, she saw the trees far off in the mountains, their tips glowing orange and gold, the signs of fall now unmistakable. She was glad that she and Aaron had a few quiet days together before they had to separate, at least for a little while. Caroline would be going back to Chicago for Lee and for her job—and Aaron was going down to Florida to meet his son. He had called Tanya's sister last night, and she'd been glad to hear from him. She truly thought Henry needed his dad. Aaron was planning to visit Henry every few weeks, so they could get acquainted. Eventually, when Henry was comfortable with him, he'd start making plans with Tanya's sister to take custody. Caroline was thrilled for him. She knew Aaron would be a wonderful dad. And she hoped to meet Henry herself before too long.

Up ahead, she could see the drawbridge leading into town, the one that had looked both familiar and different to her when she arrived two weeks ago. She'd left town as a twelve-year-old long ago, and now she was finally ready to think about how Lake Summers might fit into her future. A career at Rantzen had never been the best choice for her, and she knew she had to leave. She thought it might be nice to go back to school and get certified to be a teacher, as her mother had planned to do. What sounded even better, though, was joining, or even forming on her own, the kind of nonprofit that Lee had invented for her mock business proposal. She couldn't imagine anything more wonderful than helping bring funding to communities with public spaces like the one her mom had envisioned. Ben had seemed very knowledgeable when he was reviewing Lee's plan. She thought she might give him a call and get some advice. She couldn't help but think that Lake Summers would be a fitting place to locate such a venture.

Back in town, she pulled into a parking spot on Main Street. She had most of the day to herself and was looking forward to spending time at the Grill, helping Maxine out with Ollie, now that Gull and Jess were on their way to Lake Champlain. Aaron was on campus, having gone to work on his research even though it was a holiday, and wouldn't be home until the evening. Now that he was no longer focused on all his questions for Tanya—questions that could never have any answers—he found himself better able to move forward on his project. He had come up with some new angles for his paper, and he'd booked a meeting next week with his department head to get her input. He wanted to work on strengthening his relationship with her. He'd told Caroline last night that he liked Gorson a lot, and he liked Lake Summers.

The mentor who had advocated for him to be offered the visiting professorship was retiring next year, he'd said. He was hoping he might be offered that spot on the faculty.

The memory of their conversation made her think about his research, and the verse he'd recited to her during their first date, the one that Tanya liked. *A river flows from Eden to water the garden.* She remembered how Aaron had told her it was about separation and division, but she now thought maybe there was a whole other way to look at it. Because even though the river in the verse eventually splits into four, that didn't mean the original river was gone. No, there'd be a little bit of the original river in all four subsequent rivers. So the verse wasn't about separation at all. It was about continuation.

The first river lived on the in the succeeding ones. Like generations of a family. The way parents never stopped thinking about their children. And children would always have questions about the people who came before.

She got out of the car and approached the stairway to the Grill. It was hard to believe how much had happened since she and Lee had landed in Syracuse. It had been intended only as a visit, but like the river flowing from Eden, it had spurred so many new beginnings. Like Maxine and Gull, and their new life together. And the potential new route for the Lily Garden. There was the new relationship between Aaron and Henry, about to meet as father and son. And there was Lee's new beginning, as she headed closer toward college after finally showing her mom that she was growing up.

And then, of course, there was her own new beginning. As she'd watched Lee head on toward the plane, she couldn't help but see the young adult her daughter was quickly becoming. And finally loosening her grip on her daughter meant that her own life had new possibilities, too. She could imagine returning to Lake Summers for good now, finally coming back to the place she'd never stopped thinking of as home. Being surrounded all the time by the memory of her parents' love for one another. And the memory of their love for her.

She and Aaron were definitely starting down a new river, she thought as she ran up the steps of the Grill to see Maxine.

She couldn't wait to see where it would take them.

A LETTER FROM BARBARA

I want to say a huge thank you for choosing to read *The Lily Garden*. If you did enjoy it, and want to keep up to date with all my latest releases, just sign up at the following link. Your email address will never be shared and you can unsubscribe at any time.

www.bookouture.com/barbara-josselsohn

The Lily Garden took its inspiration from many sources, the most unlikely of which is the Harry Potter series by J. K. Rowling. What does a boy wizard have to do with a feel-good summer romance, you ask? A lot! You see, for me, the most poignant aspect of Harry's story is his never-ending quest to know his parents, who died when he was a baby. Yes, Harry can do extraordinary things—even vanquish his nemesis, Voldemort. But in the end, despite his magic, he cannot bring his parents back.

I've always enjoyed stories that explore families: how they evolve and grow; how they mystify and infuriate; and how they can also lead to understanding, self-awareness, and even triumph. I loved writing *The Lily Garden* because I loved delving into Caroline's story, as she and her teenage daughter visit her first home and, like Harry, confront the early, tragic loss of her parents. Writing this book gave me a new perspective about myself as both a mother and a daughter. And I hope that in reading it, you've discovered something new and important about your own family—whether it's the family you were born into or one you chose to create for yourself.

I hope you loved *The Lily Garden,* and if you did, I would be very grateful if you could write a review. I'd love to hear what you think, and it makes such a difference helping new readers to discover one of my books for the first time.

I love hearing from my readers—you can get in touch on Instagram, Twitter, Goodreads, or my website.

Thanks,
Barbara

 BarbaraSolomonJosselsohnAuthor

🐦 @BarbaraJoss

🌐 www.BarbaraSolomonJosselsohn.com

ACKNOWLEDGMENTS

The Lily Garden was such an emotional book for me to write, and I am lucky beyond words for the encouragement, support, guidance, and friendship I received along the way. While this note is short, it has a world of gratitude behind it.

First, a huge thanks to my agent, Cynthia Manson, whose wisdom, knowledge, and thoughtfulness continue to amaze me. I am so thankful, too, to my brilliant editor, Jennifer Hunt, who understood what this book could be way before I did—and somehow helped me find the story deep within the bare-bones idea I originally proposed. I can't even express how thrilled I am that she's the one I send my work to! Thanks, as always, to the incredibly talented publishing, marketing, and PR team at Bookouture, and hats off, too, to my fellow Bookouture authors—I love being in your company!

My writing community is filled with the most talented, inspiring, and generous people you could ever want to know. Thanks to Caitlin Alexander, Jimin Han, Pat Dunn, Veera Hiranandani, Diane Cohen Schneider, Jennifer Manocherian, Marcia Bradley, Patty Friedrich, Linda Avalon, Maggie Smith, Susan Schild, Tiffany Yates Martin, and Nancee Adams. An extra shout-out here to Diane, my go-to Chicago maven, for answering all my questions about the Windy City, and to Patty and Jimin for their expertise and insights into academia and campus life.

Thanks, too, to the talented writers and professionals who make up the Women's Fiction Writers Association, the Writing

Institute at Sarah Lawrence College, the Women's National Book Association, and the Scarsdale Library Writers Center. And a super-big hug to the amazing book bloggers and reviewers I'm privileged to know. It's been a treat to connect with you all over the last couple of years, both personally and professionally.

To my pal Susan Levin, a big thanks for your gardening savvy, which proved invaluable as I was writing this book. And to Julia Klein, all my gratitude for your creativity and expertise!

The fictional Gorson College in *The Lily Garden* was inspired by Colgate University in Hamilton, N.Y., consistently named one of the most beautiful campuses in the United States. My family and I adore this school and are so proud of our association with it. Thanks, too, to Alyssa Sherry, a Syracuse native who generously shared information about the most delicious dishes that Upstate New York has to offer! I also want to acknowledge Westchester Reform Temple in Scarsdale, N.Y., where I first came across the verse from Genesis that plays such a pivotal role in the novel.

Finally, as always, my deepest and most heartfelt thanks to my awesome family—my husband, Bennett; our children, David, Rachel, and Alyssa; and our amazing dog, Mo. You guys are everything to me, and I couldn't love you more!

Printed in Great Britain
by Amazon